Until We Meet Again

Jill S. Flateland

ISBN: 978-1-966012-15-3 (paperback)
ISBN: 978-1-966012-16-0 (hardcover)
ISBN: 978-1-966012-17-7 (digital)

First printing - February 2015
Second version – April 2022
Third update – September 2024

This is an original Jill S. Flateland.

Website: JillSFlateland.com

Cover illustration by Robert M. Henry.

Printed in the United States of America

10 9 8 7 6 5 4 3 2 1
First Edition

In Memory & Dedication

I dedicate this book to my fun loving aunts, Vera E. Williams and Vivian V. Lund who have shared their wisdom, humor, and blessings with me throughout my life. Together we've spent many years tracing our ancestors, sharing family traditions, and just kicking back and having fun recalling memories of days gone by.

I give special thanks and gratitude to my mother, Rosemary Williams. She faithfully read my work and lent support with honest appraisal throughout her life.

Although they have all passed on, I feel truly blessed to be a part of this special family. Like my guardian angels, they never left my side, and even today, I feel their presence in the gentle breeze, a song, a poem, and even rainbows. No matter what mistakes I've made along the way. Even when the world feels like its crumbling and nothing makes any sense, they gave me guidance, becoming super heroes to make the world safe once again. I know they loved me and have stood beside me always. For this I am truly grateful.

Acknowledgements

As I'm writing the 'Secret Series' and now Until We Meet Again, I've looked back through my life at many who have touched it along the way. I want to thank my sisters: Wendy, Debbie, Cindy, and Charlotte; my brothers: Lloyd, Jim, Phil, and Fred; and to my closest friends: Jeri Lou Maus, Kathy Brown, Renee Bergeron, and Christine Howes. It's been thrilling to weave bits of their personalities, insights, and inspirations. creating the soul of my characters. I'm sure each will recognize who they are. Jeri Lou, Kathy, Renee, and my sister Cindy have also been great editors for my novels. They fill my heart and soul with positive energy, and I appreciate their tremendous support.

I would also like to give special thanks to my illustrator, Robert M. Henry, who designed this creative cover. His talent overwhelms me when I first see his delightful covers.

As always, I am grateful for my husband, Byron, and his continued support. He is my inspiration and the love of my life.

My greatest blessings are our daughters, Kirsten Sielaff and Crystal Fletcher, and their husbands, Tim Sielaff and Jason Fletcher. Kirsten set aside time to edit my novels, making many corrections and patiently reviewing my rewrites. Her technology skills have bailed me out on many occasions. Thanks to Crystal for her great sense of humor, honest appraisal, and for supplying me with updated criminal, forensic, and pharmaceutical information I can weave into many more novels.

Our most cherished additions to the family are our granddaughter, Elsa Hana Sielaff, and grandson, Wyatt Samuel Fletcher. I hope, in years to come, they'll enjoy these books.

Last, but far from least, I give thanks to my writer's group colleagues, who I'm privileged to call my sounding board for creating this novel. They helped me refine the chapters and bring the story to life. Without them, this book would never come to fruition.

Table of Contents

Until We Meet Again

Tobias McFitzroy's old tombstone lay cracked in half and sinking under its weight in a cemetery outside a Colorado ghost town northeast of Fort Collins. The old stonemason had carved his own epitaph. It read, "Until we meet again. 1830 – 1899." Unlike most people, it didn't mean when he'd meet them in heaven. He couldn't. He hadn't made it that far.

Tobias had never been one to leave something unfinished. He knew it was madness to expect to finish the task now, more than a hundred years after his death. However, he had to save his reincarnated daughter. Her present life depended on it, and so did his soul. He'd succeed, *or what? Die trying?* A rumbling laugh worked its way through his misty throat.

No idiot, you'll remain a ghost forever. That thought silenced him. Back on task, he left the cemetery for his daily cool mug at Pops' soda fountain.

Tobias didn't have to wait long before the shop bell tinkled. A petite, brown-eyed beauty bounded through the door. The jacket of her blue scrubs billowed behind her. She slipped a stethoscope from around her neck and brushed aside her shoulder-length red hair, the same color as Molly's, his late wife.

Tobias knew she had to be the one, a rebirth of his long-lost daughter. Now he had to find a way to prove it.

Samantha McFitzroy wrapped the stethoscope in thirds, shoved it into the pocket of her scrubs, and made a beeline across the black-and-white checkerboard tile floor. She leaned over the gray marble countertop and pulled a teaspoon from the wire silverware rack. Her taste buds salivated for the flavor of thick, dark fudge. Without hesitation, she snuck a sample.

Her father stepped from behind the metal fountain. "Tempting, isn't it?"

"Oh, Pops, you startled me." Samantha gave a guilty smile and licked the spoon. She studied her father from his black spit-shined shoes on up. There was a stark contrast between his starched white apron and his golden-tanned arms. Still fit for an old military vet.

Pops cleared a banana boat dish and a soda fountain glass from the counter.

Glancing around the room, Samantha asked, "Has he been in today?"

"Who? Ivar?" Pops smiled broadly and chucked her under the chin. "His dad says you've been…shall we say dating?"

Her heart leapt at the thought of Ivar, but she wasn't ready to tell the world her feelings yet. "News to me. I'd call it more like he's following me around like a lost puppy." She gave a nervous laugh. "And I haven't bothered to fight him off for some reason." Lowering her voice to nearly a whisper, she said, "I wasn't talking about Ivar. You know who I mean."

Pops wrung out a rag and wiped off the counter. "Oh, your ghost?" He chuckled. "Yep, as usual. First, the cold mist appears, then that frosty mug. Don't know why they show up in front of the same stool even when someone's using it. Most people won't sit there anymore."

"This building used to be a saloon. Maybe he died here—"

"What an active imagination you have for a twenty-four-year-old." Pops plucked the now well-licked spoon from her hand and placed it in the sink.

She defended her thoughts. "You've seen the mist and heard the whispering sounds it makes. I've felt his presence for years, but it was nothing like the past six months. If it's not a ghost—"

"Okay, I admit, you might be right. You look as if you've had a rough day. I don't need any help this afternoon. You can run along, Sam."

"You know I hate that name. Call me Samantha."

Pops ruffled her hair.

She pulled back and frowned. "I'm not a child anymore. Just came by to see if you will be home tonight. I planned to stop over and join you and Mom for dinner."

"I thought you'd rather ride the ambulance than spend a night with your old man."

Samantha rolled her eyes. "Mom would appreciate a hot dinner for once, and I know there was still half a cake left over after my birthday party. Don't be late."

Pops picked up a soda can from the counter and raised it in a salute. "Tell her I'll be there."

Samantha crossed the room, rested her hand on the doorknob, and turned toward Pops. "By the way, it's time to get new cushions for those old stools, especially the middle one. The material is fraying at the back. I noticed a long thread tucked under the seat. The patch job looks shabby."

"Okay, Sam." Pops nodded and twisted the can in his hands. He wrinkled his nose. "This one's a dud. No pull tab." Setting it down, he turned for another and accidentally brushed the dud can from the counter. It hit the floor.

Everything happened in a split second as a rumble of an explosion rolled through the building. Samantha's mind moved in slow motion.

Her eyes widened in disbelief as a dark mist burst from the ceiling. Like a high-speed train rushing through the door, air whistled past her. Pops flew backward into a dark cloud and disintegrated.

"Pops!" she screamed above the roar.

A tongue of reddish-brown flame erupted over the counter. Intense pressure and heat burst outward and rushed toward her.

***

Samantha felt a tingling sensation. In contrast to the flash of heat, a cold, dark mist surrounded her as she flew backward through the front door's glass and landed on the sidewalk.

The store's windows shattered, bricks, and walls buckled, causing the ceiling to bow under the force of the explosion. The roof let out a loud groan before succumbing to the destruction and crashing down.

Pain ripped through her. Unable to catch her breath, she detected the pungent stench of charred wood, and a faintly sweet odor filled her nostrils.

The vapor disappeared as Samantha succumbed to the black dots that dimmed her vision.

***

Samantha awoke in total confusion. *What happened?*

Anxious voices grew from a chaotic crowd gathered nearby. "Help!" Lying under the debris, she couldn't see her surroundings. Fear heightened her awareness. The odor of wood smoke hung in the air like incense, and nearby sounds flooded her. "Help me, please. I can't get up." A fire crackled nearby, while in the distance, a siren wailed. It became louder as it raced toward her. The rhythmic high-pitched whine vibrated through her.

She heard an endless cacophony of traffic—cars honking, and radios clamoring in the background. A lower-pitched scream of a fire truck joined the cadence and blared to a stop, followed by a stampede of feet slapping the pavement. Hoses dragged along the sidewalk. A squeak followed the clang of metal as someone connected the fire hose threads to the hydrant. Water splashed, and the fire sizzled.

"Someone, please, anyone! Help." Samantha shivered as cold water seeped under her. "I'm over here."

A pulse of rotor blades overhead matched the rapid thump of her heartbeat.

Samantha rasped another shaky "Help." Her hearing was hyper-alert as she tried to figure out what was happening.

Someone tried to control the crowd. Voices came closer. "Get back."

It must be the fire chief.

A woman asked, "Possible gas explosion?"

"Nope. I checked. Gas has been disconnected," the chief said. "I haven't seen anything like this since my military days. With such a broad sweep of damage, I suspect twin explosives. Keep a log of witnesses and document everything. The cause of the explosion is unknown, but we'll treat it as a crime scene."

"Right, Chief," the woman said.

Crime scene? Who would want to blow up a fountain shop? Samantha remembered that frayed chair seat. *Was it a bomb? Could I have stopped this? Why didn't I check it out?*

A familiar voice filtered through the crowd. "No one could survive—" The voice faded as a hovering helicopter landed.

"Amos!" The fire chief yelled. "I said, get back. This area is off-limits."

Amos Vickers piped up, "Pops is my best friend. He was in the shop."

Good, Amos is here. He'll help. Samantha tried to move again, but something pinned her right side. *I still can't see anything. I have to get out of here.* "Help." Her voice sounded muffled. "Amos! I'm trapped. Front door." Her right arm throbbed and refused to cooperate. Barely able to move her left arm, she felt debris embed into her skin. It stung like hornets.

Pinned down in darkness, her mind shrieked, *I'm buried alive!* Panic grew as she fought to catch her breath, and her lungs burned as bile rose in her throat. Her mind tried to understand what had happened, but it felt like hammers pounding in her head, and something warm trickled down her cheek. Sharp pain enveloped her into a black swirl, and she entered the abyss again.

Reliving the event in her mind, her scream jarred her back to consciousness. "Help." *How long have I been here? What if they can't find me? Where's Pops?* "Help. Help!" Her voice no longer held any volume. *I wish Ivar were here. He would know what to do. Please let me live to see his face one more time.*

Something bright flickered above, slicing through raw nerve endings in her head. Squinting, Samantha turned away from a beam of light, and then it disappeared.

"Don't leave." She kicked her left foot against what remained of the door. It joined the debris that had collapsed on top of her. A moan escaped her lips.

"Something moved," a man with a deep Scottish burr said. "Shine your light over here."

"I need help," Samantha cried. "Pops needs help, too," she added, remembering how her dad disappeared as if he'd disintegrated.

"Did you hear something?" the Scotsman asked. "Yes, but it sounded like a whisper."

Hope surged through her. "Ivar! I know that's you. It's Samantha." Her shout died on her lips. Tears welled in her eyes.

A pathway of clutter lifted. "If you can hear me, make some noise. I don't see you anywhere." Ivar's concerned voice was a welcomed relief.

Her left hand clutched a chunk of brick and tapped it against the wood covering her.

"Okay, I hear you." Ivar's calm tone steadied her shattered nerves. "We'll get you out. I promise."

A board lifted, and Ivar's tanned face came into view. "Thank God, you found me." Streaks of grime smudged his cheek. His light-blue shirt, soaked in mud and soot, had a tear along one sleeve. Yet, to her, he'd never looked so handsome.

He stumbled forward, pulled away the debris in his path, and knelt at her side. "Sam!"

Her entire body relaxed with a shuddered exhalation of a long-held breath, and she cleared her throat of the knot growing there.

Ivar's fingers shook in a rare show of nerves as he pushed back a stray lock of hair from her face. "I could have lost you." He yanked a handkerchief from his pocket and pulled a glass splinter from her cheek.

His touch felt like life itself, and she smiled despite her pain.

A smear of blood appeared on the cloth after he dabbed her face. "Are you all right?"

His concerned eyes made Samantha's heart kick into overdrive. "Yeah, but Pops—"

"Step aside." A young EMT dashed forward with a rescue bag in hand. His badge was from her precinct, yet she didn't recognize him. He nudged Ivar out of the way.

Samantha reached for Ivar. "Don't leave."

Ivar stood beside her. "I'm not going anywhere."

The EMT knelt over her. "Your lips are blue. You need oxygen!" He brushed debris from her hair and placed a mask over her face. Then he grabbed her right arm to check her vital signs.

"Ouch." Samantha winced in pain.

He felt along her arm. "You have a broken wrist, and your cheek is bleeding. Do you hurt anywhere else?"

Samantha tried to speak. She ached all over, but that wasn't her primary concern. "Check on Pops."

No one responded to her pleas.

"Don't move." The EMT stood. "I'll get a backboard and be right back."

A female paramedic ran forward and dropped to her knees. "Samantha?" she asked in surprise. "I heard someone was down, but I didn't know it was you."

Samantha pulled her oxygen mask aside. "Abby, I'm glad you're on duty. Pops is inside."

Abby went about her duties without acknowledging Samantha's fear for her father. "Relax. Don't worry about a thing. You know the routine." Abby replaced the mask and babbled as she cleaned and steri-stripped the wound on Samantha's cheek. "Backboard, C-collar, the whole ten yards. I added a yard for good measure—only the best for one of our own." It was as if Abby tried to occupy Samantha's mind to keep her from worrying.

"My father needs help." Samantha's hoarse voice sounded muted under the facemask. Getting no response from Abby, she grabbed Ivar's wrist. "Pops." She pointed toward the building. "He's inside."

Ivar's cold, sweaty hand squeezed her fingers. "He's..." Ivar shook his head.

Samantha read his expression. "Oh, no, Pops dead?" A sob escaped her lips.

"Barclay, help me lift this beam and clear a path to the chopper." Ivar let go of her left hand, brushed his palms down his pant legs, and then gripped the wooden beam, lifting it partially from Sam's shoulder.

She gasped when she saw a bone fragment lying in the rubble. Samantha grabbed her arm. Thank God it wasn't hers. A tear trickled down her cheek. She choked back another sob, "Pops." Her heart beat so hard that she knew Ivar could hear it.

As if he read her mind, Ivar snapped, "Don't go there." His square jaw flexed. "It's too painful."

"Go where?" Barclay asked. "I thought you wanted help."

Ivar sighed. "Yes, I do. Lift that end. Let's move, Sam. She needs hospital care. We'll come back later for—"

"For Pops' body," Barclay continued.

Ivar gave Barclay the evil eye and cocked his head toward Samantha. "What's wrong with you?" Ivar mouthed.

Pops dead. How will I tell Mom? It had been quick. Maybe not painless, but he didn't linger. The one fear he'd expressed all of his life.

The wooden beam slowly lifted the rest of the way off Samantha, and the paramedics pulled her free from the wreckage.

"I'm sorry for your loss." Barclay avoided eye contact as he helped Abby strap Samantha to the backboard and loaded her on a gurney.

"Someone has to tell Mom." Samantha choked on the words. Her head and arm throbbed, yet she felt numb and unable to think clearly.

"I already called her," Ivar said. "She'll meet you in the emergency department."

Samantha blinked away tears. "How did Mom take the news?"

"She's a strong woman and hell-bent on keeping you safe." Ivar moved closer. "I'll ride with you."

"Where are we going?" Samantha tried to sit up, but the straps around her head prevented movement.

"We're flying to the Medical Center of the Rockies in Fort Collins."

"I don't need a chopper, and neither does Pops. I'll ride to MCR in the ambulance."

"We're flying. It's a precautionary measure." Ivar's jaw clenched, refusing to take 'no' as an answer.

"I'm fine," Samantha insisted. "It's just a broken arm. My head's clearing, my vision is only slightly blurred, and I can move both legs. I'm a paramedic. I know what signs to look for."

His fingers laced through hers. "It's a trauma center, and the Fort Collins police can protect you."

"What about you?" Samantha squinted up into his ice-blue eyes. "You're a cop. Can't you keep me safe?"

Ivar cleared his throat. "Too close to the victims. Better to stay neutral."

"They killed Pops, and you're dumping me into some stranger's care?" Samantha glared. "I expected more from you."

"Sorry." Ivar let go of her hand. He grabbed the foot end of the gurney and then nodded to Abby.

Samantha felt him stumble through the wasteland into the street, now filled with flashing red-and-blue lights. Firefighters and a crowd of bystanders parted like the Red Sea to let them through.

Ivar transferred the gurney into the helicopter and crawled in beside her. He grabbed a headset. "You'll need to speak to me through this microphone after we take off. Do you understand?"

Samantha nodded. "I need to find out who did this to Pops."

The door slammed shut. As they lifted, the engine drowned out Ivar's reply.

He placed a headset over her ears and then put on his. "Don't get involved with this investigation," Ivar warned. "It's too dangerous."

She opened her mouth to argue.

Ivar glared. "I mean it, Sam. This wasn't an accident. Someone planned this attack."

Molly's Diary

Bridget McFitzroy spent most of the day cleaning after Samantha's birthday party two days ago. She listened to classical music using noise-canceling headphones to make the task more palatable. When she finished with the living room, she turned off the music. *One more room, then I can reward myself with a cup of coffee and relax.*

She opened the door to Pops' office. Everything was in its place. No dust, clutter, or even a cobweb hung from the ceiling. *How does he keep his stuff so tidy?*

Gripping the door handle, she paused to make a final scan of the room. A crumpled paper wedged in the corner of his top right-hand desk drawer caught her eye. Curious, it drew her inside. *He's a bit messy, after all.*

She chuckled, opened the drawer, and pushed the paper back in place. Her hand hit a hard object. *What's this?*

Bridget knelt on the floor and opened the drawer all the way. A black cast iron lockbox sat in the far corner. She pried it out and noticed the lid lay ajar. *I haven't seen this box in years. I wonder why it's in his desk.*

Inside was an old, beige leather-bound book. The years had not been kind—the discolored pages were warped and brittle. Bridget carefully opened the cracked cover. She traced the drawing with her fingers. *Pansies.*

The title read, "Diary of Molly McDermitt McFitzroy (1852-1893)." Below the title were two hand-drawn pansies. The name Molly was scrawled under one and Tobias under the other.

A crisp, yellowed map dropped to the floor when she lifted the diary from the box. *Why was this hidden under the book?*

A cold mist blew through the room, flipping the book open to the last page. A shiver tingled up her spine as she read, "Beware. Don't trust anyone!" written in dark black ink. Bridget shuddered. *That's odd. They didn't have gel pens in those days. I wonder who added this and when.*

Her trembling fingers slid the diary back inside the cast iron container and closed the lid. It locked with a click. Bridget shoved the lockbox back into the desk drawer.

Oops, I forgot the map. With a shrug, she picked it up from the floor. *I'll ask Pops about this when he comes home.*

The phone rang.

Bridget shoved the map into her apron pocket and answered. "Hello." "Oh, Ivar, Sam's not here right now." She pulled open the middle drawer to take a message. Her hand paused before picking up a pen.

"I'm glad I finally reached you," Ivar said. "I've been calling for the last half hour."

"What do you mean you've been calling? I didn't hear the phone." She glanced toward the answering machine and saw the light blinking. It indicated she had messages. "Why didn't you call my cell?"

"I tried every number I had." Ivar sounded upset.

"Oh, you did?" She dug the phone out of her pocket. There was a voicemail. "I can never figure out how to get that app to work. Sorry, I guess I had my headph—"

"Mrs. McFitzroy, this is important," Ivar took a deep breath. "Sorry, maybe you should sit down before hearing this."

"What?" Her heart leapt as she pulled out the chair. "Okay, I'm sitting. What's wrong?"

"I'm calling about Pops' Fountain Shop. There's been an explosion—"

"Explosion?" She nearly dropped the phone. "Oh, my God. Is Pops all right?"

"He was inside the shop, and we fear the worst." Ivar's Scottish lilt grew stronger with emotion.

Tears rolled down Bridget's cheeks. "Pops' dead?" Her vision blurred. "Are you sure, Ivar?"

"I'm also calling about Sam," Ivar said, "we found her under the debris, and we're flying her to Fort Collins for treatment."

Jumping from the chair, she gasped, "Sam was there, too?" Everything started to blur. She shook her head to clear it. "How bad are her injuries?"

Ivar's strong voice remained calm and reassuring.

"I'm sorry, I missed that last sentence. Where are you taking Samantha?" Bridget's fingers shook but were poised to jot down the location. "Fort Collins MRC emergency department? I'm on my way." She nearly hung up and then gasped at Ivar's words. "What do you mean this wasn't an accident?"

"We don't have all the details yet, and I'm flying with Sam, so you be extra cautious."

"Okay, I'll be careful. Meet you at the hospital." She disconnected the call and dashed from the office. She hastily pulled off her apron and threw it in the laundry. She rummaged through her purse for the keys and bolted for the car.

Bridget drove her navy-blue Honda Accord twenty miles over the speed limit. She thought back to the old diary in Pop's desk. Her mind flooded with questions. *Why did I find it today? There was that warning on the last page. Could it have anything to do with the explosion? Why Pops? Was he involved in something dangerous?* Anxious to check on Samantha, she stepped on the gas and nearly rear-ended the vehicle in front of her.

"Move it!" Bridget pulled around the slow-moving van and floored the gas pedal to pass.

An oncoming semi blasted its horn.

Yanking the car back into traffic before the truck clipped her front end, she heaved several tiny breaths. *Easy. Sam can't lose both parents in one day.*

Her cell chirped. *Now what?* Her hand groped her pocket, dug out her old, outdated phone, and flipped it open. "Hello. Talk. Make it quick. I'm on the road."

"Bridget, honey, I called to say I love you."

"Pops?" She slammed on her brakes.

Horns honked. Lights flashed. The car behind her skidded and passed on her left.

The driver of a Toyota pickup gave her a middle-finger salute, screamed obscenities out his open window, and pulled onto the shoulder of the road.

Bridget managed to pull in behind him. "Pops, is this really you?" Her heart raced, and she could hardly breathe. "How? Where are you? Pops? Talk to me?"

The driver hopped from his truck, yelling, "What the hell's wrong with you, lady?" He yanked open her door, raised his fist then his jaw dropped. "Ma'am, are you having a coronary?"

Bridget dropped her phone as she pushed past the driver, fell to her knees, and vomited.

He knelt beside her and grabbed his phone. "I'll call for help." Glancing at the curdled mess on the ground, he stood. "Lady's having a heart attack. Highway 14, five miles east of Fort Collins."

His boots flicked up dust as he paced in front of her. "Name? Why do you want my name?" After her pause, the truck driver said, "Oh, her name. Hang on."

The driver shoved his phone toward her mouth. "What's your name?"

"Bridget McFitzroy." *Something about that man looks familiar.*

He flinched and brought the phone to his ear. "McFitzroy. You got that?" Pacing again, he looked up and down the road. "Yeah, yeah. I'm holding already."

I can't think. Bridget pulled herself onto her car's seat and grabbed her cell with trembling fingers. "Pops, are you still there?"

No answer. *Where have I seen this man before?*

The driver stood wide-eyed outside her car door. "Are you talking to Pops now?"

The man's voice was familiar. "Do you know my husband?"

"Ah, no." He stroked his goatee. "But not many people call their husband Pops."

"It's short for Papadopoulos. Not that it really matters." Pops had disconnected the call. "He's probably an angel by now." Ignoring the man, she punched calls received. The last number to appear came from Ivar. *Nothing from Pops? I'm losing my mind.*

A siren sounded in the distance. "Sorry, I can't wait. Don't die. Help will be here soon." The driver headed for his truck.

As he turned, Bridget saw a gun tucked in his waistband. *Where have I seen him before?*

"We got disconnected." Pops redialed. His return call didn't go through.

"Put down that phone." Tobias' spirit ranted. "Can't you see? This is war. Everything has literally blown up in my face."

Pops blinked and shook his head to clear the cobwebs. "What happened?"

"I barely whisked you from the shop in time. Now focus. Sam's life depends on us."

Pops squinted. "Am I a ghost, too?"

"As far as the world knows, yes. And you'll stay that way until we meet again."

"Huh?" Pops rubbed his eyes. His tattered shirt hung from his shoulders. He stared at his soot-covered hands. A sharp spasm zinged across his back. "I can't be dead. I'm in pain."

"Better that than the alternative," Tobias said. "You never believed in me before. Why are you talking to me now?"

"I guess I owe you. Why'd you save me?" Pops asked.

"Who else will serve me a fountain drink?" Tobias chuckled. "Besides, you're my grandson. You're the spitting image of your father."

"My father?" Pops frowned. "And you're how old?"

Tobias rumbled a laugh. "Yeah, I know I'm old, but all the men in our family wait until their mid-forties before having children. You did."

"Is Sam all right?"

"I don't know. She flew through the door so fast. I couldn't manage to save both of you. If I'd left you, well…bye, bye, Pops. All I could do was get her out of the store, so the blast wouldn't kill her."

"How did you get me out of the building?"

The spirit hissed. "Time warp. Your body became particles of matter. It's complicated."

"You mean like in 'Beam me up, Scotty?'" Pops rubbed his hands over his shoulders and legs, examining them to see if he was in one piece.

"Yeah, something like that."

"Then beam Sam here, too!"

"Can't. It's too late. I needed the extra energy the bomb created."

Pops cringed. "Sam is still under all that debris?"

"I doubt it. Someone's found Samantha by now."

"I sure hope so. Sam's resilient. She's a paramedic on the brink of danger most of her life, but I worry about her."

"And she's still in danger."

"Who did this?" Pops gritted his teeth. "It better not have been Maddog."

The mist roiled and grew thicker. "Maddog Parker?"

"Yeah. He's been sniffing around Sam since she was eight. He proposed to her, and he stole her bike when she refused to talk to him. I found it by the shop later that day. Both tires were slashed. Of course, he was only twelve at the time. He continued to send her flowers, unwanted gifts, and letters. When Sam became fourteen, she turned him down for a date to the prom. I nearly put a restraining order on him. He swore she'd become his wife one day. Sam has other ideas. He even had the nerve to stop by last week and asked me for her hand in marriage. I said, 'No!'"

"His great-grandpa was Fang. I swear the family is rabid."

"Please say it wasn't Maddog. He was the last customer before…" Pops' hand flew to his face as he recalled the event.

"I reckon I don't know that either, but he's why I'm hanging around. Never found my daughter once Fang came to town. I searched for years. Died trying. Keep in touch."

"Wait." Pops jumped to his feet. "Where are you going? What am I supposed to do locked up in this…where am I?"

"An abandoned depot. Cot's not the best, but it'll do. I worked here until they shut her down in 1890. I'll bring enough food so you can stay here for a good month, and you have all the major conveniences."

"A month! Are you crazy?" Pop glanced around the main office. Holding up a key and sounder, he frowned. "How do I reach you? I'm not a telegrapher."

"Not telegraphy. Telepathy." The ghost rumbled a laugh.

Pops moved into the old warming room. A typical military style cot sat in the corner. It was complete with a blanket wrapped so tight over the thin mattress that it could probably bounce a quarter a foot into the air. A metal can with a cover sat in the closet at the end of the hall.

"Don't tell me. A slop bucket?" Pops asked.

The mist chuckled. "Chemical toilet, not that you'd know the difference, and a pump for the best-tasting well-water a boy could wish for. Cold and rust-free."

"Uh-huh." Pops turned to the mist. "What happened to the major conveniences? What am I supposed to eat until we meet again?"

"You have plenty of canned food in the pantry." The mist swirled, and the temperature dropped when Pops frowned. "Punk kids nowadays. Why in my day…never mind. I'm confining you to this place. Keep the shades pulled, lantern down low, and await my return. You have a laptop with Aethernet access and that cell phone. Don't show yourself, and only use the electronics for research. God help me, but I need to work through your hands."

Feeling a twinge of guilt, Pops asked, "May I call you Gramps?"

Warmth filled the air. "The name is heaven to me. Or the closest thing to heaven I've heard in over a hundred years." The old spirit faded.

Get Me Out Of Here

Samantha's gurney wheeled into a swarm of activity. "Code Blue, ED 5, Code Blue—"

Nurses dressed in colored scrubs dashed toward a room off to her right. They nearly collided with a large red cart. A defibrillator, balanced on top, wobbled precariously as a nurse dodged around them.

"Whoa. It looks like you'll be here for a while," Abby said.

Samantha winced as a plump lady grabbed one end of the backboard and helped Abby slide Samantha onto an ED cart.

"Let me find her nurse." The lady darted out of the room.

"I'll give my report, and then I have to run. Sorry." Abby pulled out her record and followed the lady.

A few minutes later, a blonde-haired nurse bounced into the room. Not a hair out of place, yet she ran her manicured red nails over her locks. She bubbled with enthusiasm as she plucked splinters from Samantha's head and neck. "Broken right arm, lacerated right cheek, showered in glass fragments. What have I missed?"

"Headache, blurred vision, and several bruises, but I doubt I broke anything else," Samantha said in a professional manner. Reading the nurse's nametag, "Miss J. Jenkins, do you think I could get this C-collar off my neck?"

"Name's Julie. X-ray's backed up as usual. It'll be at least an hour." She placed a cuff around Samantha's upper left arm, hooked it to an automatic blood pressure machine, and put a probe on her index finger.

Next, she took her temperature with an ear probe. "B/P 122 over 76, pulse 98, temp 98.2. Pulse ox 97%. Guess you'll live." Off came the oxygen mask. "Want anything for pain? I noticed you grimace whenever you move, and your pulse is a bit high. I'll get the doctor as soon as he's free."

"He's busy. I heard 'Code Blue' called over the intercom. Just don't touch me again, and I'll be fine. Has my mother arrived yet? Her name is Bridget McFitzroy. She should be in the waiting room by now."

Julie bit her lip and twisted the gold charm wrapped around the bridge of her stethoscope. "Umm. I don't think she's… I'll go check." Like a bull in heat, Julie rushed out of the room.

"What's with her?" Ivar asked, side-stepping Julie. "Are you all right?"

"Yes, I will be as soon as they get me out of here. Can you loosen this collar?" She tugged at the offending restraint around her neck.

"Ah, Sam, don't ask me to do something you know I can't do." Ivar pulled up a chair.

"It's Samantha. Did you see Mom in the waiting room?"

"No, now that you mention it, I better see if I can find her." He left as the doctor walked in.

"Busy day, huh?" Samantha asked.

"Aren't they all?" The doctor laughed. "Fill me in on what happened."

He sat down and listened as if he had all the time in the world. Yes, he actually listened to her story. After a thorough exam, he said, "You told me, 'no allergies,' right?"

"Uh-huh." Samantha tried to nod. Taped to the backboard, she couldn't manage the small action.

"How does Demerol IV sound? It'll help ease the pain, and we'll have you down to X-ray in no time."

"Thanks." Samantha blew out a deep breath. "Can Mom and Ivar come in to see me?"

"Sure, why not?" He flashed a bright smile and left.

Julie entered the room. She had applied fresh lipstick since her last visit. "I have some Demerol for you." Bending near her ear, she whispered, "There's a cop outside who wants to see you. Should I let him in?"

"Is his name Ivar?" Samantha whispered back as if conspiring their next plot.

"No, he's Detective Colby Cage, a bomb squad investigator. I saw him talking to the policeman who escorted you to the hospital."

"My escort would be Ivar," Samantha said. "Show them both in. Is my mother with them?"

"Mmm." Julie scrunched her face and then shook her head. "No...but she's still alive."

"What?" Samantha tugged at the C-collar. "What aren't you telling me?"

"Umm, sorry, I didn't mean to upset you." Julie's face turned red as a radish. She managed to gasp, "You're Mom's in ICU."

Samantha tugged at the tape holding her head to the spinal board. "I have to go to ICU. Now."

"Julie stepped to the door. "Ivar, I need your help."

Ivar rushed into the room. "What's going on?"

"Mom's in ICU. Was she the Code Blue—"

"Yes, I know." Ivar's hands held her shoulders in place. His steady gaze calmed her. "I've already talked with the doctor and with your mom." A smile crossed his lips. "Let's get Sam to X-ray and clear her of this board."

"Yes, Sir." Julie flipped the brake off from the end of the bed and wheeled her toward the hall.

Outside the door, they met a tall, lean man with gentle green eyes that crinkled in the corners as he smiled.

Julie's face lit up as bright as the sun. "She'll be right back, Detective Cage. I promise."

"I'll wait inside for her return." His deep baritone voice made Sam's heart pound like a base drum. The detectives' chiseled face etched an imprint into her memory. *He's handsome. I want to get to know him.*

Aethernet

Pops couldn't stand the dank smell and heat of the old rundown depot any longer. Desperate to cool off, he opened a window, threw open the back door, and basked in the gentle breeze.

When the room was tolerable, he moved to the bay window and raised the shade just enough to look out at the abandoned property. The platform that once graced the area between the depot and the tracks had rotted away long ago. The rails lay rusty, almost covered with cinders and mud. A clump of maple trees shaded the west windows from the afternoon sun.

Bored, Pops opened his laptop computer and waited for it to boot up. Although Sam did most of the net surfing in the family, he knew a few programs. Without much thought, his fingers pecked at the keyboard. "What am I supposed to research?"

An hourglass symbol appeared and flipped for nearly a minute before anything else appeared on the screen. Pops typed, "Come to think of it, how did you connect to the Internet in an abandoned town?" What can one expect at such a remote location?

"Aethernet" popped onto the screen.

Pops fingers pecked across the keyboard. "Never heard of that system."

The computer hummed softly. "It's a spiritual link between the two of us," Tobias responded. "Use it with caution. Now let's get to work."

"Wait. Any news about Sam?" Pops asked.

"She's safe for now, but I want to figure out why this happened. Need to know everything you can find on Fang Parker."

"Such as?" Pops typed. "Do I need to go to Ancestry.com?"

"No. What do you know about Jack Slade?"

Pops scratched his head. "Never heard of him." With two index fingers, he labored to add, "How are we communicating again? Is this Google program email?"

"Never mind the details."

"How can you type with no fingers?"

His keyboard leapt into the air.

Pops grabbed it before it flew across the room. "Calm down. I'm just asking."

"In 1892, Overland Trail stage line fired one of their managers, Jack Slade. Everyone knew he led a gang, but no one could prove it."

"Can you prove it now? Is that our job?" Pops wondered how this information had anything to do with today.

"I don't know how Fang got mixed up with that critter or if he ever even met Slade, but after Jack's death, Fang got hold of a lot of money and bought a silver mine. I suspect he paid for it with an old army payroll from the 1860s. How else would you get that much dough?"

"Fang must be dead by now. He couldn't have bombed the shop." Pop ran his hand over his chin when he received no reply.

"Is Fang his real name?" Pop tried again.

Frustrated after waiting ten minutes, he got up and stretched. "How can I look up an obit without knowing his name?"

The screen chirped a reply. "Fang died October 12, 1909, in Leadville, Colorado."

Pops' jaw dropped. "I didn't even type the question. If you can hear me, why make me do all that work?"

The screen went blank. The shade over the window zipped back in place when a breeze tore through the depot. It ripped the lantern mantle, and the light went out.

"Gramps?" Sitting alone in the dark, Pops added, "Sorry. It's been a long day."

Unable to replace the mantle, he lay on the cot in the dark—nightmares of Sam in danger filled his sleep.

Discharged

The doctor applied a cast from the knuckles of Samantha's right hand to three inches above her bent elbow. A dull ache nudged her senses, but she refused more pain meds. "I want to see Mom ASAP."

Julie helped Samantha back into the wheelchair. "You'll be discharged shortly. Remember, Detective Cage, has a few more questions."

A warm feeling spread over her then she remembered her mom in ICU. "I would have already answered them if you hadn't wheeled me away to the cast room. Now we have to go back to X-ray for a repeat film." Samantha's pain went up another notch. Her mood reflected her misery.

Julie crossed her arms and frowned.

"Sorry I'm so snippy," Samantha said. "Please hurry, I have to see Mom."

Thirty minutes later, Samantha returned to her room. Detective Cage was nowhere in sight. She blew out a sigh of relief. Then she spied a note on her pillow. "Now what?" She snatched the paper in her left hand and read:

"Sam,

"I got called away on a possible drug case. See you in my office at eight o'clock tomorrow morning. Detective Cage and I will investigate the crime scene. We're meeting with the fire chief and the state fire marshal at 6 p.m. I stopped by to see your mother. She's resting. They suspect an irregular heartbeat. No evidence of a heart attack. "See you, Ivar."

Disappointed that she wouldn't see him again until the morning, she remembered something else. *Oh great. Now, how do I get home?*

Samantha found her damp and soot-coated clothes balled up in a plastic bag in a rack at the end of the gurney. After removing everything from the bag, one shoe was missing. She searched the room and found it under a chair.

It wasn't easy, but she managed to slip on her jeans and zip them. With a groan, she pulled a couple of mud-crusted clumps of cloth from her Nikes. *Socks are overrated.* She dropped them in the trash and shoved her bare feet into her shoes.

Julie entered the room with discharge instructions and a prescription for Vicodin.

"Great. You're here just in time to help me with my shirt."

"Let's get rid of the IV first." Julie placed the papers on the overbed table and removed the IV catheter. She applied pressure and patched the wound with a cotton ball and tape. "Now, hand me your shirt."

The cast didn't fit into the sleeve.

"Just cut the seam open," Samantha said. "These are ready for the rag bag."

Julie made the designer adaptations. "You look as if someone dragged you down the street behind their BMW."

"Thanks. It's a new look for me, but I'll get over it. Where do I sign?"

"Bottom line." Julie handed her a pen. "I heard about your father. Sorry for your loss."

Tears threatened to spill. "It's hard to believe he's gone." Samantha asked for directions to the ICU.

"Your mom's on the second floor, ICU-3," Julie said. "You can visit for only five minutes every hour. Oh, that's right. I was supposed to give you her car keys and purse."

Julie dashed from the room and returned with a black leather bag. "Check to see if the keys are inside."

"I wondered how I'd get home." She found the keys on top of the heap.

"Don't drive after taking the pain meds." Julie walked with her to the ED doors and pressed the automatic button. "Take care."

Without a backward glance, Samantha headed for the lobby elevator and punched the up arrow.

Dark Men

The boss gazed down from his stealth helicopter at a seedy bank of the jagged shoreline along the Columbia coast and shuddered at the filth. After landing on a patch of dried grass, he emerged to the stench of fish brine and rotting trash. *You'd think I'd get used to these dilapidated villages.*

He had learned of the smuggled shipment earlier that afternoon via a coded message from General Gonzales. It didn't give him much time to orchestrate the job and then negotiate his secret flight. He had to time it just right to return from the Caribbean coast for a major event in Denver.

Dressed in all black, he put on his night-vision goggles and hid among the shadows. He advanced through the grass laced with dew and saw the unloaded ship from afar.

The boss switched on his lapel speaker to hear what went on at the docks.

A drug-sniffing dog nudged one coffee crate, but the local agent, Troy, tugged on the leash and guided the German shepherd away from the stash.

Troy's dark eyes glanced toward the ship's captain. He nodded toward the crates and herded his team's inspection down the shipyard away from the special delivery.

"Nice job," the boss whispered to himself in satisfaction. "Maybe I'll let this one live." Dedicated men were hard to find.

Everything needed precise timing. There would be only fifteen minutes to create the distraction and retrieve the hidden cocaine.

"Morning, Troy." The old sea captain's voice crackled through the boss's speaker. The captain bumped against Troy and slipped a note into his pocket. "See you next week. We're scheduled for Tuesday minus two."

Turning, the captain joined a cluster of sailors loading the drug-laced crates onto a speedboat. They spoke Spanish with a variety of thick accents.

"Cover them," the captain warned. "Fill the empty spaces on shore with the dummy crates."

"Aye, captain." The men moved in unison without another word.

"Ten minutes," he cautioned his men.

The boss smiled at his handpicked crew. They never asked questions. Never wondered why they sailed at night or why every delivery arrived on shore during the wee hours of the morning. They only cared about the money they'd make when they returned across the sea for the next shipment.

"Seven minutes and counting," the captain whispered.

The crew boarded the ship and cast off.

Early-morning fires came to life as the villagers began to wake.

The sky lit a scarlet red.

Troy drew his tattered cloak tighter around his body and glanced up as General Gonzales approached in his military regalia—sharp creases formed along his camo-colored uniform. Three stars decorated his shoulder. An AK-47 was draped across his arm. "Storm's coming from the east."

Troy passed on the note he'd received from the sea captain. "News from the tower?"

"Perhaps," the general's voice lowered. "Five minutes. Be away from here." The decorated general climbed aboard the speedboat.

Troy quickened his pace and disappeared into the black truck parked nearby. He took out the detonator and drove to the pre-designated spot.

The boss glanced at his watch. "Thirty seconds."

Soon, a resounding whoosh burst through the boss's speaker. He chuckled as he recalled a similar sound at Pops' Soda Fountain. *Too bad about Pops, but he was in the way.*

The shoreline erupted into a world of grit, and sea spray swirled like a tornado. Crates, fishnets, and shredded boats flew into the air.

The explosion is right on time. The boss watched the villagers rush from their huts. Sirens blasted in the distance, and the speedboat was nowhere in sight. An aroma of burned coffee beans wafted through the air as the boss returned to his helicopter.

"Mission accomplished," he received in code from the general.

The boss didn't reply. He had to get back to the States to give another charity performance that night.

More Bad News

The next morning, Samantha couldn't tell if the conference room at the police station was too hot or too cold.

Detective Cage extended his hand, smiled, and gazed into her eyes. It generated enough heat to scorch the soles of her shoes.

A glance at Ivar's narrowed blue eyes sent cold shivers down her spine.

Avoiding the decision, she charged forward with the burning question that kept her awake most of the night. "Did you find Pops?"

"Not exactly," Ivar said.

Detective Cage frowned. "The bone we found at the scene was a female's ulna."

"How can that be? I was the only female in the store at the time, and I have all of my body parts."

Cage winked. He slowly scanned his gaze from her heeled shoes to her eyes. "That you do." His wolfish grin let her know that he'd eat her alive.

"Stop it!" Samantha felt her face flush.

"Was Pops seeing another woman?" Cage asked. "Maybe she hid when she saw you coming."

"No. Pops loves my mom. He'd never have an affair."

As the implication hit home, she stepped in front of the detective. Standing toe-to-toe, she glared at the man. "Don't you dare bring this up to Mother." Samantha poked her finger into his chest for emphasis. "She's already in ICU with a heart problem, and she doesn't need to worry about Pops' fidelity."

Cage looked down at her finger and smiled.

Outraged, she shoved him back with the palm of her hand. "There has to be another explanation." Samantha lowered her voice. "I just don't know what it is yet."

Ivar snickered under his breath but didn't make eye contact. "Colby, stop teasing. You know that bone was old. Let's start from the beginning. What do you remember from the time you entered the shop?"

Samantha cradled her cast in its sling and doubled over at the memory of Pops disappearing before her eyes.

Ivar reached for her and eased her into a chair. "Maybe this is too much, too soon." His hand rested possessively on her shoulder. "Would you like something to drink?"

"Water. Ice cold." Samantha's breath hitched, but she refused to cry.

Detective Cage pulled a chair next to hers as Ivar left the room. "I'm sorry for your loss."

Her fists clenched. "Will everyone stop saying that?" Samantha turned her face away from the detective. "Mom told me last night that Pops called her on her cell phone. Maybe he's alive. I'm not willing to say he's dead until I see *his* bones."

"This is difficult," Cage said. "My investigation hinges on the facts. You were the only one there who can give them to me. So you walked into the shop, and what did you see?"

Samantha bit the corner of her lip. "Pops cleaning the counter after Maddog left."

"Who is Maddog?"

"This guy who's had a crush on me for years. He won't leave me alone. He follows me everywhere."

Ivar entered the room with ice water and handed her the glass.

"Go on," Cage said.

Samantha gazed at the floor. "You'll think I'm crazy."

"I already know you're a little crazy. I love that about you." Ivar laughed off the tension. "You're going to mention the ghost, right?"

Samantha drank the whole glass of water and set it on the table. She decided to tell all and let the chips fall where they may. "His name is Tobias."

Cage glanced sidewise at Ivar, arched his eyebrows, and then turned back to stare at her. "What else?"

To her surprise, Detective Cage didn't laugh at her. Tapping a finger on her chin, Samantha slowly raised her head. "I smelled wood smoke…and something sweet."

The detective wrote down every word she said. "Sweet. That's a clue. The chief said the fire burst from the counter. Everything seemed to blow outward from that area. You mentioned a frayed cord or thread at the back of the middle stool. I wonder… "Do you have the chief's report from last night's meeting?"

Ivar stepped around the corner behind the desk and pulled out a manila folder.

Cage took the file. "Unfortunately, the blast damaged some of the evidence, but the bomb has traces of a professional hit. Our investigation shows there were two sources of fire, one at the counter and another along the ceiling. We used this scenario in the military."

Talking about the fire made Samantha more relaxed. Asking questions helped satisfy her curiosity. "How do they know there was a second source of fire in the ceiling?"

"The beam that fell on you had rounded edges," Cage said.

Samantha leaned forward. "And that means what?"

"The fire surrounded the beam," Cage explained. "The rounded edge was further from the flame, so the fire started from the alley side of the building. What color was the smoke?"

Samantha closed her eyes and relived the scene. "At first, it turned reddish-brown, then it burst into flames, and I flew out the door."

"Nitric acid or a byproduct of nitrates." Cage nodded as he read further. "Says here it was a rapid burn fire. The can of soda without the pull tab could have been an accelerant. A char pattern showed alligatoring and irregular blister marks on the beam that collapsed over the counter."

"What's alligatoring?" Samantha asked.

"Shiny patches on charred wood," Cage said. "The irregular marks usually mean splashing of an accelerant along the area."

"When can I go back to the shop?"

"Not until we complete our investigation." Cage flipped to the next page of the report. "Says the chief noted the gas was shut off."

"We haven't used gas for years," Samantha said. "Mom's scared of leaks since her father died of carbon monoxide poisoning. Could the fire have been an accident?"

A chorus of "No," echoed in unison.

"Why would someone blow up Pops' shop? We don't have any enemies."

"Good question," Ivar said. "Did Pops meet anyone new or change his routine in any way recently?"

Samantha thought for a moment. "I guess you need to ask Mom."

"Did he have any financial problems that you're aware of?" Ivar asked.

"He owed a bet to his best friend after losing a chess game to him the other night. I think it was ten bucks. That's big money for Pops." Samantha laughed, recalling his penny-pinching ways.

"Who's his best friend?" Cage asked.

"Amos Vickers, but he has plenty of money. Ten dollars means nothing to him. He knows he'll get paid. Seriously, I can't think of anyone who'd want to hurt Pops."

"How was his relationship with your mother?" Cage asked.

"They've been married for twenty-five years. I've never seen them have a major fight." Samantha frowned. "Wait. Did they only find one bone in the rubble?"

"So far, I believe that's true," Ivar said.

"That doesn't make any sense. If my father had a mistress with him," Samantha held up a hand, and cleared her throat, "that would make two people inside the building, so more bones should be present."

Ivar's cell phone rang. He glanced at the caller ID. "It's the fire chief. I'll take it outside. Hello. Officer Rexall."

Samantha hopped to her feet. "Did they find Pops?"

Ivar cocked his head toward Cage and darted for the hall. A creak echoed in the room as he opened and closed the door behind him.

Samantha dashed to catch up to Ivar.

"Wait!" Cage called after her. "If he wanted us to hear the conversation, he'd have stayed here to talk."

Samantha didn't hesitate. She flung the door open. It slammed after her. "Ivar!"

Peering up one side of the hall and then the other, Ivar had disappeared. "Dang it."

Mysterious Bones

Fire chief Martinelli stood outside the fountain shop's remains and barked orders to his team. "Did you call the medical examiner?"

A sketch artist peered up from his work. "ME's on her way."

"Did you finish the 3-D mockup?"

"Yup," the artist said. "Just flagging the landmarks and entering measurements."

"Roxy, did you get all the photos you need?" Martinelli asked.

Brushing a sleeve over the sweat on her brow, Roxy nodded. "Yeah, at least until we move the evidence. Not much left except bones. Fragmented ones at that."

"What do you expect when things are blown apart?" Martinelli asked.

Roxy shot a few more photos outside the building. "Where did they come from?"

"Must have been in the ceiling. We need more information to be certain."

"I'm glad I had the video camera running when the rear of the building collapsed," Roxy said. "However, with all that dust, I'm not sure how clear the images will be."

"At least the camera didn't get damaged during the crash."

A siren blasted and whined to a stop.

Ivar stepped out of his car and walked over to Chief Martinelli. "What's up? I had to abandon a meeting with Miss McFitzroy. She's going to fume for months."

"She didn't follow you, did she? We don't need any looky-loos right now," Martinelli said. "The scene's a mess, and it gets more interesting by the minute."

The passenger door opened, and Detective Cage joined the crowd. "No, we left her at the station."

Roxy tapped the chief on his shoulder and held out the digital camera. "See that guy in the gray windbreaker?"

Martinelli flipped open the LCD display, studied the screen, and glanced up. "Yeah, where is he?"

"Just crossed the street. He's by the corner bakery. I saw him here yesterday during the fire. One of the first to arrive at the scene. Got his photo on my 35-mm camera, too, so there's evidence if needed."

"Good job, Roxy. Keep an eye on him. Show that photo to Officer Rexall and the detective."

Ivar squinted at the display. "I can't see a thing. Too much light." He pulled the camera into the shade of a now brown, crispy maple tree. "Oh, I see what you mean. He caught my eye, too. Yesterday, he was dressed in a black hoodie, too hot for the weather."

Ivar passed the camera to the detective, then dropped his shades from the top of his head and crossed the street.

A white van with a medical examiner logo on the door pulled to the curb. A petite, raven-haired woman slid from the front seat. "What do we have, Chief Martinelli?"

"Bones." He liked Angela Claymen's quiet, no-nonsense manner of doing business. "More bones than make up two people. Maybe four or five bodies, but it's your specialty, not mine."

"Are they human or animal?" Angela asked.

"I'm sure they're human." The chief removed his hat and swiped at the soot caked along his creased forehead with a rag that hung from his belt. "Not a whole skeleton, but fragments; maybe you can put together a complete set." After wiping his hand on the rag, he lifted the tape for the ME to enter and replaced his hat.

"Not a pretty site." Angela fished in her pocket and shoved her narrow hands into a pair of latex gloves. "Did you get all the photos you need before we move the evidence?"

"I've taken videos and photos." Roxy mounted the video camera onto a tripod and bent down next to the sea of white bones floating among the dark soot. "I'll record everything as you pack them up. My assistant has another camera. He'll follow you to the van and shoot photos of the surrounding area."

Angela opened her ME box. "Let's get to work. I'll do most of my research back at the lab." Looking up at the chief, she added, "The dirt and ashes go, too, for forensics. Are you through here?"

Chief Martinelli nodded. "We'll add to the chalk lines as the ashes are removed."

"I heard Pops was in the store at the time of the explosion," Angela said. "I see only bone fragments. No blood, tissue, or organs…I think these have been around for a while. What about Pops?"

Martinelli scratched the day's growth on his chin. "We'll send a cadaver dog in to see if we found everything, but for now, take these to the lab."

"If all goes well, you'll have my preliminary report by the end of tomorrow. I don't know how long before I'll have the final results."

"Fine. I'll send some help to load the remains." Chief Martinelli motioned to Cage. "Take a look before we move anything. Where did Officer Rexall head off to?"

"I last saw Ivar crossing the street." Cage ducked under the tape. "I thought he planned to talk to the guy in the gray windbreaker, but I don't see either of them now."

Famished

Samantha found the ICU secretary at the front desk. "Where is Mrs. McFitzroy?"

The secretary typed on the computer keyboard and lifted her head. "She moved to telemetry. Room 210."

"Why wasn't I notified?"

Shrugging her shoulders, the secretary repeated, "You'll find her in 210. Sorry for the inconvenience." The ICU phone rang, and the secretary picked up the call.

Samantha's stomach grumbled. She hadn't eaten since... yesterday. Glancing at her watch, it was already 1:20. *Where did the morning go?* She trudged down the hall in search of her mother. After a tap on the closed door to room 210, she pushed inside.

"It's about time you got here," her mother said.

Samantha set a leather suitcase alongside a chair. "I brought you a few clothes."

"Thanks. I was afraid you took my car and left me here a prisoner."

"I love you, too, Mom." She bent over the raised bed and hugged the bright-faced woman.

"Did you bring my robe? Let's go to the cafeteria. I'm starving. All I've had is Jell-O and broth."

Samantha smiled. "I'm with you all the way, but can you leave this room? I mean, with that tele-unit on?"

Her mother hopped from the bed and grabbed the small suitcase. The latch snapped open with a click, and a pair of slippers dropped to the floor. Sliding her coral-painted toenails into the slippers, her mother yanked out a pink fleece robe. "Let's go."

"You surprise me. I thought you'd be more upset about Pops."

Mom shrugged. "Why should I be? I talked to him. I know he's alive."

Cage's comment about another woman flashed through Samantha's mind. Shoving it aside, she cleared her throat. "We don't know that for sure."

"I do, honey." Mom darted to the door and peeked around the corner. "All clear." Motioning for her to follow, Mom moved across the hall so fast that Samantha barely kept up.

The elevator dinged, and the doors slowly opened. "Comeon."

"You're acting as if you're making a mad escape."

Mom pulled her inside. "Makes it more fun that way?" She hit the button for the basement, and the doors slid closed.

As they entered the cafeteria, "Bridget McFitzroy, please return to your room," squawked through the overhead intercom.

"Busted!" Samantha laughed. "What do you want to eat? I'll bring it up to you."

A nurses' aide peeked into the cafeteria. "There you are. You can't leave the second floor. Your tele straight-lined, and everyone's looking for you."

"Oh, so now I'm wanted, dead or alive." Bridget leaned toward Samantha. "Make mine a cheeseburger with all the fixings."

"No, she can't have real food yet," the aide warned.

Bridget scowled.

"Best bring it in a doggy bag," the aide whispered to Samantha and winked. Turning back to her patient, she wrapped an arm around Bridget. "We'd better go back to the room."

"So not fair," Mom said before going without a fight.

"What'll you have?" the server behind the counter asked.

"Two cheeseburgers, one fries, one order of onion rings, a salad, and two cups of coffee." Samantha thought a moment. Not sure if her mom should have caffeine. "Make that one cup of coffee and a lemonade." She paid the bill. "Can you make that to go?"

"Sure thing." A cheerful food tech removed the items from the tray and stuffed them into a paper sack.

"Thanks." Samantha grabbed the bag, balanced the two drinks, one in each hand, and returned to her mother's room.

A nurse stood beside her mother's bed, frowning and giving a lecture about rules and regulations.

Mom nodded in compliance. She glanced at Samantha, eyed the bag, and shook her head.

When the nurse turned toward Samantha, Mom mouthed, "Hide the bag," then rolled her eyes and smiled broadly when the nurse returned her gaze.

"I hope you didn't bring her food from outside the hospital," the nurse said.

"Of course not," Samantha said honestly. *After all, it was from the hospital's cafeteria.* She crossed her fingers behind her back and dropped the bag onto the overbed table. "This is for me. I haven't eaten since yesterday, and I'm famished."

"All right then. I'll leave the two of you alone to chat." The nurse scurried to the door, turned, and gave one last glare at the bag. "Don't even—"

The doctor strode into the room. "I hear you've been venturing a bit today, Mrs. McFitzroy. How do you feel?"

"I'm fine. I'm hungry, and I want to go home."

"Maybe we can get you some solid food, but I'm afraid you'll need to spend another night. If you're free of any erratic heartbeats, we'll discharge you in the morning."

"Great! Bring on the food." Mom hesitated and smiled at the doctor.

Samantha handed her the lemonade. "We'll start slow and work our way up."

"Do you have any questions? No? Then I'll see you tomorrow." The doctor didn't hesitate and brushed past the nurse who stood in the doorway with her mouth agape.

"I'm glad he stopped by to chat, but I doubt he'd wait around if I really wanted to talk." Mom looked toward the door.

The nurse seemed glued to the floor.

"That will be all." Mom sipped her drink.

As soon as the nurse left, Mom grinned and broke into her cheeseburger. "Now, fill me in on your meeting this morning."

Samantha told her everything she knew, except the fact about one mysterious female bone. "Ivar had to leave, so I came to see you." *Sometimes, I think he's avoiding me.* Pulling her cell phone from her pocket, she called Ivar.

"Sam. You okay?" He seemed out of breath.

"Yeah."

"Good. I can't talk," Ivar whispered. The line went dead.

He is avoiding me. Why?

Windbreaker

Ivar crossed the street and followed the nimble man in his mid-thirties. "Sir, I'd like to have a word with you."

The man leaned over to tie his shoe. "Don't have anything to say." When he stood, the hood of his gray windbreaker dropped back to reveal a faded, purple baseball cap pulled low over his eyes. Beneath the Rocky's logo was the signature of the famed Gold Glove winner, Larry Walker.

"You're a witness to the fire at the fountain shop." Ivar closed the distance. "I saw you in the crowd yesterday."

"I don't know how it started."

Ivar held up his hand. "You're not a suspect."

"Good, then catch me later." The man spun around and sprinted down a narrow alley. A cry escaped his lips as he tripped over a trashcan, knocking it over. The knee of his dust-covered khaki trousers blossomed with a patch of bright red. Muttering under his breath, he ran with a limp.

"I just want to ask you a few questions," Ivar called after him.

The man twisted through a cedar fence behind the post office.

Ivar's phone rang. *Sam's ringtone. What's she up to now? Is she in trouble?* Torn between pursuing a potential suspect or protecting Sam, he answered. "You okay?…I can't talk." Ivar hung up. *Where the hell did he go?*

Running footsteps crunched on the other side of the fence. Ivar rushed through the narrow opening and snagged his pants on a nail. "Colby, follow that man." He glanced back across the park. The detective was nowhere in sight. "Where's Colby? I need him."

By the time Ivar tore free, the guy was at least two blocks ahead of him.

Ivar ran after the man. "Stop, police." Barely ten minutes of hot pursuit, he had dodged oncoming traffic, jumped over another fence, and weaved through thick patches of wild roses then lost the man in the windbreaker, who disappeared in the woods behind the cemetery. "Dang, I'm out of shape."

Panting, Ivar slumped over with his hands on his knees trying to take deep breaths. Sweat dripped from his brow and stung his eyes. His legs throbbed, and his arms stung where the thorns had caught his skin.

Detective Cage ambled across the park towards Ivar. "Why did he run?"

"Wish I knew," Ivar said. "Where were you? I needed backup."

"Fire Chief Martinelli's looking for you. The ME arrived, and they're packing up the bones as we speak."

"Good." Ivar gave a shudder. "At least you covered that in my absence. What did you find out?"

"I didn't see any evidence of Pops," Detective Cage said. "I'm sure there's a trace of him somewhere in that building."

"Disintegrated, I presume, but for Sam's sake, I'll keep looking." Ivar unwrapped a stick of gum, popped it into his mouth, and offered one to Cage.

"No, thanks." Officer Cage straightened to his full height. "I need to ask. Are you dating Samantha?"

"Not during the investigation," Ivar said. "It wouldn't be professional."

"I see. Then she's fair game?"

Ivar's fists clenched but he didn't answer. "There must be a reason the shop was destroyed."

"Right. Back to business." Cage patted him on the back. "Maybe it has something to do with the bones. I'd say they've been hidden away for decades."

Ivar nodded. "If anyone can discover their identity, Ms. Claymen can. She's the best ME I've ever worked with."

"I'm sure we'll track down the arsonist, but those bones are old. Where will you start?"

Ivar sighed. "I'll pull a list of missing persons' files and see if we hit a match."

Curious

Detective Colby Cage walked along the alley, scanning the destruction of Pops' burned-out soda shop. The cause of the explosion was still unknown, but he searched for any pattern recognition for more insight into the bomb.

Samantha McFitzroy stood outside the crime scene tape next to the alley studying the ruins when she spied Cage. "I guess I'm not the only one who can't sleep tonight."

Cage turned and honed in on the musical tone of an angel's voice drifting on a gentle breeze. "Is that you, Samantha?" Thick red hair graced her shoulders. *A man could tangle his hands in those silky locks.*

Samantha walked closer. "Are you looking for something special? You've been out here pacing for a while."

He smiled. *She's been watching me.* "I came back to review the damage. My thoughts are clearer when I'm alone. It's easier to imagine witnesses and relive the scene from their perspective. Each angle gives me more insight."

"You and Ivar left in a hurry this morning," Samantha said. "What did you find? Bones of a whole woman, so you can accuse Pops of an affair. I don't like being left out in the cold when it involves my family."

The tinge of anger stung Cage, but it was the truth. "Please accept my regrets for leaving in such a hurry. I didn't thank you for explaining what happened, especially since you doubted that I'd believe in your ghost." *Which I do doubt.* "Is he related to you?"

Her brown eyes glinted with flecks of gold as she stepped into the lit street. They held a hypnotic gaze. "You believed me?"

"More like you enchanted me." Detective Cage gave her his brightest grin. "You're lovely when you tamp back your anger. Was the ire aimed at Ivar or me?"

"Both." Samantha crossed her left arm under her right to support the cast and winced.

"I duly apologize." He pressed a hand across his abdomen and made a deep bow. "I wish you'd forgive me."

With a laugh light as a butterfly's wing, Samantha said, "I may grant you that wish, Detective Cage."

"That's most kind of you. I prefer Colby. It's less formal, and that's what my friends call me."

"Very well, Colby."

"May I bounce some ideas off you? I need an expert's advice about the workings of a fountain shop."

Samantha leapt the few feet between them and grabbed his arm. "I thought you'd never ask. Can I go beyond the tape? I'll point to where everything was located. I'll even reenact the last few minutes before the explosion."

"The fire marshal hasn't released the crime scene. Can we draw it out on paper?"

"I suppose so," Samantha hesitated. "I see the rest of the ceiling along that back wall collapsed since yesterday."

"That happened early this morning. It's why we ran out on you. You're right about finding more bones."

"Did you find…Pops?" Tears welled into the corner of her eyes. "I know, deep down, he couldn't have survived that blast. It blew up in his face but without his bones…well, I hoped Mom's phone call was real."

A sob broke a dam of tears, which flooded down her cheeks. She turned away and darted to her car. "Pops. Why Pops?" The keys fumbled from her fingers and fell to the ground as she tried to unlock the door.

Colby scooped them up and wrapped Samantha in his arms. "It's all right. How about some coffee, and we can talk."

"He was a remarkable man," Samantha blubbered through racking sobs. "I always called him Pops, but he was my dad."

Cage held Samantha close as her body wrenched with grief. He took out a tissue and brushed at her tears.

It took a few minutes before Samantha lifted her head from his shoulder. "Thanks, I feel a lot better." She glanced at his sleeve. "Sorry. I got your shirt wet."

"It'll dry." He didn't want to let her go, but he released her shoulders, ran his hand down her arm, and clasped the fingers of her left hand.

Composed once again, Samantha walked down the street hand in hand. "There's not much open in town at this hour."

"I have a thermos of coffee and a couple of disposable cups in my car. We can pick them up with my drawing kit and sit on a park bench if that suits you."

Samantha moved closer. "Yes, I'd like that."

"Try to relive the important details, second by second," Colby said.

They sipped coffee, and she told him everything about the explosion in great detail. She answered his questions, drew a diagram of the shop, and added where the dud soda can rolled from the counter. She described the flames and her blowing through the door, and then bolted upright, nearly spilling her coffee. "That's it. The ghost!"

"What about the ghost?" Colby asked.

"He was there. I know because Pops lifted into the air. I thought the explosion caused it, but it was too soon. You know, when everything breaks down into slow motion. That's how I just saw it. A split-second before everything erupted, Pops flew into the air and dissolved. Vanished. Gone."

Cage nodded. "Keep talking."

Samantha's eyes widened. "Then I heard, 'Bam!'" Her arms gestured. "The building shook. Glass shattered, and a blast of cold air carried me through the door."

"So, how do you know the ghost was there?"

Samantha turned abruptly. "You were there, weren't you?"

Colby got up, lifted his arm to place it on her shoulder, and paused. "Who are you talking to?"

"What happened to Pops?" Samantha demanded.

"Are you talking to that tree?" Colby asked.

"No. I'm talking to Tobias. Can't you see him? He's that mist in front of the tree."

"I don't believe in ghosts."

"Why can't you tell me? What secret?" Samantha raised her fist, ranted, and paced. "You can't keep Pops a secret! I want to know the truth. Who blew up the shop?" She turned and placed her hands on her hips. "Tobias, secrets can be dangerous."

"What secret?" Colby asked.

"Wait! Don't fade away. Show me what happened."

"What happened?" Colby peered around her. "There's no one."

"Please, what did you see?" Samantha sounded desperate.

Confused, Colby moved in front of her face, locked eyes, and frowned. "All right. We'll play it your way. Did Tobias see who set off the bomb?"

Samantha backed away and turned, demanding, "Where's Pops?"

"Pops is missing," Colby said under his breath.

Samantha continued to rant at the tree. "Wait? No. I can't wait. I want to know now!" She paused. "Fine. I'll do it your way." Samantha took another step back and bumped into Colby. "Excuse me. I have to go."

He grabbed her shoulders. "What's going on?" Colby didn't really expect an answer, but she validated his concern.

"That GHOST just admitted to a secret. I think he knows more about Pops. I need to find out what it is." Samantha moved away.

Colby reached for her. "Stay and talk to me!"

She shook her head, "I can't." In her haste to leave, she caught her ankle on the edge of the bench and nearly tripped.

Colby caught her.

"I'd love to chat, but I really have to go." Samantha moved around him.

"It's been a pleasure getting to know you, Miss McFitzroy."

"Call me Samantha."

"Yes, well then, stay safe until we meet again."

"That's his line. And I plan to meet him soon." She dashed from the park.

"No wonder Ivar enjoys your company." Watching her flee, his thoughts were no longer on the case. *You're one mysterious woman Samantha McFitzroy—intelligent, witty, and a bit, hmm, crazy. But I'd listen to whatever you have to say, even if I can't believe it. I love a challenge.*

Columbian Drug War

Santiago Castrini heard his wife call him for dinner, but he had a paper to publish. He finished setting the type and loaded the printer.

His wife stood in the doorway, tapping her foot. "Come and eat now, or there'll be no dinner."

"I'm on my way." Santiago joined his five sons and their families at the table and gave the blessing. Within minutes, he'd gobbled his food and excused himself.

"What? No dessert?" His wife called after him. "You're too skinny already."

He didn't bother to respond. Excited to return to work, he opened the door to his secret pressroom at the back of the house. Hunching his shoulders, he ducked through the door and set to work.

His ink-stained fingers pulled the first copy of the July 12th, 2023 Watch on War newspaper from the press. Sliding his bifocals from the end of his nose, he read the bold headline, 'Drug War Escalates.' "Ah, perfecto."

The war had been extremely violent these past two weeks. Two drug lords fought for dominance to overtake the cocaine market. Neither side bought off the police. They simply made them disappear.

Dedicated to his job, Santiago went the extra mile for a story. Today's news quoted two mothers who told their horrific experiences.

The first described, "My son worked for the Boss. An hour ago, a military truck pulled up to the house. A young lad entered and shot my son between the eyes. Then he turned the gun on the rest of my family. I was the only one to survive."

Santiago nearly lost his life getting the other woman's story. He wrote, "We're hiding in a bullet-riddled house that lies abandoned near a savannah at the edge of a small village in Columbia."

The woman wept. "I'm in the middle of a drug raid. Most of the people have fled. Although I see no one, I know the army watches and waits for any movement. More than thirty men have died. Their lifeless bodies rot along the roadside. Skeletons of burned-out trucks clutter the town. My son lies with the dead."

Santiago recalled that he bolted for the door once he got his story. Automatic rifles spat out bullets. A three-starred general cornered Santiago at the side of the building. Military medals graced the officer's uniform. An engraved nametag read Gonzales.

Knowing he was about to die, Santiago ducked around the bombed-out building and ran for the woods.

A single shot rang out. He dove to the ground and saw the old woman had thrown herself in the bullet's path to spare his life.

It took the rest of the day to weave his way through the woods back to the main road and home.

The door to his office opened. Santiago's eldest son, Diego, strode into the room and glanced over his shoulder. "Not again. Every time you write one of those articles, you get a death threat. Why do you put our family in danger like this?"

"I must expose those bastards. Besides, I owe it to the old woman." Santiago folded the paper and started the press run.

Diego dug through his pockets, found a cigar, and bit off the end. "I worry about you. My bodyguards might not be able to protect you this time." He took out a book of matches.

Santiago grabbed his son's treasured cigar. "Don't smoke in here. Take it outside."

"Fine." Diego snatched his cigar. He stomped to the backroom and slammed the door as he left the building.

The noise of the printing press grew louder as it ramped up the speed. He barely heard the telephone ring from the other side of the room.

Santiago stepped away from the press to answer it. "Hola."

"Diego, this is the Captain. Get out. Get out now. Boss is on his way." The line went dead.

"Who is this?" Santiago asked, but he got no answer. He slammed down the receiver. "I pushed it too far this time." He flung open the secret door to warn his family and was startled.

An AK-47 pointed at his chest. Gunfire and screams came from inside the house. The man threw something metal into the room and slammed the door.

It hardly registered with Santiago before the whole building rocked. The extreme pressure of the bomb blew him against the press. Darkness overtook him.

Am I Related?

Samantha fidgeted as she sat outside Angela Claymen's office. The ME promised to review the details of her investigation to date. It had been ten days since the examiner had collected every bone fragment from the fountain shop.

"Nervous?" Ivar asked, scooting his chair closer.

Stifling a yawn, Samantha nodded. "And tired. This gives me nightmares. Pops is missing. I have to know where he is."

Ivar's voice dropped to a whisper. "What do you mean, where he is?"

"I know people die at any age, young or old. I've heard of heaven, hell, and even purgatory. Then there's being in limbo."

Rolling his eyes, he said, "Like your ghost?"

"Exactly. I've talked to Tobias, but he refuses to tell me about Pops."

A cold breeze lifted the hair from her neck. Tobias?

Samantha clenched her fist and punched it skyward. "If Pop's not dead, you can't take him. I won't let you!"

Ivar leaned toward her.

No mist formed, so maybe it wasn't the ghost. Lowering her voice, she added, "If he's dead...he should be in heaven. I don't want Pops to linger forever on Earth and be unhappy."

"We'll know soon." Ivar reached to take her hand.

She pulled away. "I don't want you to feel sorry for me."

"I won't!" His jaw tightened, and he scooted away.

"Don't get huffy." Samantha snapped, then softened and blew out a sigh. "Mom's not taking it well either. No more before dinner chitchats. She doesn't want to talk about anything. It's been rough on her."

"I'm sorry," Ivar said. "Does she still think she spoke to Pops on her cell?"

"Absolutely swears by it," Samantha said. "Even after the doctor said it was probably a hallucination from her near-death experience."

"Pops never called or contacted either of you since?"

"Like that's going to happen." Samantha shrugged and covered her face. "He just vanished! I already told you that."

"Yet, a part of you must think he's dead. You did furnish a sample of his hair for DNA," Ivar reminded her.

"I'm so confused. I hope today settles everything. If he died, there must be at least one bone in the lot that belongs to him."

"Good morning." Angela strode into the lobby. "Let's go into the lab. I have something of interest to show you." Turning on her heel, she paused to hold the door open.

Ivar took the lead and headed down the hall.

"Thank you for seeing me," Samantha said. "I know it's unusual to meet directly with the family."

"On the contrary," Angela laid a hand on her shoulder as she walked through the door. "I prefer it."

They turned left and entered an anteroom at the end of a long hall. "There's a gown for each of you hanging on a peg." Angela donned a coat. "It's rather chilly in the lab."

The door slid open with a sucking sound. Samantha crossed her arms and gazed at the bones, now assembled neatly.

"Are all of these from Pops' shop?" Samantha stepped closer for a look.

"That's right," Angela said. Five tables had skeletal remains.

Three skeletons were much smaller, probably children.

"There were five bodies in the ceiling of the shop? How long have they been there?" Samantha turned toward Angela.

"We're still trying to answer that question, but for as long as your father owned the building," Angela said. "Probably put up in the ceiling back when it was a saloon."

"That's amazing. Which one is Pops?"

A frown crept over Angela's smooth face. "That's part of the mystery. After sorting out the puzzle of each skeleton," Angela said, "All these are female bones."

"Female?" Samantha couldn't believe her ears. "Then where's Pops?"

"I don't know quite how to say this, but the DNA sample you gave me has many exemplars in common with this female." Angela motioned with her hand to a skeleton on the middle table.

Samantha frowned. "Meaning?"

"Pops is related to this female."

"That can't be accurate." Samantha ran her eyes up each bone methodically placed from the large toe to the skull. One rib bone on the left side lay in three pieces.

Narrowing her eyes, Samantha said, "I can't believe that. With the explosion, this specimen has no soft tissue or fingerprints, and dental records probably are unavailable." Staring at the narrow-cheeked skull, she ran her fingers over her own cheekbones.

Angela picked up a file from the end of the table where the skeleton lay. "Everything you said is true. Traditional methods for forensic ID didn't help in this case because the DNA of burned bone becomes degraded."

"So you're not really sure that her DNA is a familial match to Pops." Samantha's hand hovered over the fractured rib.

"Actually, I'm 99% certain she's related," Angela said. "Since you are Pops' daughter, I'm sure she is also related to you."

Samantha frowned and backed away.

Angela continued. "I used short tandem repeat markers or STR, as we call them in the field, using sensitive and highly reliable fluorescent technology."

"I'm not sure I understand," Samantha said. "Can you clarify?"

"All humans inherit half of their genome from their biological mother and half from their father. So there are two copies of each gene in our genome."

"I learned that in biology," Ivar said.

Samantha rolled her eyes.

"Using this data, we can match parent and child, or even other relatives such as grandparents, cousins, etc. That's simplifying my explanation, but this skeleton is related to Pops."

"I wonder who she is," Samantha said. "She's tiny."

"She might be your cousin." Angela continued. "Based on the length of the femur, she stood around 4 feet, 2 inches."

"How old was she?" Samantha fingered her cheekbone again, imagining how the girl might look.

"I'd say mid-teens. Her wisdom teeth haven't erupted."

"I wish I'd asked Pops more about his family when I had a chance," Samantha said. "Does Detective Cage know about your findings?"

Ivar glanced toward Samantha and then at Angela. "I'm sure you'll send him all the details."

"I emailed my results to you earlier this morning and copied him at the same time. You'll have them by the time you return to the office."

"Thanks for the information." Samantha shook Angela's hand.

Again, a cold blast of air brushed past Samantha as she left the building. A warning flashed through her mind. Has Tobias just learned about a long-departed relative?

"What do you think, Sam?" Ivar asked.

"Think about what?"

"You haven't listened to anything I said. Thinking about Colby again?"

"Why would you say that?" Samantha squinted into the sunlight. *I wonder if Tobias is here.*

"I keep hearing how Colby asked your opinion on the fire. Now I ask if you want to have coffee to go over some issues, and you ignore me."

"Why Ivar, I think you're jealous." Samantha laughed and smoothed a stray black lock of hair from his forehead. "Ivar, I adore you."

His grin widened. He wrapped an arm around her waist and led her down the steps to his car. "Let's get that coffee." He opened the passenger door.

Turning, she skimmed her finger over the dent in his chin. "Sounds wonderful." She felt cold without his arm wrapped around her. With one foot in the car, she paused and scanned the area. A shiver went up her spine, but no mist formed. "Did you feel a draft float by?"

Twin in Town

Wendell Gordon flew to Denver International Airport for the second time in two weeks. The last time he arrived in town, he rented a Toyota pickup and was on his way for a surprise visit with his twin brother, Gary. Then that old lady having a heart attack nearly ran him off the road outside Fort Collins. Fortunately, he'd dyed his hair, grown a goatee, and worn his Kevlar vest, which plumped him up a bit, so she didn't recognize him. No doubt she'd seen his gun as he left her at the side of the road. Because of her, his plans changed. He didn't meet with his brother and left for Reno that afternoon. *That's the last time I'll be a Good Samaritan.*

This time he wised up and used an alias. He spied the airport phone and dialed. "Hey, Gary. How are you?"

"What? No collect call?" Gary sounded miffed. "When did you get out of jail? I didn't expect to hear from you for another two years."

"Yeah, bro. I got out on good behavior. Heard the old man kicked the bucket while I was in the slammer and wondered if you took that cache of silver for yourself while I was under lock and key."

"What are you talking about?" Gary asked. "You don't really believe that treasure is still around, do you?"

"Yeah, I do." Wendell tucked the receiver under his chin and glanced around the airport. "Now, all we need is the map to the mine. How about driving to Denver to get me? We can make plans on the way back to your apartment. You still living on the king's estate?"

"Wendell, don't make waves. I like my job. Amos is an okay fellow to work for. He pays well, and the perks aren't bad, either. I get to travel all over the world."

"Come to Denver and pick me up in one of his classy cars," Wendell said. "I'm sure Amos won't mind if you take a few hours to greet your bro."

"Can't today. I have to drive the boss to town for his charity celebration."

"Is that today? You'll have plenty of time to dash over and get me while he's at the event. What do you do all evening anyway? Get drunk and have a filly in the back seat of one of his convertibles?"

"No, Wendell. That's what you'd do. I'm a respected member of his extended family. No way will I let you dip your fingers in his pie."

"Oh, come on, Gary. I've grown up since our college days. How about I grab a cab and meet you downtown at the Sheridan? That's where the event's held, isn't it?"

"No. It's at the Denver Tech Center," Gary said. "I don't want the boss to see you. We look too much alike, and I know the games you love to play. Find someone else to pester."

"I'm only looking out for our share of the silver. Find the map to the mine. Since you won't pick me up at DIA, I'll be at your place first thing in the morning." Wendell hung up.

"Damn fool," Wendell muttered as he went down the escalator to catch the train to baggage claim. *We're supposed to share that silver. After all, Pa worked hard to smuggle it away from his pompous boss, Fang Parker. However, if something happened to Gary, I could have it all.*

Wendell stepped onto the train. He nudged his way to the seat and ignored everyone around him. *Who needs him? There's a score to settle. I wouldn't be in the slammer if Gary had taken the fall as planned. Why'd I ever trust him? After all, we even argued over marbles as kids, squabbled during high school, and stole each other's girlfriends. We fought over everything. I always had and probably always will.* "I'm better off without him."

"Who are you talking to?" a young lad asked as the train stopped at the A-concourse.

"Huh?" Wendell glanced up at the smiling boy. "Buzz off."

The lad backed away and grabbed his mother's hand.

The train stopped at baggage claim. The doors opened, and everyone filed out.

Must be a great job. I could be a chauffeur for the world's charity king, the prestigious Amos Vickers. It'll be easy to step into Gary's shoes. I've done it dozens of times before.

Wendell headed for Carousal 12, found his luggage, and went outside to flag down a taxi. "Denver Tech Center."

Spurs Jackson

"Tobias, I want to see my family." Sequestered sixteen days in an abandoned railroad depot was too much. Used to a king-sized bed, Pops tossed and turned on his small cot. His stomach growled. *I'll puke if I have to eat canned tuna and baked beans another day.*

Pops had spent hours on the Aethernet to find something to connect Fang with Tobias's daughter, Sara. The computer frequently needed rebooting, but he finally discovered a small, obscure memoir. "Hey, Tobias, listen to this story."

When he got no answer from the ghost, he got up and padded to the waiting room. The wooden bench had become his spare office. Copies of notes he'd printed on the back pages of old waybills he'd found stuffed in a drawer littered the workspace. The old forms had originally been used to help route each railcar from its point of origin to its destination. Today, the forms help route an old misplaced story to a great discovery that could link his fountain shop to an old saloon. Pops had written down nearly half the story but it was taking forever, so he decided to just read the memoir directly from the computer screen. "Tobias, where are you? This is important."

It took a while, but a lighter-than-usual mist filtered through the ceiling. "Whew, I made it. What did you find?"

"What took you so long?" Pops asked.

"I was resting. What do you have?" The mist's whisper was barely audible.

Pops wiped away sweat dripping down his face. "I've worked hard, but I think I found a piece of what you've been looking for. Agnes Jackson Parker gave this memoir to her son on her deathbed."

"I can't read it from here. What does it say?"

Pops pulled the computer closer. "Well, here's her story:

"Old Spurs Jackson hit a mother lode. We packed up the family and headed to Denver to quick claim his deed. Silver lined his pockets and weighed down the wagon under a false floor, making it a heavy pull for our two mules.

"I, too, was heavily laden. Due to deliver within the week, I lay on a quilt atop the treasure. Our three children sang as we rode along.

"As Spurs crossed a bridge and wound around the mountain trail, one of the rear wheels wobbled. He managed to take it slow the last mile. When we reached a knoll above a small town, Spurs pulled off the road to tighten the wheel.

"I crawled from the wagon with our girls in tow, and we went into the woods nearby to comfort ourselves. My back ached, and I had terrible cramps, so I sent the girls to be with their father. The cramps grew worse. I sat under a tree to wait. Not wanting my children to see my pain, I moved further into the woods, squatted, and gave birth to our son. To my horror, when I returned to the wagon with our newborn baby, I found our girls murdered— scalped by savages.

"Not far away, two other girls lay dead. Arrows pierced their chests. The mules were gone, and the wagon was on fire with all our belongings in flames.

"A young man galloped toward the wagon, dismounted, and ran to one of the other girls I didn't know. He knelt beside her and screamed, 'No! Jenny.' The man held her and rocked her body in his arms. 'What have they done to you?' Glancing up, he saw me. 'Who did this?'

"I don't think I answered, but he laid the girl's body on the ground and backed away.

"'Oh, her pa will kill me when he finds out. I should never have planned to run away and marry her.' He gasped when he heard my baby cry. 'Ma'am, do you know what happened?'

"I panicked and ran to the woods, calling, 'Spurs, where are you?' A large bird flew overhead, and I looked up. Spurs' lifeless body hung above me. I screamed. 'My children, my husband, everything is gone. My newborn baby has no father.'

"Deep concern creased around the man's eyes. 'Your child was just born? This is terrible. What's your name?' He came closer when I didn't answer and gently whispered, 'They call me Fang.'

"I must have recoiled at his name.

"'Don't be afraid. It's not fang like a wolf's tooth. It's a Scottish name for a shepherd. Come on. We have to get out of here.'

"'No.' I refused to budge. 'I can't leave my family like this.'

"'I'll help you if I can, but they've massacred your husband and children, my fiancée, and her friend. We have to go. They might return.'

"'Why would anyone do all this for a little silver?' I asked.

"'Did you say silver?' Fang hesitated. 'I don't think it was done for silver. I heard the government forced the Indians from their land. It appears they're taking revenge on anyone who gets in their way. They probably only wanted the mules.'

"'You can have the silver. But promise me that you'll cut down my husband. You must bury my family before the vultures pick the flesh from their bones.'

"'How much silver? No, that doesn't matter. We must get out of here.'

"I felt myself sway in the heat. 'I won't leave.'

"Fang must have seen me ready to collapse. He grabbed my elbow and led me into a thicket of trees. Overturning a stump, he patted the top. 'Sit down in the shade. Stay out of sight and care for your babe.' He handed me his bandana. 'For the infant. I'll be back.'

"Fang rode away and returned shortly with a horse hitched to a wagon. A shovel lay in the back. He cut down Spurs and spent over an hour digging a shallow hole, barely deep enough so animals wouldn't dig him up. 'It's too dangerous to dig graves for everyone,' he said, laying the girls' bodies in the fire.

"'No.' I wept bitterly for my family, but I didn't have enough energy to stop him. Later, I realized it was for the best.

"'Now, we must go!' Fang was persistent.

"I couldn't think and still refused to budge. 'Please, don't leave their bones to be eaten by wolves.'

"Fang sighed. 'I'll think of something, but if you don't come with me, I'll take the baby and throw you over my shoulder. We can't stay here any longer.'

"I realized I should be grateful. 'Thank you, for burying Spurs. As promised, I'll share my secret. There's a silver treasure hidden in that old wagon's hulk. If you're able to save it, you can keep it. In return, please care for my infant.' I placed my son in his arms and collapsed."

"Fang described what happened next."

"After Mrs. Jackson fainted, I loaded her into my wagon, held the child in my lap, and drove to my sister Marion's home for help. A few hours later, I returned to the burned-out wagon, dug through the ashes, and retrieved what I could.

"I didn't dare let Jenny's pa know what happened to her, and realizing my good fortune, I did not want to draw attention to the area. I gathered the burned bones and placed them in a blanket. As I grabbed my shovel, I saw movement from the corner of my eye. Afraid the savages had returned, I snatched the bundled blanket, threw it in the back of the wagon, and took off.

"Being a coward didn't bother me, but I couldn't lie to Mrs. Jackson. I'd have to bury the bones later. For now, I knew the perfect hiding place and raced to Father's saloon. When the coast was clear, I darted upstairs and lifted the floorboards of the old closet. I stuffed the blanket between the rafters and slid the boards back in place.

"When I returned to Marion's, I loaded the baby and Mrs. Jackson into the wagon. We continued the trek to Denver to claim the deed. Three months later, I married Agnes and raised little Spurs Fang as my own son."

***

"Wait," Pops glanced toward the mist. "Is Fang referring to my building? It used to be a saloon. Were those bones in the rafters of my Fountain Shop?"

"Maybe." Then Tobias wheezed a puff of mist over the screen. "Well, I'll be. I reckon Fang had nothing to do with old Jack Slade after all. He got his money, honestly. He sure dropped his love for Jenny when he heard about the money, though."

"I didn't see any mention of your daughter in the old woman's story."

"Sara was Jenny's best friend. I'm not sure if she was with her, but I haven't been able to find her since that day. I wonder…" The light mist seemed to whistle. "Wait. Fang took the widow to his sister's home. Her name was Marion Parker."

"Do you know her?" Pops asked.

"She married my son, Jacob. You remember your Aunt Marion, don't you?"

Pops frowned. "Did she live in Leadville?"

"Yes. For years, she took care of her elderly brother."

"If Fang died in 1909, I wasn't even born yet." Pops scratched his chin. "Was that Fang?"

"Yup. It's the map!" Tobias hesitated. "That has to be it. Someone's looking for the map to the silver mine. I should have known." Papers fluttered from the bench in the waiting room. "Do you still have my wife's diary?"

"What's that got to do with anything?" Pops frowned.

The room's temperature dropped.

Pops shivered and shook his head. "I haven't seen it in years. Dad kept it at the shop. Then, when he died, I took it home. Why?"

"Someone wants it, or maybe they want it destroyed."

"Why would anyone want an old diary destroyed?" Pops asked.

"Not the diary. The map tucked inside. The one of Fang's mine. This gives me an idea." The gust of cold air rushed through the ceiling and disappeared.

Pops called out in frustration, "Gramps? When can I go back home? Tobias? TOBIAS!"

When there was no answer, Pops shouted, "I'm not sticking around another minute." He grabbed his laptop and stormed out of the old depot.

PI Max Wright

At four o'clock on a cloudless afternoon, a retired FBI Agent, Max Wright drove along I-25 toward Fort Collins in pursuit of Wendell Gordon. Now a private investigator, Wright tracked the scum bag from Reno to Denver, and then lost his prey at the airport. Nothing short of death would stop him from avenging the murder of his godson and the only child of his former partner, Jump Sweeny. The son died of a shanking incident in Folsom Prison nine months ago while tending to the inmates.

Wendell was Sweeney's number one suspect, but the law refused to charge him with the crime. Instead, they freed the son-of-a-bitch even though he had a juvenile rap sheet as long as his arm. Wendell's crimes included auto theft, B&E, and malicious wounding of a high school student. None of those crimes counted once he became an adult. The hard-nosed, streetwise college dropout helped himself to whatever he laid his hands on. The kid hadn't been out of jail for a month and was already smuggling drugs.

Wright recalled his partner's plea for help. "Damn it. You'd think I could hunt down my own son's killer, but no. Some schmuck has dibs on my life. I'm strapped with an international drug case. Some drug lords had smuggled millions of dollars of cocaine over the U.S. border. Can you do this for me, Max? He's your godson. I owe you."

Max's bloodhound instincts led him north, following his nose to Wendell's twin.

A red convertible shot across the highway.

"Holy shit!" Max slammed on his brakes and laid on the horn. His ticker jolted, missed a beat, and then thumped wildly in his chest. "Wendell, you asshole."

The vehicle missed his fender by a hair and sped ahead at an alarming speed.

Out of habit, Max reached for the lights and siren, then remembered this was a lousy rental with nothing of value. He stepped on the gas and chased after the jerk. "Wonder where he got that car. It's a beauty. But it's in the hands of a beast."

Max's car almost ate the license plate 'CHAR8T-1' as Wendell slammed on his brakes.

The convertible nearly spun out of control as it veered right onto an exit.

The rental couldn't make the turn. Gravel spit against the passenger side as Max skidded onto the shoulder and made an illegal U-turn. He took the exit, rounded a bend onto a dirt road, and followed a cloud of dust.

Grit billowed up onto Max's windshield.

Wendell ran the stop sign at the end of the gravel road. The car swerved and then straightened onto a paved one-way-only bridge.

A motorcycle was halfway across the bridge and coming toward them.

The car's brake lights flashed. Wendell pulled to the right.

The motorcycle dodged away from the convertible but remained upright. The driver slowed and hopped from his bike before he hit the railing.

Max came to a halt. "You all right?"

"Damn tourists." The driver pushed his cycle to the end of the bridge and took off.

The convertible disappeared. Max wasn't too worried. *How far can a red car go in this small town?*

Max drove down Main Street, took a right at the church, and caught sight of the car out of the corner of his eye. It headed down an alley.

Lights flickered as a garage door opened behind a two-story building.

By the time Max caught up, Wendell had already driven the car inside, and the door closed behind the vehicle. *I have him now.*

Max parked and walked through the front door. A doctor's clinic was on the right, and a dental office was on the left.

A man in overalls looked up from mopping the hall floor. "Sorry, they closed at five. You'll have to wait until morning."

"What's upstairs?" Max asked.

"X-ray. Both offices share the equipment, but it's locked up, too."

"What about downstairs?"

"Storage," the janitor said. "Excuse me, but you're standing in my way. I want to get home in time for dinner."

Max peered through the glass window of the clinic.

"As I said, come back in the morning unless this is an emergency. Is it?"

Max turned to stare at the man. "Is it what?"

"Do you need a doc?" The janitor pulled a set of keys from his pocket. "I can use the office phone to call my sister. She's their nurse."

"No. Thanks. I need to get to the building's garage."

"No direct access from the hallway," the janitor said. "I think they reach it from their offices but I don't have those keys."

"Okay." Max went back outside and heard the door lock behind him.

The janitor stood inside the door and waved. "I'm leaving now."

Max glanced at his watch. *Five-forty.* He scanned the neighborhood for potential hazards. The area seemed quiet. No streetlights lit the alley. He used a flashlight from his key ring and headed around to the back of the building.

He checked the garage door and found it locked. A heavy-duty wooden door at the right of the building was also locked—no windows from this side. Weeds poked through cracks in the cement step. A broken liquor bottle lay on the ground. *This entrance isn't used much.*

He dug through a pocket of his baggy jeans and came up with a lock pick—no time like the present.

It took only a few seconds before the door unlocked with a gentle click. Max checked the area once again before opening the door.

Darkness met his eyes. It smelled like an old library—musty, cold, and damp.

Max slipped inside and closed the door. He paused to listen. Something scampered off to his left. Rats? This part of his job made his skin crawl.

He shuddered, put his hand over the small flashlight, and then flicked it on. The rays filtered through his fingers and lit up a wall in front of him. He moved to the left and stood at the head of narrow wooden stairs.

A rustling sound came from below.

Max pulled out his pistol, turned off the light, and felt for the railing as he descended one step at a time. He gently lowered his weight on each step to avoid creaking. A handful of cobwebs made him flinch and shake his wrist.

A faint light shone to his right. He could see the bottom three steps in the shadows. Several shelves lined the floor filled with boxes—probably *medical files*. An old EKG machine sat to the left of the stairs. Blood pressure cuffs sat on top.

The paper rustling grew louder. "F, Frederick, Fuller, G, Gardner. Shit, not this one either."

A shadow shifted in the dim light. Another box slid from the shelf.

The step creaked.

"Oh so, you took my bait," Wendell said. "Join the party, Shady Max."

Sweat dripped down Max's back despite the coolness of the basement. Thoughts of running back upstairs flashed through his mind, but a glint of light made him dive down the remaining steps as an ax blade swung from a heavy rope. He dropped his pistol. It flew under the staircase.

Wendell flipped on the light. His devilish smile beamed across his face.

"I see you stole that car. The license plate says CHAR8T-1. I'm sure Amos didn't just give it to you."

"So what're you going to do about it?" Wendell's brows rose. "You're getting old. Too old to be a cop." He leapt forward.

"I'll be older than you when you die." Max bounded to his feet and braced for an attack. He kicked the EKG machine into Wendell's path. It gave Max time to dart under the staircase, retrieve his gun, and roll to the other side.

Wendell leapt behind a bookcase.

Max ran full speed and threw his weight against the end shelf. It toppled and knocked against the next case causing a domino effect as they crashed. They just missed Wendell as he grabbed something from his pocket.

Wendell lunged forward. The glint of metal reflected off the knife.

The blade slashed through Max's right shoulder. His shooting arm hung uselessly.

Wendell jabbed again, but Max grabbed his arm and dove to the floor.

The knife struck the wall and dropped to the ground.

Max kicked it under the shelves, unable to reach it as a weapon. He sucked in shallow pants as the pain grew. Max tried to clutch his gun with his good arm but couldn't reach it. His taunter came into view. His eyes never left his attacker.

Wendell crouched low. His hand twitched. The scar on his forearm flexed.

That arm still bothers him—his brother's handy work. Max slid under a corner of the tipped bookcase. His fingers teased the gun forward until he reached it.

Wendell pulled out a Glock and backed into the darkness out of sight before Max could get off a shot.

Max adjusted the weapon in his left hand. He propped himself onto his side, swung his pistol toward the shadow, and took a few deep breaths to steady himself.

Nothing clears my brain faster than a gun pointing at close range. Max braced his arm against the case, took aim, and fired. His arm jerked. Everything went dead still.

Wendell let out a cry and fired several wild shots. The gun fell to the floor as the man swayed in the light. He swiped at his greasy hair plastered to his head in sweat. His body made a perfect target.

Max's blood pumped so fast he feared he'd bleed to death. He fired.

Wendell flinched and took a step backward. Another shot forced him to fly backward and hit the ground.

Max's pistol clicked, but it was empty. He waited a few seconds. His eyes blurred. Blood soaked his shirt and dripped down his arm. The pain got worse. He grabbed his right elbow and tried to sit up.

A scraping sound came from his left. Wendell's trance-like eyes fixated on Max.

Too late, Max realized the bullets hit a Kevlar vest.

Wendell leapt forward.

A thin cord wrapped around Max's neck. Wendell's hands shook as he pulled.

Max's meager efforts to fight back ceased as he slumped to the filthy cement floor.

***

Wendell knelt beside the old man's body. He caressed his mother's silver locket dangling from the cord he'd used to end the wretched man's life. Inside was a photo of the twins at age three. Back when they were best friends.

He emptied the old man's pockets. Then he rummaged through the files, found what he wanted, and left the warehouse.

Intruder

Samantha scooted across the front seat to Ivar's car's passenger door. "Thanks for picking me up after work. These two weeks have flown by, but it seems like forever since I last saw Pops."

Ivar leaned over and slipped his arm around her. "Want to go out for dinner tonight?"

She felt his familiar warmth. "Wish I could." Turning, she lifted his arm from around her.

"Why don't you then?"

Samantha raised the latch and slipped out of the car. "Some other time."

Ivar bolted out of the driver's side and slammed the car door.

"Don't get pissy! I'm really tired."

"Okay, I get that." Ivar moved to her side, playfully nudged her, and then linked her arm in his. They walked to the front of her condominium. "I'll swing by in the morning and bring you to work."

"Sorry. I promised to join Mom for breakfast," Samantha said. "I have my own car, and my arm feels better."

"Dinner tomorrow then," Ivar insisted. "I'm researching unsolved crimes as far back as 1910. I hope to match up the bones. We can discuss my findings."

Samantha adjusted the sling around her neck. "Are they missing persons' reports on runaway teenagers?"

"Something like that."

She felt a slight quiver run through her. *Excitement or Tobias?* "I wonder if any of them worked at the saloon."

Ivar grinned. "I hadn't thought of that. Does Pops have any old records from that time? Maybe at home or in storage?"

"I'll check with Mom. See you tomorrow." Samantha stood on her tiptoes to give him a peck on the cheek.

He turned and captured it square on his mouth. Placing his arms on each side of the door, he leaned in and trapped her with his body. He nibbled her lips, and then kissed her long and deep.

Her pent-up energy drained as she melted into him. She savored his taste.

"Please," he groaned and moved his lips to her chin, planting small, light kisses down her neck. "Remember this until we meet tomorrow." He gently backed away.

Samantha felt weak-kneed. Unable to stand without his support, she clutched his arm and opened her eyes. "I will."

Breathless and feeling drugged, she released his arm, unlocked the door, and slipped inside. She dropped her purse to the floor, closed the door, and leaned against it briefly. Recovering, she flipped the light switch.

The light didn't turn on.

"Shit!" Now, she had to climb up and replace that bulb.

Turning, she felt a cold metal object poke into her back.

"Don't scream," a man said in a low voice. "Raise your hands where I can see them."

"I can only raise one arm, dork. The other's in a sling." She gasped as the metal object jabbed her between the shoulder blades. Her arms lifted.

"I'm not playing games here. Where's the key?"

"What key?"

"To your mother's house." The gun moved to her temple.

"In my purse." She motioned with her foot to the bag on the floor.

He moved the gun and stepped in front of her. "Kick it over here. Slowly!"

The intruder still eluded her as she squinted in the darkness. "My arm is killing me. Can I put them down?"

"Not until I get the keys!"

Samantha backed slowly to the door. A faint light shone through a shaded window.

The shadowed figure came into focus. He wore a gray sweatshirt.

"Why do you want them?" She shoved the bag with one foot toward the guy, making sure it didn't quite reach him.

Without an answer, he knelt to pick up the purse with the gun still aimed at her.

Samantha slammed the elbow of her cast down on his head. The gun went off, and it flew from his hand. A bullet pierced the front window, shattering the glass.

She hit him again, and he fell to the floor.

"Samantha, are you all right?" Wood cracked, and the front door flew open.

A flash of metal swung into the hallway, followed by Detective Colby Cage. "Don't move!"

The gun was aimed at the guy in the sweatshirt.

"You!" Colby said.

"Do you know this guy?" Samantha cradled her right arm.

A pair of handcuffs snapped around the guy's wrists so fast it made her heart race. Or was it being in the same room as Colby? "Thank you for coming," she gasped. "I wasn't sure what to do."

"You handled yourself quite well, even with a wounded wing." Colby helped the dazed man to a standing position. "Turn on the light." Colby spun the man toward him. "You have the right to remain silent…"

"Light switch doesn't work. He must have tripped the breaker." Samantha moved into the living room and found a flashlight in a drawer of the TV stand. Her arm throbbed. Her head pounded, and she was in no mood for this. Returning, she stood inches from the stranger and beamed the light toward his face. "I've never seen you before. Who are you?"

The man gave a glaring smirk.

"Wait a minute. I'm a paramedic. I should check for a head injury before you take him away." Samantha held up her middle finger. "How many fingers do you see?"

"Ha, ha," the man said. "The same to you."

"Why do you want Mom's keys? You broke in here just fine. Why not break into her place?" Samantha asked. "Not that I'd wish that on her."

"I'm not saying another word until I see my lawyer." He made a zipping motion across his lips with his cuffed hands.

Colby pulled a cell from his front shirt pocket.

"Who are you calling?" Samantha asked.

"Officer Rexall. I saw him drop you off a few minutes ago, so he can't be far away.

What? He saw me kissing Ivar? Well, on the kissing scale, no one tops Ivar. Yet, Colby makes my heart race, too. He must think I'm fickle. Then again, Colby's never kissed me. She noticed he was still talking. *What did he say?*

"...surprised he didn't turn around when he heard the shot."

Colby diverted his attention to the phone. "Hello, Ivar. We have a situation at Miss McFitzroy's condo."

Colby paused. "The guy in the gray sweatshirt paid Samantha a visit."

Within minutes, she heard tires squeal outside. A car door slammed, and Ivar burst through the now-open doorway. Dashing to her side, he placed a gentle arm around her shoulders. "Did he hurt you, Sam? I could kick myself for not coming inside with you."

Colby cleared his throat. "You might want to take this guy into custody. You were hell-bent on asking him questions the other day. Here's your chance."

Samantha stepped back and stared at Ivar.

"Do you know him?"

"I have an inkling," Ivar said. "You're Terrance Rodriguez, aren't you?"

"They call me Ter." His voice came out as a growl.

"Okay, Rodriguez, Let's go." Ivar grabbed his upper arm none too gently.

"Don't forget his gun," Colby said.

"Bag it as evidence." Ivar moved to the entrance. "Search the front yard and get the slug as well."

"Shouldn't you take a photo of the damages?" Samantha asked.

Ivar grimaced and nodded. "Your phone photos might work, but it's an older model, and the last ones I saw were a bit grainy. Do you have any film in your old 35 mm?"

"It's in the closet." Samantha opened the door. She fished around the top shelf with her left hand. "It's too dark to see."

A light popped on overhead. "I screwed the bulb back in place." Colby stepped up and snagged the camera. "It's on number 14. I'll take a few shots, and we'll need to take the film as evidence. You don't have anything of importance on here, do you?"

Samantha grabbed the camera strap. "It has pictures of Pops at my birthday party. You can't have them. They're mine."

Ivar moved Ter onto the porch. "Stop bickering. Leave the film with me, and I'll make sure you get your photos. Now let's go."

While Ivar escorted Ter to his car and called in the crime, Colby snapped some photos inside the house. He used the film, rewound and removed it from the camera, and placed the roll into his pocket. He used his cell phone to take a few more shots outside. An uprooted strip of grass revealed the remains of the bullet.

Samantha called to warn her mom, but it went to voice mail. She took a couple of Tylenol and returned to the entry. A groan escaped her lips. The jamb had split away from the wall. The strike plate lay on the floor, and the door hung loosely on one hinge.

"Guess I owe you one front door," Colby said as he approached the steps and handed her the camera. "I'll have it repaired in no time." Back on his cell, he gave orders and her address. "Take care of the damage and install a new lock, pronto."

Done with the call, Colby slid the phone into his pocket. "While we wait, I'll whip us up a delicious meal. It can't be easy to cook with one arm in a cast."

"No, it's not," she agreed. "I pulled desk duty all week. They can't send in a damaged paramedic when times get tough."

"Where's the kitchen? I make a mean salad."

"I'm afraid I don't have much on hand, and the last head of lettuce molded months ago."

Colby smiled. "Not much of a cook, huh? I'm fine with take-out pizza. What toppings do you like?"

"This isn't Fort Collins," Samantha reminded him. "We don't have fast food take-out."

"Then I'll have my brother deliver it when he comes to fix the door." Out came the phone again. "Pepperoni, sausage, mushrooms, black olives, and extra cheese sound passable?"

"Does it ever!" Samantha kicked off her shoes and went into the kitchen. "Want wine with that?"

While talking with his brother, he followed her into the kitchen.

She opened the cabinet and reached to the top shelf for wine glasses. "I have Shiraz or Pinot Gris."

He disconnected the call and nudged her aside. "Shiraz for me."

She took the glasses as he handed them to her and placed them on the counter.

"Would you mind opening the bottle? My arm aches."

"Sure thing." Colby poured two glasses, and they retired to the living room.

He spent the next hour updating her on the latest events. "We're unable to track the origin of the bomb materials, and there's still no sign of Pops. We've tracked down some prints in the alley but haven't ID anyone. Nabbing this guy might be our biggest break."

Samantha set her untouched wine on the end table. "Did you hear anything more from the ME about those bones?"

"Angela's still working on it."

Samantha had to admit only a little new information except a footprint may have some bearing upon the case. "Do you know anything about Ter?"

"Nope. Just that Ivar tracked him down and lost him the other day."

Samantha grimaced. "Oh, that's who he was following when I called him."

"Do you call Ivar often while he's on the job?"

Avoiding the question, she asked, "I meant to ask, why did you come over tonight? Don't get me wrong. I'm glad you interrupted whatever Ter had in store for me, but did you have some news to share?"

Colby took a sip of wine. "I wanted to know if you ever met that ghost the other night. You left in such a hurry."

Samantha moved to the edge of the couch and picked an imaginary thread from the floor. "No. He didn't show up." Disappointed, she asked, "Is that the only reason you came here?"

"That and to ask you out to dinner." Colby grinned.

"You could have called. I've seen you use your cell phone several times since you arrived."

"But this way, I can see the sparkle in your eyes when you say yes."

Samantha felt heat flush her cheeks. A knock on the doorjamb interrupted her gaze.

"Is it safe to come inside?" A lanky blond, a younger version of his brother stood in the entry with a box of pizza in one hand

and a toolbox in the other. "You sure did a number on this door, Ma'am. I'll patch the space for now and replace it tomorrow."

Colby jumped from his seat and took the pizza. "I did the damage while rescuing a lady in distress."

"My brother is a knight in shining armor? Who would have guessed?"

"Jared, this is Samantha, a client of mine."

Client? Ouch. Oh, it's his brother. He doesn't want to let on.

"It's a pleasure." Jared laid the toolbox on the floor. "I have more equipment in the truck. Your help would be appreciated, Sir Knight."

Samantha smiled at the title. "Go ahead. I'll dish up the pizza. You'll join us, won't you, Jared?"

"I brought extra, so we'd have enough." Jared saluted, then grabbed his brother's arm and led him outside. "That's some catch. Don't let Misty know about you-know-who in there. By the way, that package you've been waiting for came in the mail today. It'll look great on her."

"Shh." Colby pulled him aside and glanced back at Samantha.

Catching a glimpse from the corner of her eye, she pretended not to notice. She rounded the corner to the kitchen and then edged her way back to listen.

"Misty doesn't like it when you're away," Jared said.

Colby whispered. "Don't worry. I'll make it up to her."

"Really?" Jared jabbed his elbow into Colby's ribs. "She's been waiting all day."

"Damn, I should have stopped by the house before coming over here," Colby said.

"You're becoming a real cad and a pain in the butt to boot, so I left you the heaviest piece of plywood."

Samantha plastered a smile on her face and met the men in the living room. "Paper plates, okay? I don't want to inconvenience the two of you any longer." Turning toward Colby, she added, "This is a nice dinner. I'm glad you invited me, but I'm terribly busy for the next five decades, so I'll see you then."

Colby's jaw dropped.

She slammed the plates on the coffee table and scooped up her purse and car keys. "I'll let myself in the back door when I return." An eerie feeling washed over Samantha as she fled from her condo.

Brown Box

Samantha unlocked her car and didn't look back. The handle nipped her fingers, cold as if it were the middle of a blizzard in January. Lucky to have the skin left on her hand, she shook her wrist and slipped into the driver's side to get the feeling back.

The door banged shut. Her car key nearly lifted from her hand, and she found the ignition. The engine roared as she felt her foot forced to the floorboards. "What's happening?"

Tires squealed. A powerful g-force pushed her body back into the seat. "Stop it!"

Her fingers gripped the steering wheel. Samantha fought to keep the car in her lane. "Stop it right now!" The car pulled to the side of the road and stopped. "Where'd you learn to drive?"

A heavy mist formed in the passenger's seat. "I didn't, but I can sure ride a horse, and that was some jackass back there."

"How long have you been here?" Samantha turned to glare at Tobias. "Did you see Ter break into my house?"

"Is that what he was doing?" Tobias asked. "I thought he was delivering a package."

"Did he have a package?"

"Well, it was some sort of brown box."

Samantha frowned. "How'd he get inside?"

"I thought you let him in. The door opened. He went inside. I didn't think it was polite to intrude, so I waited outside."

Samantha fished through her purse with her casted hand. "Damn. I don't suppose you can make my cell—" The air swirled, and a silver phone lifted from her purse.

"Thanks." Samantha snatched it out of the air. "You *can* be useful at times." She punched in Ivar's number. It rang until it went to voice mail. "Ivar, Ter left me a brown package. I don't know where he put it or what's inside but ask him. Better yet, call me ASAP." His voicemail cut off.

"I saw a package like that just before the fountain shop—"

"Don't tell me it's a bomb!" Samantha pulled into the lane and made a U-turn. "Colby and Jared are still in my house, and I don't have Colby's phone number."

She swerved around a garbage truck sitting in the middle of the street and nearly hit a mailbox. Parking across the street from her condominium, she saw Jared outside in his truck. She zipped down her window. "Where's Colby?"

Jared sauntered toward the car. "Why'd you run out on us?"

Samantha nudged her car door open. "I don't have time for this." She darted past Jared. "Colby, get out here right now."

Colby appeared in the doorway. "Back so soon?"

She ran up her sidewalk. "Did you see a brown paper box anywhere inside?"

"What are you talking about?" Colby moved down the steps.

Samantha passed him on the stairs. A cold blast hit her, causing her to fall backward then she felt herself fly through the air. The next thing she knew, Colby cradled her in his outstretched arms.

He peered down at her when a loud explosion sounded. The windows shattered, and the half-patched door blew from the hinges.

A shiver raced through her. "Not again!" Samantha dropped to her feet and clung to Colby, afraid she'd collapse. Panic snaked around her chest. It squeezed. A lump grew in her throat. Tears streamed down her cheeks as she watched her condo turn to splinters and dust. "My house."

"My pizza!" Jared said as the box flew through the window and landed at his feet.

His comment made her laugh and cry at the same time. "Gone. Everything's gone. Now, what will I do?" Samantha dropped her head into her hands. "My life is falling apart." She glanced around. "Nowhere of my own."

"You can stay at my place." Colby pulled out his cell and dialed.

Angry and frustrated that she couldn't do anything, Samantha swiped at her tears. "Are you calling 'what's her name' to ask permission? It might not be as easy to make up this time." With a deep breath, she fisted her hands and stepped away from him.

Colby frowned, shook his head, and spoke into the phone. "There's been an explosion…"

What About Mom?

Samantha forced herself to slow her breathing as she paced the street in front of her house. *Be strong. Don't frighten Mom. She'll have another episode, and this time, it might be a real heart attack.*

Her fingers shook as Samantha gripped the phone and dialed. "Mom, are you all right." Samantha's voice quivered.

"I'm fine. Why wouldn't I be? Did something—"

"Didn't you get my message?" Sirens blared in the distance and grew louder as a fire truck approached. An ambulance and two police cars followed in its wake.

"Oh my, what happened?" Mom asked. "Are you in the hospital?"

"Not this time, but I need to move back into my old room. Some creep bombed my house." Samantha said.

"So, you're unharmed, right?"

"Physically, yes. Emotionally, I'm a wreck!"

A news reporter from Greeley set up his camera and microphone. "...Firefighters have arrived. Multiple engines are at the scene. A crowd of onlookers is being cleared and forced across the street."

Samantha had to shout above the noise. "Mom, this guy wanted my key to your place. A bomb crew will be there any minute to check out your home. I want you to get out immediately until they arrive."

"Relax, dear. I'm glad you're safe. Don't worry about me. No one's been here all day. I made cookies. Why don't you join me for a late-night snack?"

"Mom, did you hear me? Get out of the house!"

The reporter moved closer to Samantha and continued his live broadcast. "Firefighters are inside. The blaze is spreading fast. An ambulance just arrived. I don't know if we have any victims."

Samantha tried to step aside.

"Wait, I think we have the owner standing by." The reporter shoved a microphone in Samantha's face.

"Get away." She ducked, shielding her cell phone, so her mom wouldn't hear the commotion.

"Someone's at the gate, Honey," Mom said. "I'll call you back." The phone line went dead.

Colby moved between Samantha and the reporter. The look he sent made the man move down the street. "Did your mom leave the building?"

"No, she's eating fresh-baked cookies, making coffee, and probably will invite the entire bomb squad to join her." Samantha shoved the phone into her pocket. "Did you get a hold of Ivar? He won't answer my calls."

"I believe he's a bit busy at the moment. Interrogating a bomb suspect takes time," Colby said. "By the way, how did you know about the box?"

Samantha rolled her eyes and gave a sheepish smile. "Guess."

"Your ghost?"

She nodded.

"That'll go over well in court."

"It's the truth. And Tobias not only saved my life but yours as well. You'd still be inside."

Colby rubbed his hand down his face and grimaced. "I'm afraid you're right. Why did you leave in such a hurry? Did you get a call from your ghost?"

"Not exactly," Samantha said. "More like a wake-up call from your brother."

"Huh? How do you communicate with…Tobias is it?"

"It's complicated." She shrugged her shoulders. "The environment around me changes. Cold air, gentle breeze, a mist appears, it varies."

"Detective Cage, the fire chief wants to talk to you," a fireman yelled from the driveway.

Another team of firefighters hooked their hoses to the hydrant down the street. Water sprayed, but the flames continued to burn.

Chief Martinelli emerged from the crowd. "You witnessed the explosion, right?"

"Yes," Colby said. "Samantha and Jared were here, too."

In a fog, Samantha heard Colby ask, "Where's Miss McFitzroy? She was here just a moment ago."

Previous Life

Samantha gazed down at a shrinking Colby. Her home, the flames, and even her neighborhood disappeared in a whirlwind. It swarmed around her and then set her down. She stood and surveyed the scene. Dust blew down her street as the pavement turned to gravel, then sand, and became woodlands.

A man covered in a layer of grit rode a black stallion and came to a halt in front of her. The man's muscles rippled as he dismounted. His craggy face creased with concern. "Name's Tobias."

It took a moment to grasp reality. "Papa?" Samantha sobbed.

"At one time, I was." He wrapped solid arms around her. "Together at last."

Her soul knew the truth, but everything seemed impossible. Words refused to utter. Her heart raced erratically. Sweat dripped down her back. Her arms felt like lead.

Tobias pointed toward the sky. Buzzards circled overhead. "I think that's why we're here." Smoke wafted through the air.

Something dead lay nearby. "Is it Pops?"

"No, dear child. He's not even a twinkle in my son's eyes. "Who then?" Expecting the worst, Samantha gathered her courage and headed toward the woods. A burned-out wagon smoldered in the distance.

A metallic odor hit her nostrils only seconds before she eyed the five corpses. Holding the sleeve of her blouse to her nose, she filtered the rank smell and struggled for breath. "Girls, three children, and two teenagers." A massacre. Savage and gut-wrenching.

"Why?" Samantha asked. Inching closer, she saw a teenage girl with long, curly red hair. A gold locket hung around her neck. Drawn to it, she knelt beside the girl. She recognized the monogram SM. Gasping, Samantha dropped the chain. "My initials."

"Yes. Sara McFitzroy. My beloved daughter." Tobias removed his hat and rolled the edges between his fingers. "I wasn't sure at first, but I had to find out, so I sent you here. You're from the same blood, a reincarnation of her. I wouldn't be able to bring you if you weren't. You've been here before, Samantha."

Coming to terms with the truth, she asked, "I'm her?"

Tobias dropped his hat and fell to his knees beside the body. "I was a fool. Locked up, drunk, and unable to convince the sheriff I had to get my daughter." He lightly touched the girl's face and then removed the locket. "If you examine her closely, you'll see a strong resemblance."

Samantha ran a finger along the contours of her face. "The bones at the ME's office. My cheekbones."

Her mind raced. Internal screams grew like a hurricane rushing through the water. Pain and trauma forced her to study Sara's body. "She's gone, you know. Heaven took her. There's no reason for you to stay, Tobias."

"I know, but I can't leave. Something holds me here, and I believe it's you."

"Do you know anything about Pops?"

"Yes, he's safe." Tobias stood and dusted his knees. "I've kept him busy the last few weeks. He researched the past and discovered information about the massacre on that laptop of his. The year was about right when Sara disappeared. Now I need to find out why your life's in danger."

"What year is this?" Samantha asked.

Tobias placed the locket into Samantha's hand. "I'd like you to have this. I gave it to Sara on her fourteenth birthday, June 5, 1899. She never made it to her fifteenth."

"June 5th is my birthday, too. I was born in 1999," Samantha said.

"I know. One hundred years after her death," Tobias said. "At least, my darling Sara lives again in you—same hair and that same smile. Even your eyes are golden brown but not as innocent as my Sara's. You're lucky to be left-handed like your great-grandfather, especially with your right arm in a cast."

Samantha rubbed her right arm. No cast in 1899.

"Will I feel any different when I return?"

"I don't think so, but I'm not an expert on the issue. I'm learning, too."

She touched Tobias on the arm, "Is this really you? I've never seen you in person during this lifetime."

Tobias picked up his hat and placed it on his head. "Time to go."

"Before we return, may I hug you one last time?"

Tears ran down his face. Tobias took her in his arms. "Sara, I've always loved you. The law can't keep me from failing you again." He caressed her hair and kissed her on the cheek.

Samantha stepped back and studied him. "How come you're a solid, living, breathing human now, but—"

"I haven't died yet. But I will be gone when we return."

"What do you mean, you'll be gone? Are you going to heaven?" Samantha asked. "Promise me you won't leave until Pops returns."

"I promise I'll do my best to bring him home safely."

"Wait," Samantha reached into her pocket to pull out her cell phone. "I want to take a picture. I need to remember everything I've seen."

The cell was missing.

"Sorry, dear. That, too, will return when you do."

"I'll make a quick sketch. Do you have a pen?" Samantha asked.

His brown eyes rolled. "I'm sure they were invented after my time."

Samantha let out a small groan. "Will I remember any of this?"

"Yes, you've known it all along. It just needed to resurface."

Samantha held up her hand. "Will the necklace stay with me?"

Tobias rubbed the scruffy beard on his chin. "I think so, but only if you choose to keep it."

"I'll cherish it forever." She carefully placed it into her pocket.

Tobias bit his lip and cleared his throat. "Do you remember what happened? Do you know who did this?"

Samantha closed her eyes. Her nightmares repeated the scene so many times, but she had no memory of the details now. "Ask me again when we return. It happened so fast, I don't think Sara understood. I'm not sure I do, even now, but I remember Jenny, the older girl next to her. I don't know the children."

Tobias turned and stared at the older girl. "Jenny Robertson. We wondered what happened to her. She fought with her mother earlier in the day. Her pa thought she ran off with her fiancé, Fang."

That's right. "She wanted to marry. Planned a secret rendezvous. Her fiancé asked her to meet him here. I walked with her when you didn't show up. It was on my way home. Fang hadn't arrived yet. We caught them attacking the girls..." The image flashed. "Tobias, get me out of here!"

The wind swirled as he held her firmly against his body, but as she reappeared on her block, he became a cold mist. The locket burned in her pocket.

"Samantha, where have you been?" Colby asked. He dashed to her side and offered his strong arm. Maybe he even noticed her tremor, but without his support, she would have fallen like a stone.

Home Sweet Home

Faces loomed in front of Samantha, but she couldn't recognize them. Voices faded to a distant drone. A bottle of water appeared. She gulped a mouthful and then splashed some on her face. "Where am I? Where's Tobias?" Her vision cleared.

Abby leaned closer. "Samantha, your blood sugar is too low.

When did you last eat?"

Smoldering flames lit the dark sky. Her home lay in ruins. The ceiling over the living room had collapsed. Her bedroom appeared to have survived at the back of the building, but her life felt swept away like the burned grass in her front yard that she sat upon.

"Here. It's juice. Drink it." Abby tapped on her cast. "Knock, knock. Are you in there? I'm talking to you."

Samantha shook her head. "Time travel's a bear. I can't seem to think."

"Time travel?" Abby asked. "I don't know what you're talking about, but Honey, this is reality. Your house burned down. Pops is still missing, and you're having a hallucination, that's all. It happens to the best of us. Now, drink up."

Colby knelt beside Samantha. "Are you okay?"

"Why me?" she asked under her breath and then gulped down the drink. "Why Pops?" She got to her feet. "Detective Cage, what did the bomb squad find at Mom's?"

"They're still inspecting the grounds." Colby stood and dusted off his knees.

"I need to check on Mom." Samantha lurched toward her car still parked across the street, halfway onto the neighbor's sidewalk.

Abby yanked her back by the sleeve. "You're in no condition to drive!"

"I'll take her," Colby said. "Jared, we're done here. I'll meet you at home. Let Little Misty out for me. She's been cooped up for too long."

"Little Misty?" Samantha asked as she climbed into the passenger's side of his white Toyota Corolla.

"Yeah, my husky. She's a beauty, but sometimes I'm so busy, I don't spend enough time with her. She gets testy. Last week, I had to bring home a treat to get her to stop ignoring me."

"You were talking to Jared about your dog?"

"Why not? He's my brother. We talk about everything."

"What was in the package?" Samantha asked.

"A new dog tag, I lost the old one. I don't dare let her out without one." Colby's eyes lit up. "Wait a minute. You thought I was talking about another girl. That's why the cold shoulder." A bud of laughter blossomed until tears ran down his cheeks.

"No, I had an errand to run. And it saved your life," Samantha said. "Don't forget it."

"I owe you that one." Colby swiped his eyes with his sleeve and started the engine. "Where to?"

Samantha gave directions, and Colby drove the car up to the outer fence of her parent's home. Her mom stood inside the gate next to the Honda, a cup of coffee in one hand, a cookie in the other.

Samantha climbed from the car, punched in the code, and the gate opened.

"You made it." Her mother dashed to her side with a hug. "There's more coffee and a plate of cookies on the picnic table in the gazebo. That is if the men haven't eaten them all by now."

"Thanks, but I came to check on you." Samantha forced a smile. "Why are you so far from the house?"

"They won't let me inside and said it was safer out here."

Colby nodded. "Usually, they clear the area, but out here in the country, you don't have many neighbors."

"Has the bomb squad finished in the house yet?" Samantha asked.

"I'll check on their progress." Colby hiked up to the two-story brick house and disappeared through the front door.

"You're pale," Mom said. "Let's sit down and talk."

Samantha followed her mother to the gazebo. The swing looked inviting. She dropped into the cushions and moved with a gentle sway.

Her mom poured a cup of coffee and handed it to Samantha. "Did they put the fire out?" Mom sat in a wicker chair by the glass-covered picnic table.

"I'm not sure. I can't understand it. The schmuck destroyed the house. Everything is a mess." Samantha ticked off items on her fingers." My clothes are gone. Furniture ruined. You have a copy of my digital files. Right? All my photos, too. Right?"

Mom nodded. "Where's your laptop?"

"I guess I should be happy. My arm ached so much today, I left it on my desk at work." Samantha got up and helped herself to a cookie and then sat down next to her mother. "You were right about talking to Pops."

"I knew it!" Mom leaned forward and whispered, "Where is he?"

"I'm not sure." Samantha rubbed the back of her neck and propped her cast on the table. "It's been a long day." After a sigh, she told her everything.

"What did you see when you and Jenny came across the family in 1899?" Mom asked.

"Don't ask. I can't face that right now. Oh, do you know if Pops has any paperwork about the shop stashed at home? Anything from the previous owner?"

"Maybe in the office or the basement. Once he comes home, he can get it for you." Mom dumped the dregs of her coffee onto her napkin.

Colby walked toward them. "All clear, Mrs. McFitzroy. There's no evidence of a bomb."

"Thank goodness," Mom said. "I'd like to go back inside, and Sam needs her rest. Can you hurry them on their way?"

Colby smiled. "I'll do my best." He packed the cookies and coffee into the back of her Honda and drove them back to the house.

"Home." Samantha smiled and grabbed her mother's arm as they went inside. "My place was only a condo. It never felt like home."

"You'll need to meet with Chief Martinelli in the morning," Colby reminded Samantha. "I'd stop by and pick you up, but I have appointments all day."

"No problem. Mom has a car. She can drop me by my place, and I'll get mine in time to go downtown. Have you heard anything from Ivar?"

"Oh, he phoned an hour ago," Mom interrupted. "He said he tried your cell phone, but you weren't answering. I told him that you were probably tied up with the fire chief."

"I know Ivar's busy. I'll leave him a message." Samantha walked Colby to the front door. "Thanks for all your help today. I'll talk to you later."

Colby leaned toward her.

Samantha felt her heart leap in anticipation. She closed her eyes.

"Detective Cage, the boss wants to talk to you," a member of the squad called out from the entry as they were leaving.

She felt his warm breath on her face, and then it was gone. Disappointment ran through her. *Maybe if he'd ever kiss me, I could compare it to Ivar's. Then I'd know for sure.*

"Duty calls." Colby followed the man outside and turned. "Good night, Samantha, Mrs. McFitzroy."

Mom waved and then stifled a yawn. She closed the door and switched off the porch light. "Clean sheets are on the bed, but you'll need a blanket from the closet. Do you need help?"

"I can manage."

"Sleep well. I'll see you in the morning." Mom kissed Samantha and headed upstairs.

Samantha went around the house, locked every door and window, and then trudged to her room. Childhood memories rushed over her. The dresser still had the lace doily her grandmother made, slightly yellow now. It lay beneath a lava lamp Samantha found it in the garage several years ago. The yellow globs rose and fell in the red liquid. It didn't provide much light, but it mesmerized her into a deep sleep.

Two Too Many

Gary Gordon jolted at the sight of the mirror reflection standing in the doorway to his kitchen.

"Howdy, dear Bro." Wendell sneered. "Thought you could get rid of me by telling me the charity gig was at the Denver Tech Center, hey?"

"Why? Did you fall for the lie?" Panic crawled through Gary's belly. He fisted his shaking hands to hide his reaction. "Guess you figured it out."

"I've had several years to figure you out." Wendell took a step closer. A glint of light reflected from the knife in his hand. "Shall we talk about the mine?"

Gary kept his eye on the knife and stepped to the counter. "Are you still fixated on the silver?"

Wendell laughed. "I know you well enough. You're still looking for that diary."

"You're drunk. Why don't you sleep it off? We'll talk about it in the morning."

"I'm sober as the day I was born." Wendell slammed the knife onto the counter. "I believe this is yours."

"How can you tell? We each have one." Gary moved around the kitchen island toward the living room door.

"It has your name on it, asshole, even though you tried to file it off."

"Not me," Gary said. "That was Pa."

"In case you don't remember, yours has a nick in the blade."

Gary gnawed on his lower lip. "Pa used my knife."

"Really?" Wendell followed Gary into the living room. "Well, I reckon he's not here to verify that, so I'll believe what I know is the truth. What happened to the map?"

"Don't know." Gary shrugged. "I saw Pa slip it in the diary when you cornered us in the mine's office. Guess Molly McFitzroy threw it out."

"Why did you do it?"

Gary swallowed the lump in his throat. "You shot Pa and paralyzed him for life."

"It was meant for you. After all, you let me go into the shaft knowing he rigged it to blow. Why?"

"He rigged it for Fang after he fired Gramps and then Pa. No more silver."

"Except for the cache that Pa managed to pilfer." Wendell took a step closer. "That's what's on the map. Right?"

"If you can find it, you can have it."

"Not so fast." Wendell held out his scarred forearm. "See that?"

"What of it?"

"You were to take the fall if we got caught. It was your repayment for this scar. But no, I took the rap while you hid away with the charity king."

"Don't threaten me," Gary said. "You nearly killed Pa."

"You were always his favorite." Wendell flexed his arm. The scar pulled into an ugly crease.

Gary tugged in a ragged breath and exhaled. "Get out!"

"I plan to stay. It's you who's leaving." Wendell's fist crumpled Gary to the floor.

Gary rolled away from a flying boot. He grabbed his twin's foot and pulled him to the floor, and then Gary wound his muscular legs around Wendell's neck and squeezed.

Wendell coiled like a snake, kicked his brother in the head, and broke free.

A brawl pursued.

Furniture crashed. Someone shattered the TV.

A loud bang on the door stopped the ruckus. "Gary! You all right?"

"I'm fine, Amos." Gary dusted off his pants, yanked open the door, and slid outside. "Just having a poker party with the boys. We didn't see eye-to-eye. Sorry about the noise."

"Did you work out the details for tomorrow?"

"All taken care of." Gary ran his bloodied hand through his hair and then flinched.

"The boys better be in good shape tomorrow. Can't have any screw-ups. You hear me?" Amos pulled out a pistol and left it on the balcony railing. "I'm leaving for the office at sunrise."

"Sure thing, Amos." Gary picked up the pistol. He opened the door. Two shots rang out. Then there was silence.

Ter's Terror

After Ivar arrested Terrance Rodriguez, he read him his Miranda Rights and loaded him into the car. As they pulled up to the police station, Ivar's phone rang, but he ignored it.

Sweat beaded on Ter's brow as Ivar escorted him to the intake desk.

"What're the charges?" the booking officer asked.

"Breaking and entering. Plus attempted murder."

"Murder?" Ter's voice trembled. "I didn't mean to fire. The pistol wouldn't have gone off if she hadn't hit me."

"It's illegal to pull a gun on an unarmed person, and your intent was perfectly clear after the B&E," Ivar said. "Book him."

"Sit down while I ask you a few personal questions," the officer said.

Ivar rubbed his temples. "Go ahead and process him, fingerprints, and photographs. You get one phone call. Do you have a lawyer?"

"No." Ter dropped onto the chair. "I can't afford a lawyer. However, I know the law. One will be provided for me."

Ivar heaved a sigh. "Great. We'll go to court and get you one. In the meantime, lock him up. It'll probably be a couple of days before we get a court hearing." He removed his hat and brushed a hand over his hair.

Ter jumped up, knocking over the chair. "Wait, I can't stay here. I don't want anyone to know that I've been captured."

Ivar shook his head. "It's a little late for that. Reporters had their cameras are running as we came through the precinct doors. It'll hit the news by nine o'clock if not sooner."

Ter's face paled. "No, they'll kill my family." Stumbling, he grabbed the desk. His breath came out in small pants. "You have to stop the news."

Ivar walked toward Ter. His normal calm demeanor swept away with those words. "Are you willing to talk? The court system doesn't move very fast. Either get a private lawyer, wait for the court to appoint one, or talk without one. You know the rules. Anything you say is admissible in court and can be held against you."

"I'll talk." Ter held up his cuffed hands, pleading. "You have to save my wife and children. They are held hostage as we speak."

"Under the circumstances, I have to make a few phone calls."

Ter turned back to the processing officer. "Take my fingerprints."

"Finish up with him and call me," Ivar said. "We'll meet in the interrogation room."

Ter picked up the chair and sat down. "Please hurry."

Ivar's cell phone rang again as he entered his office. He glanced at caller ID. "Hello, Detective."

Ivar scrambled to catch the phone that fumbled from his fingers. "Another explosion? Is Sam hurt? Was anyone else in the house?" He collapsed onto the edge of his desk. "I can't get away right now. You'll have to handle the situation. Keep me updated." The phone call disconnected, and he moved to his chair.

Ivar's hands shook. He misdialed twice before getting it right. It took close to an hour to contact the TV newsroom, halt newspaper presses, and track down a judge. No prosecutor was available tonight.

Sweat dripped from Ivar's brow as he pulled out a velvet-covered box. A gift. *Dad told me there'd be days like this.* He unhinged the lock, lifted a snub-nosed semi-automatic, and checked the safety. *From now on, I'm carrying a second gun.* He clipped a flat holster to the back of his belt and slipped the gun inside. Then he put on his jacket and left the office. Tense, irritable, and worried sick about Sam, he stepped into the interrogation room.

Ter waited. His hands still in handcuffs, he paced. "I can't believe this is happening. We left Columbia to get away from violence."

Ivar ran a hand over his chin. "How long have you been in the country?"

"Five years. I'm a citizen of the United States. I have rights."

"Sure you do. The same rights as Samantha, but you…" Ivar took a deep breath. "Want a cup of coffee."

"Sure, and remove these cuffs so I can drink it."

"Fair enough." Ivar opened the door and held up three fingers.

A few minutes later, a pudgy, balding man appeared.

"Ter, this is Brody, my partner." Ivar pulled out a chair for Ter to sit down.

"Three cups of brew." Brody set them on the table. "Cream or sugar?"

"Black." Ter held up his arms.

Ivar dug the key from his pocket and uncuffed him.

Ter rubbed his wrists and sat down. "We don't have much time. Walter may already know I'm in custody, and he'll call his boss. My wife and kids don't deserve to die, just because I failed."

Setting a tape recorder in the middle of the table, Ivar asked, "Is it all right with you if I record this interview?"

"Yes." Ter flipped on the record button. "If they kill my family, I'll be next. It might be the only witness report you'll have."

"Fine. The following is an interview with Terrance Rodriguez, Officer Ivar Rexall, and Officer Brody Dunsty. The date is June 24, 1923, at 7:42 p.m." Ivar repeated, "For the record, Mr. Rodriguez agrees to this recording."

"What can you tell me about the bomb at the fountain shop at 2:38 P.M. on June 7, 1923?"

"I didn't know what was in the package. I just delivered it and a can of soda to the shop at a certain time as requested," Ter said. "Walter vowed he'd kill my wife if I didn't follow his instructions to the letter."

Ivar rubbed his aching knee, an old football injury that plagued him when he'd been on his feet too long. "Describe the package."

"A small, brown box about six by six square." Ter tapped his foot and fidgeted. "It didn't rattle. I shook it gently. Now that I think of it, that was really dumb. The bomb could have gone off in my hands."

"How much did it weigh?"

"Not more than a few pounds."

"What did you do with the package?" Ivar asked.

"I dropped it into the rain gutter outside of the shop. No one was in the alley. I had to stand on a trashcan to reach the drain. Walter said to put it in the middle. I did my best, but I think it was closer to the street than the rear of the building. That's probably why the back remained standing so long."

"Where did you place the soda can?"

"I walked inside the shop, glanced around, and slipped it on the counter along with some other cans."

"Is that all you did?" Ivar leaned closer.

"Well, no. I was supposed to pull something from the middle stool. I couldn't find anything except a long thread. I pulled it free and tucked it back into the cushion."

"Was anyone else in the fountain shop when you entered the building?"

"Maddog was eating a banana split and talking to Pops." Sweat dripped down Ter's cheek. He ran a hand over his face and wiped the moisture onto his pants.

"His name is Duke Parker," Ivar said. "I went to school with him. Did anyone else see you?"

"I don't think so. Samantha came to the shop just after Duke left."

"Did you see anyone else?"

Ter tapped his fingers on the table and then hesitated. "I don't know for sure when people started arriving. My thoughts were on Pam and my kids. After the blast, the whole town showed up."

"What did you do after you delivered the package?" Ivar asked.

"Can we hurry this up?"

"Answer the question."

Ter took a gulp of coffee. "As soon as I delivered it, I hung around for half an hour to see what happened as instructed. I couldn't believe it when the building exploded. I wondered if I'd caused it, but the box was so small. The Coke can was the old kind without the pop top."

"Why did you return to the scene the following morning?"

"I was hunting for Walter. He took my wife and kids. I sure as heck didn't want to talk to you."

"Tell me what happened," Ivar said.

"As soon as I returned home after the explosion, I found the garage door open, and the car was missing. I didn't know if my wife had escaped and taken the children or if they'd been kidnapped."

"So, did she escape?"

Ter shook his head. "My gut clenched as I ran into the house.

It was so quiet. A puddle of coffee lay on the kitchen floor. My wife would never leave a mess. I searched through the rest of the house, but no one was there. Not even a note. When I went to the back door, I heard Fluff Ball. I found her in the kennel, sitting on the freezer. I know the kids would have taken the cat with them. Walter must have said no."

"Did you find Walter?" Ivar asked.

"No! I haven't seen him since the seventh, but he calls me every day. Sometimes, he lets me talk to Pam. Other times, he gives me orders. Today, he ordered me to deliver a brown box to Miss McFitzroy's home. I refused at first, but he put my wife on the phone. The kids are safe, but I think he hit my wife. She cried and begged me to do whatever the man asked. She hinted that Walter's in trouble, too. Poor bastard probably has someone threatening his wife and kid, too. Walter will kill my family if ordered to do so."

"Was the package the same as you delivered to the shop?"

"This soda was a Root Beer. Otherwise, the box was the same. I suspected it was another bomb. I handled it with more caution."

"Did Walter ask you to do any other errands?" Ivar asked.

"Two days ago, I was to check on those bones they found at the shop. I dressed in a white coat and entered the lab, but I couldn't find any records. People talked about the bones, though. I gather they are old, all females. I can't imagine what bearing they have with anything today; just something that the bomb uncovered."

"Anything else?" Ivar got up to limp around and work the kinks out.

"I was supposed to get Mrs. McFitzroy's key from Samantha, but I failed that mission, too."

"Why did you need the key?"

"Don't know," Ter said. "Walter only told me to get the key. I suppose I'll have further orders waiting."

"Who else is involved?"

"Don't know that either. I wish it wasn't me. I'm sure Walter feels the same way. He sweats like a pig. Smells like one, too."

"What else can you tell me about Walter?"

"He's about my age, thirty-five. Wears faded blue jeans and a black vest over a black T-shirt. I saw him in scrubs once. Weighs about 170 pounds, maybe an inch or two taller than me, 6 foot 1 or 2 inches."

"That fits the description of a lot of men," Brody interjected. "Does he have any distinguishing marks?"

"There's a tattoo of the American Flag on his left forearm. When he gets nervous, he pumps his fist to watch the flag wave."

"I'll bring in a sketch artist when we're done here," Ivar said.

"Guess I should have contacted the police earlier. When I ran from you that morning, I was scared spitless. They have my family. Who knows what they're doing to them? I feel like I'm on a short electrical cord that going to zap me any second."

"Who is Walter's boss?" Ivar asked.

"Haven't a clue," Ter said. "He talks to Walter by cell phone. Maybe if you track him down, Walter will give you the boss's number. I can't imagine what they wanted with some Podunk fountain shop, much less why they'd injure the McFitzroys."

"How did you get selected for the job?" Ivar asked.

"I wish I knew. Look, I've told you everything I know. Can't you help me out here? Save my family, I'm begging you."

"Why did you point a gun at Samantha?" Ivar asked.

"To get her out of the house. I was afraid the brown box was another bomb, and I didn't want anyone else to get hurt."

Ivar took a deep breath and let it out slowly. "If you were afraid for her life, why didn't you fess up when I cuffed you? Maybe we could have saved her home."

Ter's jaw dropped. His eyes flew open. "Oh, my God! Did it explode already? Was anyone hurt?"

"I don't know many details, but I know Sam wasn't hurt."

"Walter said to go back and watch tomorrow at 10 a.m. I thought she'd be at work, and I planned to call in an anonymous tip."

"But you went ahead and planted the bomb."

"Sort of. It must have been the can of soda, but how can that be? I brought the brown box inside. Afraid it would go off; I took it outside and left it by the living room window under a shrub. The soda I set in the living room next to an empty Dr. Pepper can."

"Did you see anyone as you entered Miss McFitzroy's house?"

"No neighbors gawked out their windows if that's what you mean," Ter said. "They might have been watching, but it was dinnertime, so most were probably eating."

"Do you have any idea where your family was taken?"

"Believe me, I've searched. I checked the airlines, train station, bus station, and every back alley from here to Fort Collins. I can't find them. I'm scared to death that he'll hurt them. So please, don't let the reporters tell anyone I'm here."

"We'll do everything in our power to rescue your family. I've contacted the Denver Post, the Rocky Mountain News, and Channel 12. They've agreed to hold off their news release for another 24 hours. After that, I'm not sure what I can do."

Ter's hands shook. His breath came out in small pants.

"What else?" Brody asked.

"Let my family know that I love them." Tears filled Ter's eyes. "If I die, be sure to hunt down Walter H. Scrubbs. Or at least that's the name he used. Call in the sketch artist."

"This concludes our interview with Terrance Rodriguez." Ivar shut off the recorder.

Brody left the room to get the artist.

"Thanks for the information," Ivar said.

Ter asked, "How do I arrange for bail?"

Help From a Friend

Samantha climbed from her mother's car in front of her burned-out condo. "Thanks for dropping me off, Mom. I'll see you later today."

Amos Vickers walked toward the Honda. "Morning, Bridget.

Sam."

Mom rolled down her window. "You're up early. It's barely sunrise."

"I heard the terrible news and had to stop by to see if there's anything I can do for my old pal's family."

"Thanks, Amos," Mom said. "I see you got a new car."

"Yeah, someone stole my other red convertible."

"Do you have plans for tonight?" Bridget asked. "Why don't you and Linda stop over for dinner? You can tell us about your vacation to South America. It'll help take my mind off all that's happened recently."

"Sorry, not tonight. I'm a guest speaker for the African Charity Event in Denver. We've raised four million so far."

"I don't know what the poor people would do without your generosity."

Grinning, Amos pulled himself to his full height. "It's not what I do for them. It's what we can accomplish when we work together."

"I know you're busy." Mom returned his smile. "We'll get together some night during your free time."

"Free time? It won't be the same. I'll sure miss playing those hot games of chess with Pops. Maybe you'd like to stop by for a game now and then, Sam."

"Sounds like fun, Uncle Amos, but I have to find Pops."

"I heard he was in the shop when it blew up. Terrible, just terrible. When's the funeral?"

"Funeral?" Mom asked. "Why would—"

"No plans yet." Samantha eyed her mother and sent a warning look. "We're waiting to see if..." Glancing down, she kicked at a rock fluttering on the ground. A gust of cold air blew the hair from her shoulders. *Tobias.*

"Oh, that's right. They haven't found his body," Amos said. "I understand. Well, we still have fond memories of Pops—maybe just a memorial service. If you need any financial help, let me know. You can give me the key, and I could go through his safe-deposit box."

"Why would she do that?" Samantha glared at him.

"Ah." Amos' eyes darted between mother and daughter. "I know how difficult last wills and testaments can be. The bank's always willing to help out." He leaned into the Honda window and kissed Mom on the cheek. "Think about it, Bridget. You know you can always count on me to lend a helping hand."

"Thanks. See you soon." Mom's window rolled up, and she made a U-turn, and then drove away.

"Good to see you, Sam. I'm sorry to hear about your condo. Thank God you're safe. I wonder what the bomber was looking for?"

Samantha's eyes narrowed. "Why would you ask that? Was there something in my house they would want other than me?"

Amos shook his head. "No, it was just a thought that crossed my mind. Think nothing of it. I'd better run. It'll be another busy day." He climbed into his new red convertible and rocketed away leaving skid marks in his wake.

"That was odd," Ivar said as he stepped from her burned-out property.

"When did you get here?" Samantha asked.

"I parked down the street and walked around the block to get a better view. Can you give me a ride to my car? I want to talk to you."

"Hop in." Samantha slid into the driver's side. Her hand flinched when it brushed against the steering wheel. "It's hot in here." She opened the windows.

Ivar climbed into the car. "Thanks for the lift."

"What did Ter have to say?" Samantha started the engine.

Buckling his seatbelt, Ivar paused at her question. "It's complicated. Come down to the station to talk. I think he's posted bail by now."

Samantha's jaw dropped. "You let him go? He might have killed Pops. He bombed the shop, not to mention my house, and destroyed everything I own. How could you?"

"As I said, it's complicated."

"I've got all the time in the world." She leaned toward him and scowled. "As a matter of fact, I'm on a month's leave from work. They think I need time to recuperate." Her tone grew more condescending. "I wonder why that is. Maybe because my whole world's falling apart, and the man who caused it will be free to do more damage?"

Ivar didn't answer.

"Colby never would have let him go." Samantha gunned the engine and pulled behind Ivar's cop car. "Get out!"

"Don't be like that, Sam."

"Samantha. The name's Samantha. Some people are so dense. I have to go, so get out!"

Ivar reached around her and locked her car door. "Not until you understand the truth."

"What truth?" She put her car in neutral and turned toward him. "Do you know where I can find Pops?"

"No."

Did Ter bomb the shop?"

"He thinks so."

"Did Ter bomb my house?"

"I'm sure he did."

"Then, why let him get away?" Samantha put up her hands in frustration. "And don't tell me it's complicated. I want to know everything Ter told you."

"I can't share that information."

"Then get out." Samantha pushed Ivar's shoulder and tried to get him to budge.

Rock solid, he refused to move.

"That's your car, isn't it?" Samantha crossed her arms over her chest in disgust.

"Yup." Ivar's dimples grew deeper with that grin plastered across his face.

She inhaled his soft, masculine scent. It brought back fond memories. She wasn't in the mood for that. "You going to get out?"

"I don't think so. Not just yet." Ivar's eyes darkened with a hint of steel gray. She'd only seen that once before. And they'd nearly fallen in bed together.

Mixed emotions flooded her mind, wanting him, yet angry. "Well, I can't sit here all day." She spun around and popped open the lock on her door. "If you won't leave, I will."

Ivar grabbed her arm and pulled her toward him. "Trust me, okay?"

"I did up until you let Ter go free." Her hand reached for the latch.

Ivar wrapped her in his arms and pulled her close. "I have my reasons." He leaned in and hovered over her mouth.

His warm breath mingled with hers. She curled her arm around his neck. Their lips locked. The kiss was long and deep. It made her heart flutter.

He released her and moved to the door. "Don't get involved."

A small gasp escaped her lips. "Uh-huh." Her eyes blinked. "I mean, no. Yes, I trust you. No, I must get involved."

"Your life's in danger."

"Yeah, now that Ter is back on the streets!" Samantha glared.

"It's not like that."

"Really, Ivar? Cuz if Ter bombed both places, he's going to pay!" She put her car in gear. "Time to get out."

"Wait." Ivar placed his hand on hers, now resting on the gearshift. "His wife and kids are being held hostage."

Samantha leaned against the steering wheel. A deep breath escaped her lips. "Shit, what bastard would do that?"

"The stakes are high." Ivar gave her fingers a gentle squeeze. "This ups the ante. Stay clear." He got out of the car and slammed the door. Leaning in the window, he added, "Promise me."

"All right." Samantha managed to say. "I'll stop looking for Pops. Now, I have to get my laptop from work. I'll see you later."

Heading to his car, he called over his shoulder, "Don't do anything foolish."

Samantha's hands shook as she clutched the wheel. Heart racing, she tried to slow her breathing. She ran the tip of her tongue over her lips and could still feel the lingering tingle from their kiss.

Her focus returned. The tires squealed as she took off. Samantha swore not to look for Pops, but nothing would stop her from tracking the bomber.

Tailing Ter

Samantha sat in her idling car and watched Ter leave the station. His face, drawn and pale, glistened with sweat.

Ter wiped his brow, glanced around him, and then slipped into his vehicle and parked two cars up from hers.

She waited until he pulled out and followed at a safe distance. It wasn't easy. Traffic was heavy as they got on the main highway. Samantha nearly lost him twice but managed to tail him to Fort Collins.

He parked in front of a two-story brick building along a side road, and then he used his cell phone. Slipping the phone into his pocket, he stepped out of his car and ran to the garage. His fingers tapped a code into the automatic door opener.

The garage door opened, and he darted inside.

Samantha noted the house numbers along the side of the front entrance and called her mother. "I need a huge favor. Can you go online and look up this address? I need to know who owns the house."

"Okay." Before her mother could get the information, Ter backed out of the garage in a white truck. The door closed behind him.

"Shoot." Samantha ducked as he drove past her.

"What is it, honey?" her mother asked.

"Keep looking and call me back. I'm on the move again."

Ter drove around the block twice, headed back on Highway 14, and then south on Highway 85.

Mom called back with the phone number and the name of the owner.

"Text me, and I'll check it out later." The car in front of Samantha pulled onto a side road, leaving her following directly behind Ter's truck. "I can't let him see me." She slowed and let another car pass.

"Can't let who see you?" her mother asked.

The pickup's right blinker lit up as Ter slowed to a stop. "Where's he going?"

"Who, honey? Should I call Ivar?"

"No! I'm supposed to be at the office getting my laptop and then going home. Whatever you do, do not call Ivar."

"But Sam." Her mother's voice trembled.

"He's pulling off the road." The dirt trail extended deep into the woods. "I need to find a way to follow without him seeing me."

"Now you're scaring me."

"Gotta go." Samantha pulled the phone from her ear.

Her mother shouted, "Wait! Let Ivar do his job and come home. I don't want anything to happen to you."

"Don't worry. I'll call back soon." Samantha disconnected the call and drove slowly down the path, hoping Ter didn't notice her. She pulled off the road to wait. *As long as I can see his dust, I can follow.*

Samantha inched her car forward in Ter's wake until the cloud of kicked-up gravel disappeared. *No. I can't lose him.* Samantha pulled back onto the road and sped closer. Rounding the corner at 30 mph, she caught a glimpse of the white pickup parked along the side of the road. She passed the truck.

No one was inside.

She peered into her rearview mirror and saw that Ter was on foot.

There was nowhere safe to park, so she drove down the hill and off the path. Her car bumped over the rough terrain. Samantha pulled in between a group of boulders and a small outcrop of cottonwood trees. Glancing back to the trail, she was sure no one would see her car.

She ran across the foxtail grass, stumbling into unseen holes and over hidden rocks until she came to the rise.

Ter stood by an old wood shack with a tin roof. He reached above the door, grabbed something, probably a key, and then fumbled with the lock. The door opened, and he ducked inside.

Once Ter entered, she jogged the distance to the back of the building and placed her ear on the outside wall. It sounded as if he was talking to someone. No reply. Must be on the phone.

"Is the family safe?" Ter asked. "I'm fine. ...jail and ... messages..." His words muffled and trailed off.

Samantha crept closer to the back door, chanced a peek through the cracked window, and his voice became clear.

"Give me a hint. Where is Walter hiding you?" Nodding, he tucked the phone between his ear and shoulder and opened the fridge door. He pulled out a soda and nudged the door shut with his elbow. Ter pulled the tab and gulped. "Did he hit you again?"

Slamming the can onto the counter, he moved out of Samantha's line of sight.

Samantha crept to another window. His arm snaked along a shelf near the ceiling and pulled out a gun. He moved again, and she returned to the broken window.

"Honey, stop crying." Ter opened a drawer. He loaded the gun and shoved it into the back of his waistband.

"I already told you. I'm fine. Let me talk to Tommy." Ter's face grimaced. His fists clenched. "Walter put Tommy on the phone. I want to know my kids are okay."

He left Samantha's line of sight again, so she ducked to be safe and listened.

"Do it, Walter! I'm not going to…Shit! It's nearly noon. There's no way I can get that key by one-thirty." Ter paused. "Okay! I'll get it by three. I'll do as you say, but don't touch my family! First, let me talk to my son."

When she chanced another peek, Ter paced the small kitchen. "Tommy? Are you taking care of your sister?" "Good. Do you remember our first ball game?" "What fun. We should do that little venture again sometime soon." He crossed his fingers and then nodded. "That's my boy. Protect Lisa. I love you, too."

His face suddenly grew fierce, "Wait, Walter!" Ter jerked the cell from his ear and flung it across the room. The phone broke in two. He swore at Walter. "Damn it. Look what you made me do!" Scooping up the pieces, he tried to fit them together again. After punching the numbers several times, he cussed and tossed the cell into the trash. "Gotta get a phone."

Ter glanced up and his fierce eyes locked on Samantha. "Stupid woman!" He dashed for the door. "Wait! I need to talk to you."

Samantha bolted across the field. Running at top speed, she lost sight of him. Tufts of grass blurred as she zigzagged around rocks and saplings.

Footsteps thundered after her.

Her heart pounded at each step… breaths shortened. She became dizzy. Can't stop!

"What are you doing out here?" Ter yelled. His raspy breaths grew louder.

Where did I park? She looked behind her.

Ter had narrowed the distance.

She kept running.

A loud pop sounded.

She fell forward and landed on the ground. Her arm throbbed. Grit flew into her eyes. Closing them, she rolled on the ground and tumbled down the hill.

The footsteps stopped.

When she opened her eyes, Ter stood over her. His gun pointed at her chest.

"Don't shoot!" Samantha curled into a fetal position and hoped he wouldn't fire.

"Why did you follow me?" Ter didn't even seem winded.

"Why are you trying to kill me?"

"I'm not." Ter motioned with his gun. "Get up."

What would Ivar do? Samantha rolled to her side and kicked at his leg, but he leapt away.

"Try that again. I'll shoot."

A numb, hollow feeling engulfed her. *No one knows where I am except Mother.* Memories of Ivar flashed through her mind. *My last conversation made it clear. Do not call for help.* Dread swallowed her whole and took her as a prisoner.

"Get up." Ter's voice rasped. "This has been a hell of a week. Don't test my patience!"

"All right, I'm not going to fight you." Her arm throbbed. The restraint strap had torn, and the cloth ripped to shreds. Her eyes widened when she saw a black streak across the gouged plaster. "You nicked my cast."

"Lucky shot." Ter grabbed her good arm and lifted her to her feet. "Move it!"

The cast grew too heavy to hold up without the sling. She jerked forward.

"More like it," Ter said. "Now, let's go into the shack and chat." He kept the gun pointed at her back as she stumbled ahead of him.

Samantha paused and shook her head. Everything sounded far away.

The gun barrel nudged her back. "I said, 'Move it!'"

"Careful with that gun," Samantha said. "Remember what happened last time?"

He nudged her again. "I don't want to hurt you, but I will if you give me no other choice. Come on, move!"

"I'm moving." She lifted her right arm and held it close to her waist. "Do you have anything for pain?" Rubbing the cast, it cracked open. "Oops, I need some duct tape to put this back together."

"Duct tape is a good idea. Keep walking," Ter said. "I'll get you what you need, but you're going to hand over your keys when we get inside, and I'm going to leave you here. I'll come back for you tomorrow."

"What?" Samantha asked. "You can't leave me out here by myself. There's nothing around for miles."

"Exactly, Miss McFitzroy. Be glad I only shot your cast." Ter opened the shack door and held it with his foot while he motioned for her to enter. This time, he gave her a nudge with his elbow to coax her inside. "I have Ibuprofen. I hope that's good enough. Duct tape is in the drawer."

Samantha squinted into the dark room until her eyes adjusted to the low light.

Ter moved inside. "You still haven't answered me. Why are you here?"

"Why did you bomb the shop?"

He dug through several items in the cupboard over the sink. "Here it is." Ter set the Ibuprofen bottle on the counter and poured a glass of water. "Drink up, then hand me your keys."

"Are you trying to cover up some deadly crime?" Samantha fumbled with the childproof cap. "You destroyed my home!" She couldn't line up the top to the arrow on the bottle.

"Sorry about that." Ter grabbed the bottle from her, twisted the cap off, poured out two tablets, and set them on the counter. "I'll leave it open, so help yourself if you need some later."

Squinting in disbelief, she reread the medication's bottle label and cautiously took the pills. "Thanks." Samantha swallowed them with the water.

Ter rummaged through the drawer and found a roll of duct tape. He handed it to her.

She struggled to free the end of the roll and held it up. "Would you mind cutting off a piece?"

He groaned. "Keys first."

Samantha pulled the key ring from her pocket. "This key opened the door to my condo, not that I need it anymore. Anyone can get inside after your last visit."

"And the key to your Mother's?" Ter asked.

Samantha frowned. "What do you need it for?"

"I'll take all of them." Ter snatched the key ring and pushed her into a chair. He leaned over her, one arm on either side, pinning her down. Piercing gray eyes narrowed. "Which KEY is it?" His fist raised.

"The red, white, and blue one," Samantha spat back.

"To what door?"

"Back garage door."

Ter stood up and studied the squatty round barreled key.

"If you hurt Mom or set another bomb, I swear I'll get even."

"I'll try not to hurt anyone else." Ter frowned. "I've never seen a key like this."

"You can find one at any Ace Hardware." Samantha cupped her broken cast, trying to ease the pain.

"Doubt that. Is the garage attached to the house? I have to get into the house." She nodded, so he pocketed the keys and tore off a piece of duct tape. "I suppose you want me to wrap the cast, too?"

"That would be nice."

Ter pulled the cracked cast back together and wrapped tape around it.

"Nice job." Samantha got up from the chair and walked closer to the door. "I might be able to get you a position as an EMT when you get out of prison."

Ter grimaced. "I don't plan to return to jail until I free my family." He dashed up behind her and spun her around. "Now, hand over your phone. I can't run the risk of you calling anyone."

Fishing through her pants pocket, she asked, "Do you know where they have your family?"

"Not yet, but my son's working on it."

"What do you mean?" Samantha turned away from Ter and walked to the table while removing the Sim card from her cell.

"I don't have time to chat," Ter said. "Hopefully, I'll live long enough to return, but your life is in danger, and someday you may thank me."

"So you're not going to kill me?" Samantha asked.

"I'm already charged with attempted murder because of you."

"But I thought YOU wanted to hurt me."

"Not me, but my boss, whoever he is, will harm you if given a chance."

"Then take me with you," Samantha said. "I'll help you find your family."

"In case you haven't noticed, it's dangerous having you around." Ter grabbed her phone and pocketed it. "I'm better off searching on my own."

Her head throbbed nearly as much as her arm. "How long do I have to be here?" Samantha sat in an armchair, rested her elbow on the table, and glanced around the small room.

"Until I return. I'm not sure for how long, but to be on the safe side, stay put. I need your shoes so you won't try to run. You know there's nowhere to go."

"My shoes? You have Mom's key and my cell phone. Now, you want my shoes?"

"Come on, quit stalling. Where did you park your car? I don't want anyone to see it."

Sighing, Samantha kicked off her sneakers. "No one will find it."

"I will." Ter snatched her shoes and tossed them toward the door, spun around, and picked up the duct tape. He grabbed her left arm.

Samantha tried to get up. "No, please don't."

Ter brought the tape down over her wrist and wrapped it around the arm of the chair. He tore off two more strips. "Now your legs."

Samantha jerked from the chair, stood on one foot, and lashed out with the other.

He ducked as her cast swung toward his head and captured her leg mid-kick. He shoved her ankle next to the chair leg and taped it over her jeans. Then he grabbed the other leg as she squirmed, still trying to deck him with her cast, and tipped the chair back.

Samantha landed in the chair seat with a thud. "Don't do this! Please, I'll be good."

Ter didn't pause. He finished taping down her legs and stood to inspect his work.

"I hope you rot in jail," she screamed and thrashed in place.

"They'll have to catch me first." Ter grabbed her right arm as it rammed into the back of the chair.

"Not my cast. How will I eat or take those pills you so kindly set out for me?"

Ter's hands fisted at his side. He grimaced and let out a low moan. "Call me stupid." He opened the fridge and pulled out a bottle of water, shoved it to the inside of her casted hand, and taped her fingers around it. "Now, if you want a drink, open the bottle by using your teeth." He put the ibuprofen on the table. Then he taped the area of her cast near the elbow to the chair back, leaving enough slack for her to get the water bottle to her mouth. "If you know what's good for you, stay put!" "I'll scream."

Ter glanced back. "Go ahead and yell. There's no one around to hear you." He grabbed her shoes and left the shack. The door slammed behind him, and the lock clicked.

On Her Own

Ter grabbed his jacket from the back of his cab and slipped it on to cover his gun. Sam's vehicle was nowhere in sight. Glancing back at the house, he heard Samantha screaming. "Save your voice. No one can hear you," he shouted back and climbed into his truck. "I don't need any more complications in my life."

Starting the engine, he inched down the hill, watching for Sam's car. After a mile, with no car in sight, he turned around.

Matted grass led into the woods. Why *didn't I see that before?* It was easier to spot in this direction.

He pulled the truck behind a boulder. With a sigh, he opened his door and dropped to the ground. Ter circled Samantha's car, ran his hand under the fender, and found a spare key in a magnetic holder. Pocketing it, he checked the backseat and trunk for anything she might use to escape. Satisfied that he'd left nothing of value behind, he returned to his truck and drove away.

***

Angry, ready to rip Ter apart, Samantha thrashed against her restraints. They didn't budge. Leaning forward, she balanced on the balls of her feet. She hopped up and down, banged the chair on the floor, and hoped to break it. The chair teetered several times, but it didn't even crack.

All the activity, pulling, and twisting only made the restraints tighter. The fingers on her left hand tingled. Only her right arm moved, and that wasn't by much. *I have to get out of here! What's he going to do to Mom?*

She felt a rush of adrenaline—flushed and hot. Yet her hands turned ice cold. They trembled.

Gray spots clouded her vision. *Can't breathe!* Air rushed out in rapid pants. A dull roar grew in her ears. *Don't pass out.* Samantha shut her eyes and focused. *Stop hyperventilating.*

After several deep breaths, she calmed her racing heart. Frantically searching the room for something to cut the tape, she spied a fork on the edge of the sink. Images of hopping her chair around the kitchen island to the sink vaporized as reality set in. *I'll never make it that far.*

Samantha gritted her teeth and clenched her left hand into a fist. "How do I free myself?" She remembered last year's self-defense class. *Why didn't I pay more attention? Restraints. I know they covered that. But duct tape?*

"Think!" She closed her eyes and concentrated. The demonstration came clearly into her mind. Her instructor had both wrists taped, one over the other. He lifted his arms overhead. With great force, he brought them down while twisting and pulling his wrists apart. The tape tore. So did the skin on his wrists, but he was free. *My arms aren't taped together, but maybe…*

She lifted her right arm, but the plastered cast limited her movement. Her upper arm budged from the back rung of the chair as she leaned forward, but not enough to reach her ankles or left wrist.

The tape wound around the bottled water and immobilized her fingers. Only her right thumb was free to move. Her left wrist seemed glued to the arm of the chair. Sweat dripped down her spine.

She leaned forward, lifted the chair, and planned to jump her way to the counter, but on the second hop, it tipped. "Ouch!" Landing on her right side, she rolled with momentum. Her vision blurred until she blinked away the tears.

The chair leg creaked when she moved. Samantha kicked with all her strength. A jagged piece of wood broke free near her knee but stayed attached to her right ankle.

She lifted her leg toward the arm of the chair. Unfortunately, the jagged edge wedged itself along the outside of her leg. No matter how she twisted, she couldn't ram the stick high enough to free her arms. *No leverage.*

She inched herself across the floor and jammed the toe of her restrained leg against the table pedestal.

Samantha slumped over and tried to grab the end of the tape around her cast with her teeth. She got a mouthful of plaster.

With a deep breath, she propped her casted elbow with her freed knee, raising it higher as she hunched forward. A corner of tape came loose near her elbow. Samantha yanked her right arm up and down, gradually getting more movement. She nibbled at the tape's edge with her teeth. It grabbed her lip, making it bleed, but the tape didn't stick as tight. She leaned over and finally teased the tape away.

Once her right arm was free, she peeled the tape from her fingers using her left hand. Then she freed her left wrist, reached down, and untaped her other leg.

"I did it!" *Ivar would be proud.*

Samantha stretched and rubbed her wrists. Blood dripped from her lip, which she blotted on a napkin. "Okay, now to get away."

She leaned against the table and eyed Ter's cell phone in the trash. *Maybe...* She picked up the two pieces and tried to put them together. The cell lit up intermittently. Unable to get a dial tone, she continued to manipulate the cover. When she held it in one position, voice mail came up. Samantha listened to the first message.

A male's voice said, "Meet today at 1:30 p.m. Usual place, bring the key, or your wife will bear the brunt..." The phone crackled and cut out.

Where did he put that duct tape? The roll lay on the counter. Samantha padded over, pulled a small strip from the roll, and used her teeth to tear the tape. She sat on another chair, stuck one end to the table's edge, and toiled for several minutes, getting the phone to work again. Holding the parts carefully, she taped them together and got voice mail.

This time, the message continued. "...brunt of my wrath. The call ended, and another message followed. This time a female's voice said, "Ter, I heard you're in jail. Call me ASAP. No, Walter—"

A man said, "Give me that. The boss doesn't have much patience. He wants that key. Make sure you get it."

A woman cried, "Ter, do as he says." Something chimed in the background and the call ended. "You have no more messages."

I need to write this down. Samantha held the phone to her ear and got up to find a pen and paper.

Samantha searched the drawer. She found a pencil and a business card. The bank logo on the card looked familiar. Sure enough, Amos Vickers' name appeared at the bottom. She flipped over the card, replayed the voice-mail message, and scribbled down everything word-for-word.

"Those chimes. Where have I heard them before?" The message repeated. "…wants that key…" sent a shiver down her spine.

"The key! I have to call Mom." Samantha dialed. An automatic recording said, "No more minutes, so she tried an emergency number."

No luck there, either. *You would think I could at least call 911 without minutes. Someone should change that.* Samantha fished in her pocket for her Sim card. She turned over the cell phone and discovered tape across the back. She had to disassemble her patch job. Not an easy task with one hand, but she managed to pull off a portion of the tape. The back cover wouldn't budge. Now what? She shook her head. Think.

Samantha reached into her pocket, found a coin, and then wedged it under the lid, but it was too thick. Maybe a screwdriver. She rummaged through the drawer that had held the duct tape.

No luck. Those chimes were Gary's ringtone. That's where I've heard them. I heard it at the bank last week. Is Gary Gordon behind this? No, Doesn't make sense. Anyone could have that ringtone. She tried a few more drawers and found a table knife among the silverware. The blade slid the cover free, and she replaced the Sim with her own card.

Again, no dial tone appeared when she got it back together.

Okay, start over. Samantha removed her patchwork, tore off a new piece of tape, and stuck it to the counter. She fumbled with the parts until it lit up and retaped the phone. The dial tone sounded at intermittent intervals. Scrolling down her contact list, she found 'Mom' and pressed the button.

"Samantha, I'm glad you called." Her mother's voice rose in an unusual tone.

Samantha gasped. "Mom, you're in danger?" Ter couldn't possibly have reached Mom's house yet.

The phone crackled, and her mom's voice faded.

"Hello? Are you there? Ter has your key."

"…fire…come home now…Amos—" the phone died.

Frustrated, Samantha repeatedly tried but couldn't get it to work. *Did someone set fire mom's home? No, she wouldn't have been that calm, not that she was calm.* "Amos? Amos Vickers?" Her mind raced as she tried to figure out the disjointed message.

Panicked, Samantha checked above the doorjamb, hoping there was a spare key.

Nothing.

She checked every drawer in the house and peered through the cracked glass. She grabbed the busted chair and rammed it through the window. A shard punctured her foot, and she remembered she had no shoes.

Samantha hobbled back to the table. She sat down, removed her stockings, and pulled slivers of glass out of the bottom of her feet. *I saw a first-aid kit a moment ago.* After searching a few cupboards, she found the box and got a Band-Aid to cover the cut.

She hunted through the hall closet and found a pair of boots. They were too big but better than nothing. A roll of paper towels stood on the counter next to the fridge. She tore off a sheet, ripped it in two, and stuffed the toes of the boots to make them fit.

She shoved the cell phone into her pocket and grabbed a soda and a bottled water from the fridge. Anxious to get home, she ducked through the window and ran down the hill.

The back door to her car was open.

Samantha unlocked and slammed the back door shut.

She placed the drinks into the passenger's seat. *Oh, right. No keys.* Scuff marks streaked the rear of the car. It wasn't easy, but she slipped between the trees and ran her fingers along the back fender. The magnetic box was gone. *Maybe the driver's side.* She hoped she'd put it there instead.

"Ahh, Ter, you took the spare key. I have to get home!" She paced for a few minutes, hoping to come up with a plan. Something would come to her. It always did.

Stamping around to the driver's door, she flung it open, and popped the trunk. *I don't have time to wait for inspiration.*

Under the spare tire, she found her tool kit. She removed a set of screwdrivers, slammed the trunk, and slid back into the car.

Recalling an incident last year, she set to work. *I wonder if I can expose the ignition switch.* She unfastened the screws that held the plastic trim on the steering column.

Samantha carefully separated the electrical wires from the switch as Pops had done. Then, she put the slotted screwdriver into the ignition. *Okay, this better work.*

Her seatbelt snapped in place. She turned the screwdriver.

"Too small." She tried another screwdriver. Three tries later, the engine roared.

"Yes!" She shoved the car into reverse, backed onto the trail, and headed for town. *I hope Mom's home is still there.*

Lost in the Woods

Pops regretted leaving the comforts of the depot behind. He spent the night in an abandoned hotel and awoke early. The chill of morning air seeped through him. He rubbed his shoulders to generate some heat. *If I don't get home soon, I could freeze to death out here.*

He found an old quilt in an upstairs closet, wrapped it around him as a jacket, and went outside to use the outhouse. His stomach growled. *Some of those canned beans sure sound good right about now. A pump would be nice, too.*

Pops rummaged through the kitchen for a morsel of food—nothing but cobwebs, dust bunnies, and bare cupboards. He moved to the pantry. Some grub-infested flour, a can of sardines with no expiration date, and a beer can—*beer and sardines—my favorite.* He nestled in a corner, away from the drafty, broken window, and ate what felt like his last meal.

Buck up, old boy. I used to march all day in freezing rain through mine-filled rice paddies without complaint. I can't believe how soft I've gotten.

Pops debated taking the quilt with him. *It's not mine, but no one else is using it. Then again, it's too heavy to lug around, especially with this laptop.* He shook his head in disgust, folded the quilt, and put it back in the closet where he'd found it. *God only knows why I'm so attached to this computer.*

He went back into the kitchen, picked up his trash, and went outside. He dumped the empty cans in a rusty trash barrel behind the hotel and set out for home.

Pops hiked for hours. The gravel road turned into a dusty trail. It narrowed into a footpath.

Heavy clouds grew across the sky. The sting of crisp mountain air made him shiver. *I should have taken that quilt and left this blasted laptop behind.* It felt as if the computer weighed a ton. He shifted it from under one arm to the other. Pop's tongue felt thick and stuck to the roof of his mouth. He licked his lips. "Water." He searched up and down the trail. Not a trickle was in sight.

No one had passed him in two days. *Leaving the depot was one of the dumbest things I've ever done.* He walked further into the woods to get out of the sun.

Pops found a stump near a fork in the road and sat for a few minutes. Taking the last stick of gum from his pocket, he bit into the peppermint flavor. His mouth watered briefly, satisfying his thirst. *I can't stay here all night.* He wadded the wrapper and put it into his pants pocket.

Now, he had to decide which path to take. The left fork appeared more promising, so Pops hoisted himself from the stump and moved on. Although he hummed off-key, it quelled his growing concern.

The trail's twists and turns went uphill and down. Exhausted, Pops paused near a sawed-off stump. *I'll rest a moment.*

A wadded gum wrapper lay on the ground next to his feet. He jammed his hand into his pocket and found a hole. A groan escaped his lips. *I can't believe it. I'm walking in circles.*

In desperation, he called, "Gramps, are you out there?"

No reply. Not even a ruffle of leaves nearby to give him an indication that the ghost heard his plea. *Maybe I should have followed the railroad tracks rather than the dirt path, but I thought it would lead to a road.*

Pops took the right fork this time, hoping to find his way back to the highway. The torturous climb took him around curves and down a steep hill along a ravine filled with water. The rougher it got, the more Pops realized he had made several wrong turns along the way.

Unable to carry the laptop in his arms any longer, he tucked the shirttails into his pants, opened his shirt, and slipped the computer next to his chest. He re-buttoned his top. The laptop rested on his belt and waistband, leaving his arms free.

The brush grew thicker. The ledge shrunk to barely enough room to set one foot in front of the other. "Turn back," screamed in his ears, but he didn't dare for fear of falling into the water below.

Pops stepped on loose gravel and flailed as the ground gave way beneath his weight. He fell from the edge of the ravine toward several trees.

"Tobias, help!" Believing he was a goner, for sure, he reached out and grasped for several limbs. They broke like sticks until he landed on the top of an evergreen tree. Flesh ripped from his palms. His hands burned. Blood dripped from his forehead and blurred his vision, but he'd saved his computer.

Hanging on for his life, he peered out at the water rushing over the jagged rocks below. *If I ever believed in a God, I do now. Please send Tobias to rescue me.*

Still nothing.

His heart pounded. A lump formed in his throat. Pops felt ashamed. All his military training dashed to the wayside. His commander's voice echoed in his mind. "Take responsibility for your actions, son."

"Yes, sir." He almost saluted. He inched forward and stepped onto a lower limb. Taking one toehold at a time, he climbed down the tree to the water's edge. With cupped hands, he doused his face, and rinsed his mouth to quench his thirst. Out of breath, he lay down to rest.

The wind echoed through the ravine. The snap of wood jarred his memory. It transported him back to Vietnam. Fear clutched his soul. He crouched among the long grass and listened for gunfire. *None came.* He inched himself to a standing position. His head spun, and he lost his balance for a moment.

A jagged breath escaped his lungs. *I'm trapped.* Shadows of fallen comrades lay scattered on the ground around him. He swore he saw Amos' brother among them. Blown to bits by a grenade, the man had sacrificed his life to save his buddies.

Raw panic rushed through him. Pops jogged along the creek and clawed his way through the rocks, anything to get out of the ravine. "I can't stay here."

He refused to become a POW again.

A low whine grew louder.

Pops stopped to listen. *Is it a chopper? Friend or foe? Or the wind blowing through the treetops?* His hands shook, and his teeth chattered.

He didn't think so. They weren't moving enough to make the sound.

The sun hung low in the sky. It would be dark soon. "God, I *have* to get out of here!"

A loud howl came through the narrow valley.

Pops blinked. The bitter breeze snapped him to attention—feeling like a frozen statue, his vision cleared. No rice paddies. Only a deep gulch. Gravel whipped into his face. "Tobias?"

A light gray mist hovered. "Do I have to rescue you again?

Can't you stay put?"

"I'm sorry, Gramps. I wanted to check on my family. Can't I go home?" Pops lifted on the wind. "Where are you taking me?"

Searching for Sam

Colby's phone vibrated as he walked out of the Fort Collins office. A quick flick of his wrist brought the cell to his ear. "Detective Cage." Pausing mid-step, he frowned. "So, Ivar, which is it? A fire or another bomb? For a small town, you sure have your problems."

"Three crimes in nearly as many weeks," Ivar said. "I can't figure out why this is happening. I remember a year ago when the greatest excitement was Maddog getting a ticket for parking in front of a fire hydrant."

Colby dashed across the street to his car. "Was anyone injured? Wait, don't tell me it's Bridget McFitzroy."

"No, but I'm putting her and Sam in protective custody," Ivar said.

"Then who?" Colby climbed into his car and gunned the engine.

"Pops' best friend, Amos Vickers."

"The philanthropist?" Colby asked. "Was he killed?"

"No, fortunately, Amos wasn't home. The fire mainly damaged his garage, and his wife's Mercedes is a heap of molten metal. The fire destroyed three classic cars, too. His home's intact, at least for now. The firemen are still fighting to contain the flames."

"I'm on my way," Colby said. "Where are you now?"

"I'm pulling up to McFitzroy's home. Sam isn't going to be happy when I whisk them away, but I'm not taking any chances."

"Where are you taking them?" Colby pulled into traffic and headed for Hwy 14.

"I know a place where they'll be safe."

Chuckling, Colby said, "You're not even going to tell me, are you?"

"I have a hunch that you'll track her down. But why make it easy on you? I know Sam can't stop talking about you. You're like candy to her right now, but like most sweets, they dissolve or turn sour with time."

Colby heard a car door slam and pictured Ivar's jaws tighten with his bitter comment. "We'll see who she chooses. After you kidnap her, I'll be the man of her dreams, so do your job, and I'll do mine." He disconnected.

***

Twenty minutes later, Bridget McFitzroy hesitated before opening her door, walked outside, and let the screen door close behind her. "Oh, good afternoon, Ivar. How may I help you?" She sounded relieved.

"I'm here to protect you and Sam. Is she home?"

A frown appeared on her face. Bridget crossed her arms in front of her chest and tapped her foot. "Like you protected the Vickers' estate?"

"You know I can't predict the future," Ivar protested.

"No. Maybe not, but Amos is the most generous, loved, and admired man in the world. How could this happen?" Tears filled her eyes.

Ivar didn't flinch.

She ran a sleeve over her face. "His wife doesn't deserve this either. I spent the last hour with Linda, trying to comfort her. What's going on in this town? You're the law. Do something!"

"That's why I'm here, Ma'am." Ivar took a step closer to the screen and reached for the latch.

"Sam's not here."

Ivar was startled by the comment and jerked back. "Hasn't she come home yet? She was going by work to pick up her laptop and return home. That was early this morning."

Bridget glanced at the porch floor and bit her lip. "I know, but she made other plans."

"So you've heard from her?" Ivar glared. "Where is she?"

"Umm, I'm not sure where she is at the moment." Bridget turned back toward the door. "I'll let her know you're looking for her when she returns."

"Wait!" Ivar blocked Bridget. "You and Sam are in danger. Someone destroyed your property, attempted murder, not once, but twice, and now went after Pops' best friend. I want to know why."

"So do I." Bridget reached around him. She bumped the screen door against Ivar.

He refused to move.

"Are you arresting me?"

Ivar rolled his eyes. "No! I'm *protecting* you and Sam. I'll let you go inside under one condition. Pack a bag and come with me. You're going on vacation until this is resolved."

"As much as I respect you, Officer Rexall, it'll be a cold day in hell before I leave my home under your orders." Bridget was a foot shorter than Ivar; however, she nudged him aside, slipped inside, and slammed the door in his face. Clicking the lock, she leaned against the door, panting. A mutter crossed her lips. "I hope Sam's safe because I just pissed off her protector."

Ivar pounded frantically. "Where's Sam?"

When she didn't open up, he darted down the steps and disappeared around the corner of her house. Bridget ran to the back door and bolted it as Ivar wiggled the knob.

"I'm losing my patience," he yelled.

"Get a court order to evict me, but I'm not leaving!" Bridget shouted back.

"Fine," Ivar huffed. "You stay, but I want to know where Sam is."

"I wish I knew," Bridget said under her breath.

Ivar's voice calmed. "When did you last talk to her?"

"A few hours ago, she will be home soon." Bridget crossed her fingers and said under her breath, "At least, I hope so. I wish Pops was here."

The curtains fluttered as a cold breeze blew through the kitchen, and a gray mist hovered near the ceiling. A whistling whisper drifted in the air, "Follow me."

Unsure if she understood, Bridget stood still and listened.

The mist moved across the room to the side door leading to the attached garage.

Intrigued, she followed quietly behind and watched the fog briefly gather and disappear through the door. She turned the knob, stepped into the garage, and paused.

Bridget heard gravel crunch as Ivar left the building. *Good, he must have gotten discouraged.* The noise receded and a car door slammed out front. Wheels squealed on the driveway pavement as the engine whined.

Bridget flinched at a dinging sound and realized it came from her car. The driver's door swung open for her to enter.

The mist filled the passenger's side of the front seat. "Let's go."

Bridget went back into the house, grabbed her purse, and fished out her keys. She climbed into the car, pulled down the visor, and punched the remote button. When the garage door lifted, she backed out and closed the door.

"I can't believe I'm doing this." Shivering, Bridget reached around to the back seat and grabbed her sweater, slipped it on, and buckled her seatbelt. "I guess you'd be Tobias?"

"Sorry." The heater turned on. "I'm not the warm, loving great-grandfather-in-law type."

"Let's just say you're one cool guy." Bridget laughed. "Can you take me to Pops?"

Her right foot floored the gas pedal, and the car jerked to the right.

Bridget fought for control of the steering wheel. "Umm, it might be better if I drive and you navigate." She stopped before the gate, waited for it to open, and turned right. Once on the open road, Tobias took control of the car again. No matter what Bridget did, she couldn't seem to change their course.

"I think I'm getting the hang of this," Tobias said. The car straightened and the engine slowed as they drove down the gravel road. "Trust me."

Bridget wasn't sure if this was a wise decision to let a ghost drive, but she had no clue where they were headed, and she had to admit Tobias was keeping the car in the correct lane, so she sat back and let him drive. She asked, "How's Pops?"

"He's not doing well. I need your help."

Her heart raced. She leaned forward and peered toward the mist. "Was he injured during the blast?"

Tobias hesitated. "No."

"Okay, then what happened?"

"I have to concentrate on my driving to take you to him." Tobias took over the controls.

After nearly an hour, Bridget snapped, "How much farther? I want to see Pops."

"I think we're close."

Bridget frowned. "You never told me what happened to Pops."

"He left my hiding place and fell down a ravine. I couldn't get enough lift and dropped him along the road. Ruined his computer, and he will not speak to me."

"You dropped him?" Bridget gasped. "How high from the ground was he?"

"Umm, good question."

"Is he unconscious?" Bridget asked.

The car sped up. "Not anymore."

She grabbed the wheel so tightly that her knuckles turned white. "Where is he?" Her voice quivered with fear. "Take me to him, now!"

The mist moved over her, and the car shuddered. A high-pitched whine pierced her ears.

"Gull darn it. I can't lift both you and the car," Tobias hissed.

Her whole body vibrated until Bridget thought her teeth would crack. She closed her eyes and clenched her jaw. "Tobias, what's happening?"

The car came to a halt, and the wind caught her hair as the window zipped down. When Bridget opened her eyes, she found herself in the air. The parked car sat below her alongside the road. In a panic, she squeezed her eyes shut again and held her breath.

Landing gently, she lay on the grass and regained her senses.

Something brushed through her hair. A warm hand stroked her cheek.

"Bridget, I'm glad to see you," Pops said, "but now we're both lost."

Tobias' laugh rumbled. "Kids nowadays just don't get it. I'm protecting both of you."

Bridget got to her knees and knelt beside her husband. "Are you all right? I've been worried sick." She kissed his anxious face and lips and held on to his arm.

Pops sat under a tree, his back propped against the trunk. "Other than my ankle, a few bruises, and a bit scuffed up, I'm fine." Pops pulled up his pant leg. A large scab covered his knee. Scrape marks ran down his shin. His ankle puffed over his sneaker, twice its normal size. "My elbows are scabbed, too."

"We'd better clean them and check that ankle. It might be broken." Bridget looked around. There were only trees and grass. She heard rushing water in the distance. "Where are we?"

"Not far from the ravine I fell into," Pops said. "At least I'm back on level ground."

"Tobias, take us to my car," Bridget said.

When there was no response, Bridget called again. "Tobias, where are you?"

She got up and studied the area. "Feisty old fart. Where'd he go?"

"Have you heard from Sam?"

"Umm. Yes." A cold breeze whipped up the gravel around them. "Tobias, if that's you, I need my car," Bridget said. "It's parked a little ways from here."

"Well, that's not quite true." Tobias' chilly blast passed them. "I couldn't lift the car, so I sort of drove it after I dropped you off. I guess I need more lessons before I try again."

Bridget turned toward the breeze. Her eyes narrowed into a scowl. "What happened to my car?"

"Ah, you needed a new one anyway. That Honda was an '88."

"Did anyone get hurt?" Bridget asked with concern.

"Only my pride, but I think the car's totaled."

"Great," Pops said. "First my shop, now your car; what else can go wrong?"

Bridget paused. "There's Samantha's condo."

"What about her condo?"

"It blew up," Bridget said. "Gone, destroyed like our shop."

Pops struggled to get up. "Was Sam hurt?"

"She has a broken arm. That happened after the shop blew up, but no other injuries."

Pops wobbled a bit as he limped forward and crushed her to him. "What a relief, she's alive."

Bridget hugged him and pushed back. "There's more. Early this morning, someone burned down Amos's garage."

Pops' face paled. "Was Amos hurt?"

"No, he went to work early. Linda was still sleeping when it happened."

"Which garage was it?" Amos asked. "Where he keeps his classics?"

Bridget nodded. "That's the one, and Linda had her Mercedes parked in there. I went over as soon as Linda called. Then she had to give statements to the police and fire chief, so I went home."

"What's happening?" Pops asked. "I didn't think we had any enemies."

"What do we do now?" Bridget asked.

Pops whispered in her ear, "Whatever we do, let's not let Tobias know."

"I heard that," Tobias said. "I can even read your thoughts, so you can't hide anything from me."

"Good, then tell me where Sam is at this moment," Bridget said. "Ivar's looking for her."

"He's not the only one," Tobias said. "Unfortunately, I can't be in two places at once, so I'm not sure where she is."

"Find her and bring her here so we can fight this together," Pops said.

"That's what I was doing," Tobias retorted. "Now that Samantha moved back home, I thought I might be able to wrap up a few details, but nooo…you had to venture out on your own."

"Okay, okay!" Pops said.

"Not only venture. You had to lose your way."

"I was trying to get home."

The mist grew darker. "Then you fell into that ravine."

"All right," Pops shouted.

"And panicked. Thinking you're back in Vietnam."

"Enough! It was a dumb idea. What do we do now?"

"First, find a place for you to stay. It'll be dark soon, and I can't keep you warm."

Pops said, "Take us back to the depot. It was warm there. I can sleep on a bench in the waiting room, and Bridget can have the cot."

"Without the extra energy from the blast, I can't carry you that far," Tobias said. "I need my rest. I'm slowing down and can't keep popping from one place to another—"

"You get tired?" Bridget asked out of curiosity. "I never would have guessed."

"I've been around for over one hundred years," Tobias said. "This spirit isn't as strong as it used to be."

"How often do you rest?" Bridget asked.

"Every few months I need a week's rest. It's been nearly six months since my last break. Since I found out that my family was in danger."

"You can't leave now," Pops said. "A week is a long time."

"If I don't leave now, I might not be able to return even that soon." Tobias' voice grew weaker. "I'll be grounded for who knows how long."

"Sam's in trouble," Bridget said. "She's tailing Ter."

Tobias groaned. "I knew it."

Bridget gasped, "Oh. That's right. She mentioned something about my key. Why would anyone want to get into our house?"

"To plant a bomb?" Pops' voice cracked.

"He broke into Samantha's," Bridget said. "I'm sure he could break into our house, too. What's so special about that key? Tobias, do you know?"

The air remained still and warm. No answer came.

"Tobias!" Pops called out. When there was no reply, he leaned against a tree. "He must have gone to find Sam. Find me a stick, so I can walk. Maybe we can find shelter for the night."

Grounded

Back in the unkempt cemetery, Tobias' spirit hovered over the weed patch that surrounded his broken tombstone. The rusty fence had fallen down along the road. His wife's stone leaned at a thirty-degree angle. Three-foot tall, purple-headed Russian thistles grew from its base. *What a shame no family member comes here to oversee our resting place. I need to talk to Pops about that.*

His spirit dropped even lower to the ground. Tobias couldn't fight the pull back into his earthly body, dead to the world. The heaviness dragged him down until he could no longer materialize into a mist, much less take someone with him. *I don't have time to rest.*

Unable to resist, his soul needed a place to reflect, time to regenerate and revive his ghostly powers.

Unfortunately, Samantha was out there somewhere at danger's door. He'd lost contact with her when he felt a panicked tug from Pops. His strength waned, not even enough to whisk Pops from the ravine. Unable to blink the Honda, along with Bridget, he had to leave it on the roadside.

"I'm a failure, Molly," he said to his wife lying in the coffin next to him. "I found Sara, only to lose her reincarnated soul once again." Remembering his wife's loving smile, his gloom grew deeper. "Will I ever see you again?"

Darkness overtook him. Tobias couldn't move. He recalled the last time this happened, over one hundred years ago, when he searched in vane for Sara. "I can't rest here again for thirty years. Samantha needs me."

Mom's Missing

Samantha's car skidded to a stop at the first business available to call home. "If anything happens to Mom, it's my fault."

She checked the clock. *One-forty. Ter couldn't possibly get back to town, deliver the key, and drive out to Mom's in such a short timeframe. Could he?* Clenching her fists, she let out a groan and hopped from the car, making sure to keep the engine running since she had no key. *Maybe he can.*

Her mind played tug of war. *Call 911. What will I tell them? That I think Mom's in danger. What if they get there and nothing's happened? Wait. Ter said three o'clock. I may still have time.*

Samantha dug through her pockets and came up with two quarters. Her engine idled as she dashed to the payphone and tapped in the home number. Voicemail picked up. "Mom, if you're there, you're in danger. Ter has my key to the garage door. Call Ivar and leave the house." The machine ate her coin.

With shaky fingers, she inserted her last quarter and phoned Ivar's cell.

It also went to voice mail. "Ivar. I'm stuck at a pay phone a good hour away from home. Mom's in danger. Ter has the garage door key. I'm afraid he's heading to her house. Please check on her ASAP." She flicked down the receiver and remembered. Hoping the call hadn't disconnected, she added, "Oh, you can't call me on my cell. Ter stole it. I put my chip in his phone, but it's dead."

An automated message cut in. "Please insert twenty-five cents."

"I'm counting on you. Thanks, Bye."

Samantha blurted over the mechanical operator and hung up.

Samantha blew out a breath and dashed back to the car. *Ivar will check on Mom.*

Pulling onto the main road, she drove five miles over the speed limit heading home. She dialed through the radio stations until the local news confirmed the fire was at the Vickers' estate.

Maybe Mom's over at Linda's.

Every station repeated the same information, so she flipped off the radio. Her hand tapped the steering wheel. *I'm sure that's where Mom is. I'll swing into work, pick up my laptop, and look up Vickers' number.*

Unanswered questions cluttered her mind. Driving on autopilot, she missed the turnoff to work and had to make a U-turn to the parking lot.

Abby lifted her head as Samantha dashed into her office. "Hi, Sam. Have you heard the news?"

Samantha's heart leapt. *Did something happen to Mom?* Before she could reply, Abby chattered on. "Someone burned down Vickers' garage."

"Oh right. I know." Samantha rubbed her sweaty palm on her t-shirt, grabbed the phone, and punched in the home number.

"We had a devil of a time finding Amos this morning," Abby said.

Samantha pulled out a chair and sat with her legs crossed. Her foot swung nervously. "Amos was waiting at my old condo."

"I didn't know that." Abby leaned forward. "However, he seemed more upset about the loss of his old cars than he did about Linda. He said, 'Someone stole my convertible, and now my babies are destroyed.'"

"I can only imagine how upset he must be." The call got a busy signal. *Good, Mom's home.* Samantha felt her shoulders relax as she focused back on Abby's words. "His cars were like children to him. Every Saturday morning, he buffed and polished those beauties."

"I'm sure they're well insured," Abby said. "The chauffeur's apartment was totally leveled. They found Gary's body in the rubble."

Samantha's gut twisted. "Gary has worked for Amos for as long as I can remember." Her finger hit redial, but the call rang four times before going to voicemail. *Now, where is she?* She opened her desk drawer and dug out a phone book.

"I wonder who's behind these crimes." Abby wouldn't shut up.

"It's still early in the investigation." Samantha looked up Vickers' number and dialed. "I'm sure Ivar will figure it out."

On the second ring, Linda picked up the call. "Hello."

"Hi, Linda. I heard about—"

"Sam. Thanks for calling. I'm fine, but I have to run. Things are really hectic. It's great to hear from you."

"Wait. I need to talk to Mom."

"Bridget's not here." Linda sounded concerned. "She left before noon."

"The line was busy when I called home. Did Mom call—" Dial tone buzzed in her ear. Samantha stared at the phone. "Where is she?" Panic cinched her like a drawstring.

"Oh, by the way, Ivar wants you to call him." Abby passed her a yellow sticky. "He stopped by a couple of hours ago and was surprised that your laptop was still here."

Samantha slammed down the receiver and took the paper. "Did he mention anything about Mom?"

"Yeah. She was upset with him for some reason. Ivar didn't stay long."

Samantha shoved her computer mouse into her pants pocket. "What time was that?" Sam unplugged her laptop and grabbed the cord.

Abby rubbed her chin. "I don't know. Around one, maybe one-thirty, I guess."

Samantha let out a gasp. The string pulled tighter around her chest. A lump formed in her throat. She moved for the door.

"Ivar said your mom was worried about Linda."

Samantha paused. "Right. She left around noon."

"Maybe she's on her way back to Linda's," Abby said.

"I sure hope so." Samantha scooted into the hallway.

Abby followed. "Don't forget to call Ivar."

"Do me a favor and phone him for me. Tell him to meet me at Mom's home. I'm afraid Ter is heading there, too." Samantha balanced her computer in her left arm and scurried for the entrance.

"If Ter reaches your Mom's before Ivar comes, aren't you in danger?" Abby asked.

"Maybe," Samantha said, "but if you call, Ivar will be there soon." She left the office.

In the shadow of the Rocky Mountains, the afternoon sun shone in her eyes, so she put on her shades. *Ivar must have gotten my message by now. Dang it, I should have talked to him. Wait. Why am I worried? I asked Abby to call. Besides, she would have told me if anything had happened to Mom.*

Samantha rolled down her car window. The cool air soothed her tormented soul. Once she was on the main road, she turned on the radio.

"...a two-alarm fire at the Vickers Estate at 8:42 A.M... *Already heard that.* She flipped through a few stations until she found an update.

"Police arrested 26-year-old Duke Parker, Jr. at 2:50 this afternoon on suspicion of arson. Young Parker goes by the name Maddog.

"Witnesses told detectives they observed Parker running from the estate carrying a gas can. A blast occurred only moments after seeing the accused flee Vicker's estate. Charred bones found at the chauffeur's residence are awaiting DNA results and further testing by the medical examiner. Detective Colby Cage, a bomb inspector from Fort Collins, is currently investigating the scene."

Samantha turned up the volume.

"Parker was in possession of a packet of marijuana at the time of his arrest. Links to recent crimes in the area are pending. Parker was the last customer at the town's Soda Fountain prior to an explosion, more than two weeks ago. He's also being questioned regarding an explosion that destroyed a condo."

Samantha's hand tightened on the stick as she shifted to fourth gear. "No. It was Ter, not Maddog."

"Parker was charged with a Class A misdemeanor for possession of marijuana. He faces potential charges of a Class B felony arson, and Class D felony for criminal recklessness in connection with the fire earlier this morning. A possible homicide is pending further research. This case remains open for active investigation. Anyone with additional information—"

Samantha shut off the radio. *I bet Mom was on her way to Linda's when I called.* Flexing her aching fingers, she decided to swing by the Vickers'. They lived only four miles from home, and she had to drive right past the estate. *If Ter reaches the house, Ivar will be there to greet him.*

As Samantha reached Vickers, floodlights illuminated the scene. Looky-loos camped out along the road, making it difficult to drive onto the property. The garage still smoldered. Detective Cage's vehicle sat in front of the house.

Samantha turned down the drive, half-expecting to see her mother's Honda, but it wasn't there.

There was no sign of Ivar's police car, either. *I wonder what he's up to.*

An officer put up his hand.

Samantha slowed to a stop and rolled down her window. "Good evening."

"State your business, Ma'am."

Samantha stifled a chuckle at his formal reply. "I'm checking on Mrs. Vickers."

Linda opened the front door. "It's okay, officer."

The officer opened Samantha's car door and backed away. "Thanks." She got out of the car and took the porch steps two at a time.

Hello, Sam." Linda motioned to her. "Come in. It's wonderful you stopped by. Amos has been so busy lately, I rarely see him, and with all the excitement, my mind's spinning."

"Have you heard from Mom?"

"No, Honey. I told you that she wasn't here when you called." Linda frowned, then, like a light switched to on, she beamed. "Why don't you phone her? She can join us for dinner."

Samantha followed Linda into Amos's office. Rows of files lined his desk.

"Have a seat," Linda said. "I'll get us a cup of tea."

"Thanks, but I need to reach Mom. If she doesn't answer, I have to run."

Linda flitted out of the door without a reply.

Samantha dropped into the cushioned leather chair. A file marked 'Bank loans' caught her attention as she dialed home. Once again, voice mail picked up the call. In frustration, she slammed the receiver. The cord hooked on the corner of the file and knocked it to the floor. Papers scattered.

"Are you all right?" Linda called from the hallway.

"Fine. I'm just clumsy." Samantha shoved the papers back into the manila folder. All except for one page. Terrance Rodriguez's name was scribbled at the top of the sheet. *Amos must be doing some investigation on his own.*

Footsteps headed down the hallway.

Linda's voice bubbled with joy. "Honey, I'm so glad you're home."

"I can't stay. I need my tux before the charity dinner tonight."

Samantha ran her eyes down the page to a yellow sticky. The names Pam, Tommy, and Lisa were scrawled in the same handwriting. *That's odd.* She pocketed the page and barely had time to replace the file on his desk.

Amos burst through the door. "Sam, what are you doing here?"

She hopped from his chair. "I had to call home. No answer though, so I'd better run."

Amos stepped closer and grinned. "I haven't talked to you in ages."

"How about tomorrow for breakfast?" Samantha inched her way around the other side of the desk.

"I'll be out of town. So much is going on in the world, and now this in my own backyard." He glanced at his watch and crossed his arms. "Oh, but I don't have time right now." His eyes peered over at his desk.

"Sorry, I can't stay. I have to run," Samantha spoke up. "Linda, want breakfast over at our house tomorrow?"

Linda appeared at the office doorway. "I wish I could, Samantha, but I'm taking Amos to the airport. It's hard to get around without his chauffeur."

Samantha lowered her head. "I heard the news. Terrible, just terrible." She gave Amos a peck on the cheek, hugged Linda, and headed for the door. "I'll have Mom get in touch."

"Thanks, honey," Linda called after her.

Amos mentioned something, but Samantha slammed the front door without waiting to hear what he said. No one was around. *The officer must have dispersed the looky-loos.* Colby's car was gone. She climbed into hers and made a U-turn, and drove to her mother's home.

Maddog's Lawyer

Nervous energy poured off Ivar as he searched his desk for his cell phone. He chewed gum and tapped his fingers on his leg as he strode across the office. *I know I left it here to charge. I can't find anything lately. Lack of sleep, fear for Sam's life, and the unknown whereabouts of Pops may have something to do with it.*

While pawing through papers on his desk, his cell chirped. He tracked the sound. His phone lay on the floor, still attached to the charger. His head banged on the edge of the desk as he ducked to get it. "Officer Rexall."

"This is Abby. Sam just left the office. She's worried about her mother and wants you to swing by the house."

Ivar rubbed the knob blossoming on his crown. "Okay, I'll check it out."

"Thanks." Abby hung up.

He pocketed the phone and slipped his jacket on to hide the snub nose tucked into the waistband of his pants.

Ivar's partner caught him in the lobby. "Maddog lawyered up." Brody bit into a jellyroll the size of a baseball. A glop dripped down his chin. He scooped it up. "Cherry, my favorite." Then he licked each of his pudgy fingers.

Ivar sighed. "So who's his lawyer?"

"I am." A spit-shined pair of shoes entered the room.

Ivar followed the feet up the razor-creased trousers, three-piece black pinstriped suit, burgundy tie, and gray button-down collar. The weathered face of Duke Parker Sr. grinned down at Ivar.

"My boy's innocent, and I'll prove it. Not only that, but I'll prove someone deliberately planted marijuana on him to make the drug charge stick."

Ivar recalled Parker during the days when he and Maddog played as teammates during high school football. He remembered those fierce gray eyes bore through him. Echoes of the tongue-lashing he'd given his son after he fumbled the ball during the last three minutes of the game plagued him. The team lost only one game the whole season, but Coach Parker never let them live it down.

As a coach or an attorney, Ivar feared those accusing eyes.

Brody came around the corner, nearly ran into the lawyer, and dropped his jellyroll with a splat across the floor.

Exactly how Ivar felt, grime on the floor, but he summoned his courage and stepped up to the senior Parker. "Good afternoon, Sir. I thought you dealt only in estate cases. I've never seen you work with criminal law before."

"I'm not really in the mood to split hairs." Duke stood even straighter. It reminded Ivar of a man with a bat up his butt.

"Get my boy out of jail. I posted bail. He'll be here for court. By the way, you might want these phone records from his cell phone. It proves the boy ran out of gas. His first call was to Gary Gordon. Text message even got a reply from our dead chauffeur telling Jr. to come by to pick up a can of gas." Duke dropped the file on Ivar's desk. "See you in court."

Ivar motioned to Brody. "Check to make sure his bail is cleared and release Maddog in his father's custody."

Brody stepped over his roll and scampered out of the room.

Ivar held out his hand. "It's nice to see you again."

Duke turned his back. "The hell it is, boy. You won't have my son to kick around much longer." The silver-haired patriarch left the office.

Shattered

The automatic lights flicked on as Samantha approached the gate to her parent's home, but the house remained dark. "Where is Mom?" She leaned over the box, punched the code to open the gate, and drove through. The lights along the gravel road didn't illuminate either. Gravel crunched beneath her wheels.

A deer glanced up from eating grass by the pond and darted into her path. Slamming on the brakes, she barely missed the doe.

The garage door was open when Samantha drove up to the house. Odd that her mom's car was missing. She always closed the garage and locked up when she left home.

Instead of driving inside, she decided to play it safe and drove around to the back of the house. She parked facing the road, ready for a rapid getaway.

Nothing seemed to move or catch her attention. Surely, her mother hadn't gone to bed yet. It was barely eight-thirty. The power couldn't be out. The gate worked. *Why didn't the motion detectors flood the area with light?*

She reached into the glove compartment and took out her heavy-duty flashlight. *I should wait outside and call Ivar.* One glance at the dead, patched cell phone covered in duct tape told her the option was moot. She pocketed the relic and hoped that Abby called him. *He'll be here soon.*

Samantha switched off the overhead light and exited the car.

The back door to the house remained locked. She slid along the rear of the building and peered through the window above the sink. A faint glow radiated around the refrigerator. *Mom would never leave it open.* Samantha's stomach growled. She hadn't eaten since breakfast.

A shadow crossed the room.

Samantha gripped the flashlight, crouched, and moved behind the attached garage. Two trashcans sat at the edge of the house by the patio. Although they stunk, she emptied the less full one and turned it upside-down. She hid under the can and waited.

A door slammed, and something clinked onto the concrete, not far from her hiding place.

Samantha's heart thudded. Holding her breath, she feared she'd been spotted.

Footsteps ran along the concrete, past the trashcan, and onto the grass. A clatter in the yard told her the patio umbrella fell over. Someone had been in the house and was now in the backyard with her. She didn't want to move, but her mother might be in danger. Samantha lifted the trashcan a few inches and waited.

It was quiet.

She moved slightly to her left, back toward the house.

Still nothing, so she raised the can higher.

Something forced it back to the ground. "Stay put," a muffled male voice said.

Alarmed, Samantha thought she recognized the tenor's voice, but wasn't sure.

"No," a deeper voice called from the backyard. "We have to get out of here. Maybe it was the cop."

"But we haven't found it yet," the familiar tenor again.

Deep voice answered. "Keep looking. I'm outta here."

"Where did you park the car?"

"Find your own ride to town," deep voice said.

"You're not leaving without me."

The backyard fence rattled, and receding footsteps crunched along the gravel. A car door slammed, and an engine roared in retreat. It paused. She heard the familiar groan as the metal gate opened.

How'd he know the code to get through the main entrance? Samantha waited for a few moments and breathed a sigh of relief. She inched up the trashcan and then hesitated when she saw a pair of sturdy legs in sneakers standing beside her.

"You can come out now. He's gone. But you have me to deal with." The can lifted above her head.

Grabbing her flashlight in her left hand, she swung it with all her might. She caught his shin and knocked him over.

"Damn it, Sam. I should have known you'd do that." Ter glared at her. He sat on the ground and rubbed his leg.

Samantha hovered over him. "Where's Mom?" She braced for an attack.

He didn't move.

She leaned closer. "Did you hurt MOM?"

"No one's home, except you." Ter brushed himself off and stood.

"What were you looking for?"

He limped to the back door. "I have to check in with Walter."

Samantha turned on the flashlight and searched the backyard. The patio table and umbrella had been overturned, but everything else was in order. She flicked the light in Ter's face.

He ducked. "Shut that off." His watch alarm beeped. "I have to call right now, or Pam's life is in danger."

Something glinted in the light. *My keys.* She picked up the shiny metal objects and pocketed them. "Let me help you find your wife and family."

"No." The back door was ajar. Ter went inside.

Samantha followed and flicked on the lights. Finding the emergency breaker off, she restored the power. "Where's Mom?"

"I told you, she's not here."

"I don't believe you. The phone was busy when I called." Samantha rushed through the living room and ran upstairs to her mother's bedroom.

The radio was on low. She barely noticed the chatter in the background as she studied the room in total chaos. The dresser drawers lay scattered and emptied onto the floor. The mattress sat flipped up on end against the wall. Clothes were in a heap on the floor in the closet. Only wire hangers hung on the rod. The top shelf now lay bare, no longer neatly stacked with sweaters and hats.

Her ears perked up when Denver's mayor introduced the guest of honor, Amos Vickers. Rounds of applause interrupted the man's praises.

Amos' voice came across as warm and folksy. He waxed on. "Together we can change the world."

"You're not the only one," Samantha said. "Look at this place." She called down the stairs, "What were you looking for?"

Samantha stopped by her room. Shock filled her when she found it neat and tidy, just as she'd left it. She slipped on a pair of running shoes. When she returned to the landing, she overheard Ter and inched forward to see what he was doing.

"We've searched everywhere. There's no map, but we found the diary. He's delivering it as you asked… No. She wasn't home… How should I know?" Ter paced the floor. "I told you. Sam's held up in my hunting lodge."

The front window shattered. Ter flew backward; his hand clutched his chest. Blood oozed between his fingers.

He must have hit the speaker button, and the deep voice said, "That's for involving the cops." The line went dead.

Samantha ran down the stairs toward Ter.

Headlights flashed through the broken window. A car turned around in the driveway and sped away.

"Holy shit!" Paramedic mode kicked in. She grabbed the towel covering the coffee table and held it tightly to his chest with her casted elbow.

Ter's breath came out in jagged pants. "Save Pam."

Ter's deathbed face jolted her. "Hang on. I'll get help." She dashed to the hall closet, grabbed a scarf, and knelt beside him.

"Kids…got away." His voice became a whisper. "Remem…" A whistling wheeze and pink froth bubbled from his lips. "Ball game," dissolved on his lips.

Samantha's fingers shook as she wrapped the scarf around his chest to hold the towel in place. She grabbed the phone from the floor and dialed 911. A small silver vial crunched beneath her knee.

"What's the nature of your emergency?"

"Need ambulance. Man down. Chest wound." A burning sensation filled her lungs and stole her breath.

"Name, please," the operator said.

"Sam…antha."

"Address?" the operator said.

"McFitzroy's." Samantha's thoughts became fuzzy. "304 ah." Her mind's fog grew thicker. "Can't think."

"Calm down and tell me what's wrong," the operator said.

Tears flooded her eyes. "Garlic smell."

"Can you move the wounded?"

"Right." Samantha dropped the phone.

Dazed, she went to autopilot mode. "Chest wound." Grabbing Ter's torso, she rolled him onto the runner by the couch and pulled the rug across the floor to the front entry.

Samantha flung open the door. She shook her head to clear her mind and breathed in the fresh air. A loose flap along the threshold caught on her foot and tripped her. She climbed to her knees and pulled the runner outside. The motion detector lit up the porch light.

"Ter, are you all right?"

He didn't respond. His lips were blue, and blood trickled from his chest.

"Check pressure dressing." Samantha pulled the scarf tighter to his chest.

His breaths were barely visible, so she rolled him over onto his wounded side. His body weight would have to create the needed added pressure against the wound.

Her mind drifted. *Tired, so tired.*

Yawning, she sat beside Ter. *Think.* Samantha responded to her inner voice. "Check vitals." She took his pulse. "Nine, ten, twelve." She jerked upright. "That can't be right." Stretching, she counted again. "Thirty-eight, thirty-nine, ten, eleven."

Samantha blinked open her eyes. *What was I doing?* She leaned against the railing. Her hearing went from a dull roar and then faded.

Bridget's Honda

Detective Cage flipped on his signal and turned off Highway 14. He hadn't driven far when a navy-blue Honda caught his eye. Its front end had wrapped around a large tree trunk.

Colby's vehicle slid to the left as he slammed on his brakes, but he managed to pull in behind the wreck. He grabbed his radio. "Auto accident. Unknown injuries..."

With flashlight in hand, he climbed from the car.

The Honda's hood folded back on itself like an accordion, and the windshield shattered into a starburst over the driver's side.

An eerie feeling crept through him. *I know this car.* "Samantha! Mrs. McFitzroy!" He darted to the driver's window. The deployed airbags now drooped. "Can you hear me?"

The radiator hissed, but there was no reply.

Colby pulled open the driver's door. "Anyone in there?" He flipped on the flashlight and searched both the front and back seats.

No one was inside the car.

Moving to the glove compartment, he found a registration card. "Bridget McFitzroy."

"Mrs. McFitzroy! Samantha! Can you hear me?" He searched the area around the wreck. Colby pulled out his cell and speed-dialed a number. The phone rang once.

"Officer Rexall."

"Ivar, what happened? You said you were going to protect the McFitzroys. I just found Bridget's car at the intersection of Highways 14 and 257."

"That can't be," Ivar said. "I saw Bridget a little over an hour ago."

"Did you see her car?" Colby asked.

"I thought it was in her garage, but maybe Samantha drove it." Ivar's voice faded. "…me phone messages…"

"What did you say?"

"Sam wasn't home when I got there. She sent me phone messages, but my phone was charging, and I didn't get them until a few minutes ago. Is she hurt?"

"I didn't find anyone in the car," Colby replied. "I don't see any footprints outside on the gravel."

Sirens drowned Ivar's reply.

"I didn't copy that. Repeat."

"I'll call the house and check with Bridget," Ivar blurted. "Wait, something's coming across the radio." Dial tone ended the call.

Poisonous Gas

Ivar and Brody were first to reach the McFitzroy's house. Ivar threw open his door and leapt from the car. He dashed to the porch yelling, "What part of don't do anything stupid, didn't you understand? You just couldn't trust me." His fists clenched and unclenched.

Then he saw her. His heart collided with his chest. The shame he felt made him cringe. He closed his eyes in prayer. His soul screamed, but only a meager groan reached his lips. "What happened?"

Samantha had collapsed over Ter. Neither responded.

"Sam?" Ivar knelt beside her and gently shook her. "Oh, God, Sam!" He flipped her onto her back to check for wounds. Blood covered her hands and was smeared across her chest. "I'm an idiot!" A lump choked his throat. His hands shook. A jagged breath escaped, letting out his exasperation as guilt and anger boiled his blood.

"Ivar! Did you hear me?" Brody knelt over Ter. "This one's critical!"

Ivar lifted his head. Unable to find a wound on Sam, he reluctantly moved. "It's Terrance. We only posted bail a few hours ago. I wonder who did this and if it was because he talked to us?"

"And we haven't found his family yet." Brody placed his finger over Ter's neck. "Faint pulse and slow."

An ambulance arrived. Abby hopped from the cab, grabbed her medical bag, and climbed the stairs. "What's the story?" She dropped to her knees. "Sam. Again?"

Ivar rolled Ter onto his back. "She's alive, but this one's barely breathing. Chest wound."

Abby's partner darted up the steps.

"Now that you're here, I'll see if there's anyone else inside." Brody headed for the car and returned with a gas mask.

Abby motioned to her partner. "Check on that guy. He's barely breathing."

The partner dropped his medical box next to Ter. After removing the scarf and soaked towel from the wound, he cut away his shirt and applied a pressure dressing.

Ter's chest crackled beneath the paramedic's fingers. "There's an air leak. Probable collapsed lung." Pulling out a stethoscope, he took Ter's vital signs.

Ivar read the paramedic's nametag. "Emit, I know CPR."

"Great. We're going to need it. I don't get a blood pressure." He pulled out an endotracheal tube. "Once I insert this, be ready with compressions."

Ivar knelt next to Ter. "Ready when you are."

Emit inserted the E-T tube and listened to each lung with his stethoscope. Only the left lung rose as he bagged Ter. "Right lung's collapsed. Okay, start compressions."

Ivar positioned his hands on the man's sternum and pumped his chest.

Emit taped the tube in place, started an IV, and injected epinephrine into the port.

They maintained CPR.

Abby placed an oxygen mask over Samantha's face. "Can you hear me?" She continued talking even though Sam didn't answer. "We're short-handed now that you're on leave. I'm stuck on call." She took Samantha's vital signs and started an IV.

"I got a pulse," Emit said. "Let's get them to the hospital. He needs a chest tube."

Ivar called out, "Brody, we need help transporting the victims."

The balding man appeared in the doorway and pulled off his gas mask. "Someone sure ransacked the place." He passed Ivar on his way to the ambulance and returned with a backboard. The men rolled Ter onto it and loaded him onto a stretcher. Then they returned for Samantha.

She raised a hand to her head.

The fire truck pulled up alongside the ambulance as they loaded Samantha.

Chief Martinelli hopped to the ground. "Sorry, we're late. Single car accident on Highway 14. Blue Honda totaled. You'll need to take another route."

Samantha's eyes fluttered open. "Ivar? Who's car?"

"No one was inside," Martinelli said.

Ivar squeezed Samantha's hand. "I'll talk to you soon. They'll take good care of you."

"Wait. Tommy."

"Who?" Ivar backed away from the end of the ambulance.

"Ter's kid."

"What about Tommy?" Ivar asked.

Samantha narrowed her eyes and turned her head from side to side. "Mind's fuzzy." She brought her hand to her face and caught the IV tubing in her hair. "Where did that come from?"

"Just rest. Everything will come clear soon." Ivar patted her leg and started to close the door.

"No. Wait," Samantha reached for him. "Tommy. Escaped.

Ballgame."

"Where are they?" Ivar asked.

Her haunted eyes blinked.

Ivar frowned. "Ball game? Doesn't make sense. I'll talk to Ter when he wakes up."

Emit motioned to Abby. "You take the back. I'll drive."

Abby moved beside Ter. "Red lights and siren. He's not responding."

Ivar's troubled gaze lingered on Samantha. "I swear I'll find the person who did this." He closed the back doors of the ambulance and tapped twice, signifying they were good to go. "Take good care of Sam."

The engine roared to life. Red lights flashed, and the siren wailed as they drove away.

Ivar stopped by his car and grabbed his mask.

"What kind of gas are we dealing with here?" Brody asked. "Sam reported a garlic smell." Ivar adjusted the strap on his mask.

"Sulfur mustard or arsine, come to mind, but they're used in chemical warfare. Why would anyone use them here?"

Chief Martinelli walked to the door with the officers. "A garlic odor was reported during a natural gas leak. But Sam told me that her mother refused to use gas even at the soda shop."

"I thought natural gas smelled like rotten eggs," Ivar said.

"That it does, but I've heard reports of a garlic odor before an explosion," Martinelli said. "Let's check out the house before we have another disaster."

Safety Shack

Tommy wrapped his arms around his younger sister. Leaning over her curly blonde locks, he rested his head on hers. She'd turn five next month if they survived the night.

He sat on a stump along the road to rest.

Lisa curled up on his lap. It reminded him that he was her big brother and protector. He'd promised his father he'd always look out for her.

Her small heart-shaped face turned up. "I'm hungry." Lisa tugged on his sleeve. "Can't we go home?"

"Not yet. We have to save Mommy. Walter will hit her again when he finds out we're gone."

Lisa snuggled closer to him. "It's cold out here."

He wrapped his arms around her.

"We've walked forever." Lisa rubbed her eyes. "Can't we find somewhere to sleep?"

Tommy shifted his weight. He peered up and down the empty roadside. "The hunting lodge can't be far now."

A man hobbled up the path. He leaned heavily on a woman's arm. A tree limb was in his other hand.

Tommy gasped and stood up, pushing Lisa behind him. "Stay away. We're not going back with you!"

The man stopped a few feet from Tommy and collapsed on the stump where he had been sitting. "Good evening, son."

The woman knelt. "Hello, little one. You're out late."

Lisa stood next to Tommy, shivering.

The lady took off her sweater and held it out to Lisa. "My name's Bridget. What's your name?"

"Lisa, but I can't talk to dangers." She reached for the sweater and then pulled back.

"She means strangers, but thanks," Tommy said. He snatched the sweater and wrapped it around Lisa's shoulders.

The man smiled. "Yes, it can be dangerous. My name's Pops. Who are you, young man?"

"None of your beeswax." He grabbed Lisa's hand and pulled her away.

Pops chuckled, "Beeswax? I haven't heard that phrase in ages."

"Gramps says it all the time," the boy said, "and he's younger than you. Come on, Lisa."

"Don't go," Bridget said. "We're not going to hurt you. We're out here in the cold, stranded just like you are. Maybe we can find somewhere to rest together."

"That's what strangers would say," Tommy retorted and backed away even more.

"Suit yourself," Pops said. "I'm ready for a nap." He bent down and rubbed his swollen ankle. "I wish we had something to eat."

"Me, too." Lisa squirmed away from Tommy's hand.

"How did you get all the way out here?" Bridget asked.

Tommy grabbed tightly to Lisa's hand even though she tugged him closer. "We can't tell you that."

Lisa stood her ground. "We're going to Daddy's shack, but Tommy don't know where it is,"

"I do know where it is," Tommy said. "I just haven't found the sign that says 35 yet."

Pops rubbed his chin. "We came across a 35 sign. It's not far from here."

"Really?" Tommy put his hands on his hips. "Are you telling me the truth?"

Pops chuckled. "I never lie. How far away is the shack from the road?"

Tommy stepped closer and stood on his tiptoes. "It's too dark to tell. I've never walked there before. Daddy always drove."

"I didn't see a shack, but let's take a look." Pops pointed in the direction he came from. "It's not far."

Bridget put out her arm and Pops pulled himself back to his feet.

"What happened to your leg?" Tommy asked.

"I fell and sprained my ankle, but I can still get around with some help."

Tommy hesitated. "How do I know if we can trust you?"

"I reckon you'll have to take a risk." Pops walked beside Bridget.

Lisa put her hand on Bridget's other arm. "You're not a danger anymore."

"Thank you. I'm pleased to have you as my friend." Bridget paused and tied the sleeves of the sweater around Lisa's neck. "We have to stick together."

"Okay," Lisa said. "Daddy always has food at his lodge."

"I'm starving." Tommy walked ahead a few steps but turned frequently to check on Lisa.

They hiked another five minutes before coming across the sign. "How far from here?" Pops asked.

Tommy scratched his head. "I don't see it, but a car came through here not long ago. See how the weeds are smashed to the ground."

"You've got a good eye," Pops said. "Let's follow the tracks." He stumbled on the rough path and leaned on Bridget.

"I don't like these weeds." Lisa whimpered.

"Don't cry. It can't be much farther," Tommy said. "Want a piggyback ride?" He knelt on one knee.

Lisa climbed on Tommy's back and wrapped her body around him. "Giddy up."

He galloped in a circle. It made her stop crying.

Moonlight glinted off a tin roof in the distance. "I see it!" Tommy exclaimed. He raced ahead to the door, panting the farther he went. "Whoa, time to dismount. This horsy is tired." He eased Lisa's arms from his shoulders.

The key is up there." Tommy pointed to the jamb above the door. "I can't reach it."

"I'll get it." Pops ran his fingers above the jamb. "Nope, I don't feel anything."

"It has to be there," Tommy said. He climbed up the trellis alongside the door. "You're right. It's gone." Tommy slid back to the ground.

Is there a back door?" Bridget asked.

"Uh-huh, I know where it is." Lisa ran around the corner of the building.

"Wait up." Tommy followed his sister.

"Oh, no. Look, Tommy." Lisa grabbed his hand and pulled him to the back of the building. "Somebody threw a chair through the window. It's all broked. Daddy's gonna be mad."

"Oh, good," Tommy shouted. "I'll climb in and get the spare key."

A few minutes later, the light came on, and the front door swung open. Tommy grinned. "Let's eat."

Lisa ran up to Tommy and hugged him. "I knew you'd save me."

Pops, winded from the walk, leaned against the door. "May we spend the night here, Master Tommy?"

Bridget stood in the doorway and peeked inside the shack. "Look at the floor. It's full of broken glass and wood splinters. Did you cut yourself going through the window?"

"Nah," Tommy peered around the room. "Someone's been in here. It wasn't like this the last time I came with Daddy."

"This place needs a woman's hand." Bridget pulled Lisa away from the window. "I'll cook us some dinner. Do you want to help?"

Lisa nodded and tugged her arm. "Kitchen's this way."

Pops picked up a medicine bottle from the table. "Ibuprofen. Just what I need." He shook out a couple of pills and swallowed them.

Bridget plucked a pair of bloody socks off the floor. "Sam has a pair, just like this." She moved toward the back of the house and tossed it on the washing machine where a few other dirty clothes lay. A broom rested between the washer and dryer. "I'll sweep up this mess. Pops can patch the window in the morning."

Tommy opened the fridge. "There's plenty of food."

"Let's see what I can whip up." Bridget set to work cooking and cleaning.

Pops let out a moan and sat on the couch. He put his foot up on the ottoman. "I'll sleep here for the night. You can have the cot, and the children can sleep in their usual beds."

Bridget found a few cubes in an ice tray and made an ice pack for Pops' ankle. Then she made sandwiches and opened a can of baked beans and a bag of potato chips.

After eating, Lisa yawned. "I'm going to sleep."

Tommy and Bridget tucked her into bed.

"Can you tell me what you're doing out here all alone?" Bridget asked.

Tommy shook his head and moved down the hall. "I have to save Mom in the morning, so I need to get some sleep." He opened his door and went inside. "It's a matter of life or death."

Red Lights and Siren

Samantha removed the oxygen mask. Her mind spun.

"I'm losing him." Abby rapped her knuckles on the partition between the cab and the back of the vehicle. "Can't you get this wagon to go any faster?"

Emit's only answer was to take a corner on two wheels, knocking over the IV pole, and tossing the cart from one side of the ambulance to the other.

Samantha unstrapped herself from the bench seat and grabbed the drug box. "What's his monitor show?"

"Irregular." Abby flipped the screen toward Sam. "Was tachy, now brady at around 30 per minute."

"Up the IV. Are you running Ringers?"

"Of course." Abby opened the flow.

"Put that sandbag on his chest. We have to stop the air from leaking and collapsing his other lung." Samantha fished through the box, grabbed a pre-filled syringe, and popped the top. She inserted the needle into the IV port and smashed on the plunger. "Atropine in."

"You're supposed to be a patient," Abby chastised.

"Yeah, well, it doesn't look good for Ter. He has to make it.

He has two little kids."

"At least he has a pulse now." Abby continued to bag Ter.

"Gunshot wound." Samantha wrote notes on the chart. Rapid-fire medicalese flowed from her head to her hand. Samantha snagged the tubing attached to her arm as she set down the chart. "I don't need this stinking IV." She picked at the edge of the tape.

"Wait," Abby said. "You better cap it. They'll need to draw blood in the ED."

"Oh, all right. She replaced the tubing with a plug. "Happy?"

Abby nodded. "What happened at the house?"

Samantha grimaced. "Gunshot wound to the chest. Possible poisoning."

"That's obvious," Abby said.

"Did you draw blood when you started Ter's IV?"

"Ask Emit. I worked on you," Abby said.

Samantha glanced at the monitor. "Tachycardia with inverted T-waves. I'll run a full EKG and transmit it to ED."

"We should be there by now!" Abby yelled at the driver, "Move it!"

A lump flew into Samantha's throat. "He's fibrillating. Get the paddles."

Abby fought to remove the sandbag and tape. His chest was soaked in blood. She gave a pre-cordial thump, but there was no change in the rhythm.

Samantha grabbed the sheet and wiped off the blood.

Abby gelled the defibrillator paddles, planted one squarely over the breastbone, and the other near the left armpit. The whine rose in tone as the paddles charged. "Clear."

Ter's body arched as the shock hit him. The monitor spiked and went back to a wavy line.

"Again!" Samantha shouted. She gave another quick swipe of his chest with the towel.

Abby gelled and reapplied the paddles. "Kick it up a notch."

Samantha upped the defibrillator to 300 joules. The whine grew to a higher pitch.

"Clear." Abby pressed her thumbs over the paddle buttons. Another spike and the line returned to a rapid but normal rhythm."

Samantha felt his carotid. "There's a pulse." Her thumb popped the cap off another syringe. "Bolus of lidocaine on board. I'll start a drip."

"Blood pressure is 80 over 50," Abby said.

"Better get that sandbag back in place." Samantha hung a lidocaine drip. "I can't stop the bleeding."

Abby set to work patching the wound.

The ambulance lurched to a stop.

"Are we there?" Abby looked hopeful.

Emit blasted his horn.

Samantha glanced out the window. "Not yet." A black Ford sat in the middle of the road at a forty-five-degree angle. "Some schmuck's blocking the way."

"We're running code three against traffic," Abby shouted over the siren. "Why won't he move?"

Emit swung the ambulance into the left lane and rounded the car.

"Did you get his license number?" Abby asked.

"I don't need to." Sam glanced back at the old Ford. No one was inside. "It's Maddog's car. I wonder what it's doing out here? I thought Maddog was in jail."

"Probably posted bail by now," Abby said.

"Why didn't we chopper Ter to Fort Collins?" Samantha asked.

"Ivar tried, but Big Meadows fire is burning out of control. Too much smoke in the air. On top of that, Chief Martinelli said something about a car accident en route."

"So, which hospital are we going to?" Samantha asked.

The siren died as Emit pulled in front of the ED.

"I guess that answers my question."

Medical personnel magically appeared. The back doors of the ambulance flew open. Two nurses grabbed Ter's gurney, while the doctor took over the airway. The emergency team whisked him through the hospital's double doors.

"Samantha, you're next," Abby said. "Thanks for your help, but we can't report it." When Sam didn't move, Abby tried again. "The doctor needs to examine you. That gas caused you to lose consciousness. It could have other side effects."

"I'm not going in. Mom's missing," Samantha said. "I have things to do."

Emit rounded the back of the ambulance. "Not on my watch. You're going into that ED. On the count of five, you'll go on your own two feet or over my shoulders. Which will it be? One, two, three, four, five."

Samantha's body lifted from the back of the ambulance, and crumpled over Emit's broad shoulders.

"Put me down!" Samantha cried, but she was afraid her cast might hurt him if she thrashed too much.

Emit did put her down, but not until she was ED-3. He set her on the cart and put his beefy arms on either side of her.

"You can't make me stay here," Samantha said.

I'm not making you do anything, but you'll see a doctor before I leave this room." Emit took off his jacket.

She knew that he planned to stay.

"What happened to your IV?"

"I put in a buffalo cap, so I could take care of Ter."

"You didn't do that," Emit insisted. "You sat on the bench the whole way here. Abby gave the meds. She wrote the document, and she was in charge of both of you. Do you understand?"

A nurse came into the room. Without saying a word, she rummaged in the cabinet beside the sink and pulled out a chest tube, thoracotomy tray, and Pleur-evac.

"Are they for Ter?" Samantha asked, knowing they were.

The nurse didn't answer and left the room.

"I wonder if anyone saw you haul me in here."

"What? I didn't do that." Emit gave a sly smile. "I think that gas causes lack of judgment, paranoia, and hallucinations."

"Fine, blackmail me," Samantha said. "I did exactly as you say. I know you're covering my backside. The boss would have my hide for my actions. I'm here now, so I guess I'll stay. You're free to leave."

"Not going unless I get a call." Emit sat on the chair by the bed.

"If that's the case, do me a favor."

"What would that look like?" Emit's bulky arms crossed tightly over his chest.

"Check on Ter. I know he has a punctured lung, a gunshot wound, and massive blood loss, but will he make it?"

"You did your best," Emit said. "This hospital is a level two trauma center. Leave the rest up to the docs. They'll handle it."

"I feel responsible." Gray dots floated before her eyes. She shook her head and continued. "He wouldn't have been in the house if I hadn't allowed him to use the phone."

The radio squawked in the main ED.

Emit went to the door. "Chopper's coming in. Guess they can't make it to Fort Collins and are routing all emergencies to this hospital." He left the room.

Samantha's hearing faded in and out. She took a deep breath and shook her head.

Emit returned shortly and grabbed his jacket from the chair. "Gotta go. Captain says a car skidded across the highway, causing a seven-car pileup. It doesn't make sense."

A terrible edge sounded in his voice. "What's wrong?" Samantha asked.

"Driver's dead." Emit ran a hand over his face. "I just spoke to him earlier today."

"Wait," Samantha hopped from the cart. "Emit?" She followed him out of the room into the busy ED. "Who was the driver?"

"Detective Colby Cage."

Time Flies

The floor smacked against Samantha's face. Her cheek burned. The plaster cast chipped at her elbow, sending pain down her arm into her wrist.

"I didn't see that coming." Someone rolled her to her back. "Did you just faint?"

Samantha tried to speak. Sounds echoed through her mind.

"Sam, did you faint?" he repeated.

She groaned. Unable to focus, a man hovered over her. As her vision cleared, it was Emit, but he looked different.

"Talk to me."

Dried blood spots peppered his shirt. "Did you pass out?"

"No, I nosedived on purpose." Samantha blinked a few times.

"What do you think?" Blood dripped from her chin.

"Dr. Clark, I need help, a nurse called from Ter's room."

"Is he all right?" Samantha asked.

"Ter's in ICU," Emit said. "On a vent, but still alive."

"There's no ICU in the ED?"

"What are you babbling about?" Emit asked.

A male nurse dashed to her side and helped Emit get Samantha back on the cart. "Should I restrain her?" the nurse asked. "She's been acting weird for the past two hours."

"No, she'll behave. Emit narrowed his eyes and glared down at her. "Won't you."

It wasn't a question, but an order. Samantha felt a tear slip from her eye and mix with the bloody mess now soaking her gown. *When did I put on a gown?* "Did he say two hours?"

Emit frowned with concern. "Yeah, I had to leave for a while. I was shocked to see you leap off the end of the cart when I came around the corner."

"I don't remember doing that," Samantha said.

The nurse wadded a few gauze strips and held them around Samantha's nostril putting pressure against the bone at the bridge of her nose.

"Ouch, that hurts." Samantha pushed away his hand. She noticed a wavy red and white tattoo on his left forearm.

The nurse yanked his jacket sleeve down before she could make out the object. "If you're going to take over the job, hold tight, so it stops bleeding."

"I know what to do." Samantha tried to read his nametag. It had flipped over, so all she could see was the magnetic strip across the plastic back.

"What kind of gas were you exposed to?" Emit asked.

"How would I know?" Samantha grabbed a handful of tissue and blotted her nose.

"It might cause bleeding," Emit pulled out his cell phone. "One moment."

"You can't use your phone in here," the nurse said.

"Don't go anywhere." Emit glowered at her to make his point. "I'm going outside to call Ivar."

"Good. I want to know where he is. Two hours?" Samantha glanced at her watch. More like three if she recalled the time they arrived. "Why don't I remember anything?"

Hell of a Day

The lights on top of Ivar's car flashed red and blue as he raced to the latest crime scene. His thoughts ran wild. "What a mess. Sam's been poisoned, and I can't even be with her."

His current workload invaded his mind. Arson started the day at Amos Vickers' garage, resulting in a dead body, irreplaceable vehicles destroyed, and then a confrontation with Bridget McFitzroy. He had arrested Maddog Parker and charged him with arson, only to release him in his father's custody.

Colby called about Bridget McFitzroy's car wreck, but Bridget was missing, and her home was ransacked. Ivar had no idea what happened to Pops either. Someone shot his only suspect in two local bombings, and Ter might not live. Ter's wife and children were also missing and still being held hostage. And then Colby's death, which complicated everything. Now, someone broke into the medical clinic downtown, trashed the basement warehouse, and Ivar was assigned to investigate.

Ivar barely heard his phone above the shrill siren. "Who's calling now? Don't I have enough to deal with?" The smell of burned rubber wafted through his vent as he pulled to the side of the road and grabbed his phone. "Officer Rexall."

A whispered voice said, "This is Emit, the EMT who brought Samantha McFitzroy to the hospital. I'm not sure what's going on. She's very confused. What type of gas—"

Ivar groaned, "I don't know. Call Chief Martinelli! He's the expert."

"I spoke to him earlier," Emit snapped. "He said it wasn't anything he's familiar with. Who else should I call?"

"Poison control. Just watch over Sam. Don't let her out of your sight. Can you do that one little item for now?"

"Why do you think I'm calling?" Emit's voice sounded exasperated.

***

A small group of nurses huddled outside on a smoke break.

They glanced up at Emit's loud comment.

Emit lowered his voice. "About Colby—"

Julie Jenkins called out in concern, "You're talking about Detective Cage, aren't you?" Her puffy red eyes blinked back a tear. "Poor guy. I can't believe he's dead. I spoke to him just the other day when I floated to Fort Collins' Emergency Department."

"Yeah, rotten luck." Emit turned his back to the group.

Ivar's voice cracked. "What about Colby? Surely, you could handle the situation."

"We cleared the accident."

"I hope you did more than that," Ivar snapped.

"Ah, you mean with his body?"

"I knew you were talking about the detective," Julie said from behind Emit.

He sighed and peered at her over his shoulder. "I'll talk to you later."

Julie smiled and nodded. "Okay."

"Talk to me now!" Ivar sounded upset. "I've already pulled off the highway."

Emit moved to the parking lot. "I wasn't talking to you."

"Who *are* you talking to?" Ivar asked. "I thought you were with Sam."

"I'm outside the emergency department. They won't let me use my phone indoors." Emit lowered his voice. "About Colby…he's really banged up. I smuggled him in the back door to the ME's office. Angela put his leg in a cast. She says he needs rehab. Are you sure he should go missing for a while?"

"I've made all the arrangements. Only you, Angela, and I know that he's alive. Find a nurse or someone you can trust for his rehab."

***

A cold draft and a light mist filled Ivar's car. "Now what?"

The mist cleared as fast as it had appeared, leaving a note lying on the seat.

"Gotta go." Ivar disconnected Emit's call.

Ivar snagged the paper and read, "Need your help. Come to cemetery. Tobias."

"Shit. Now I'm getting demands from a ghost. What else can go wrong?"

"Officer Rexall, where are you?" came across his radio. "We just found a body under the stairs leading to the medical clinic basement."

Bridget rose early and knelt over Pops, who was still sleeping on the couch. "Wake up, honey. I'm going to get help."

"No." Pops grabbed her arm and pulled her close. "The weather is miserable. It rained all night. Wait here until my ankle gets better. It can't be more than a few days, and we're safe here. We can watch over the children and make sure no one harms them."

Bridget patted his arm and stood. "What about Samantha?"

A bolt of lightning flashed, followed by a rumble of thunder.

She switched on the lamp sitting on the magazine rack, but nothing happened. "I guess the bulb's burned out."

"I bet the power's off. Try the kitchen light." Pops swung his legs over the couch and sat up. He shivered and pulled the blanket around him. "I better build a fire."

"I'll do it. There's some wood on the porch." Bridget moved into the kitchen and flipped the light switch. "No electricity."

Pops hobbled over to the counter and found a flashlight in one of the drawers. "Take this and come with me."

Bridget took the light. "You know Samantha could be in danger. I'm sure she was tracking someone when she called."

"That was yesterday." Pops piled several cut logs in a canvas bag and started to drag it through the doorway, limping as he walked. "Tobias will look out for her, and if he doesn't, I know Ivar will."

"Wait, let me get that." Bridget handed Pops the light, grabbed the bag, and hauled it inside. "You haven't been home lately. Too much is happening. I'm leaving right after breakfast. You take care of the children." She set the bag down and opened the door to the wood stove sitting between the kitchen and living area.

"It's freezing out there," Pops said. "I walked for miles without seeing one car." He took hold of her hands. "You know I love Sam, but she has people looking out for her. I'm not going to let you risk your life while trying to rescue mine. And if the children try to leave, I can't stop them. My ankle won't allow it."

"I saw a radio on the kitchen counter," Bridget said. "Let's get some breakfast and listen to the news. Then we'll decide."

Tommy hurried into the room. "If you leave, I'm going, too." He went to the closet and put on his jacket. "Lisa can stay here with Pops."

"No, Tommy," Bridget said. "We don't have enough food or warm clothes for both to leave."

"Then I'll go by myself. I have to save Mom."

"Let's eat before making any decisions." Pops crumpled a paper towel and placed it into the stove. "I'll start a fire while you make breakfast."

Tommy threw his coat on the floor. "You can't stop me, but I better eat before I go."

Pops shook his head. "I hope the radio runs on batteries."

"It does." Tommy darted into the kitchen, clicked on the power switch, and dialed to a station full of static. "We don't get much up here, but this is Dad's favorite."

"…rain today and most of tomorrow."

Pops lit the fire and closed the door to the stove. "Nice day to stay indoors. What's for breakfast?"

Bridget whipped up some pancakes.

Lisa joined them at the table. "I want Mommy."

"I know, honey." Bridget picked up Lisa and propped the little girl on her lap. "They'll find your mommy. I promise."

As Bridget washed the dishes, a news flash came across the radio. "Police have rescued a woman believed to be Pamela Rodriguez. They found her alive and well in a farmhouse three miles from town. Her kidnapper eluded capture."

Tommy jumped up and down. "Mommy's free!"

"Now, will you agree to stay here until the storm blows over?" Pops asked.

"I guess, but I want to see her as soon as it stops raining."

Lisa put her hand in Tommy's. "Me, too."

"I found a deck of cards." Pops shuffled over to the table. "Who wants to play Old Maid?"

Lisa pulled Tommy to the table. "We do."

Bridget smiled. "I'll make some popcorn."

Going Underground

Two days later, Colby Cage pressed the crease between his eyes to ease his headache. "What do you mean the body found at the Vickers' estate is not Gary Gordon's?"

The ME replied, "I don't know who it is yet. DNA has familial matches, but it's not Gary. Did he have anyone staying with him?"

"Not according to Mr. Vickers," Colby said.

"I researched Gary's family," Angela said. "Both parents are dead, but he has a twin brother. His name is Wendell. I'm not sure how to contact him. I understand the state penitentiary recently released him from Folsom Prison."

"Do you think the victim is Wendell?"

"I considered that, but when I checked jaw remnants against Wendell's dental record, there was no match."

"All right." Colby heaved a sigh. "I'll add it to my list. Thanks for the information, but let's keep the identity to ourselves for the time being."

"I've already sent the information to Ivar," she said.

"Of course. That makes sense, but no one else should know until I've done more research."

"Okay. Must be difficult working undercover," Angela said.

"What really gets me is Ivar quashed any contact with Samantha. How's she doing?"

"I think she's still in the hospital, but I'm not privy to any information. Take care, and let me know if anything new develops."

There was a click and then a dial tone.

Colby's leg throbbed, but he refused to pop any more of those blasted pain pills and fog his mind.

He spent the next two hours researching reports, photos, and following up on the remains of Vickers' vintage cars. Nothing could be identified. Burned-out parts littered the garage, but key pieces were missing.

He knew the insurance company would have to pay out several million dollars, and they would refuse to pay off the funds until his final report. He'd already worked on the case for a few days and wasn't making much headway.

Amos told him that he wanted the investigation wrapped up ASAP. He had to leave the country on another humanitarian mission.

A rap at the door startled the detective. *Who could that be? No one knows I'm here.*

An envelope slid through the mail slot.

"It's me, your private nurse. Open up." A female voice said.

Colby lifted his casted leg from the footstool, eased himself up from the chair, and grabbed his crutches. With an awkward gait, he made his way across the room and snatched the envelope. It smelled of Lavender.

"It's legit," the woman said. "Ivar sent me."

"He sent a private nurse?" Colby spoke in a low voice and pried open the flap.

The note confirmed it.

Colby unlocked the deadbolt and opened the door. His jaw dropped and then snapped shut. "Come in. I thought you worked in the emergency department."

Julie Jenkins walked into the room. "I'm a temp. Travel to wherever they need me."

"I get it. It's called moonlighting." Colby chuckled.

Private nurse Julie ran her ruby red-tipped finger gently across his cheek. "That's quite a shiner you have."

"The better to squint at you with."

She flashed a smile and slipped out of her raincoat, revealing long, silky legs. Her eyes shut briefly. Dark lashes brushed against her rosy cheeks. "Are you in a lot of pain?"

"Probably not as much as I would have been if I'd gone over that steep cliff."

"Let's get to work." She took his hand and led him to the ottoman. "Have a seat."

With great effort, he obliged her request. He ached all over.

Tired to the bone, his eyes drifted shut.

"You're emotionally drained." Julie moved around to his back. "Too much tension. You can't take a hot soak with that cast, so I'll help you relax." She leaned against him and unbuttoned his shirt.

Her warm breath washed over the nape of his neck as she pushed his shirt aside. Her fingers felt like magic as she rubbed his shoulders. She moved down his back with deep kneading motions. Then Julie slid her palm below his waistband.

Colby wordlessly took her hand and pulled her around to face him. "I'm not sure, but I think you're seducing me. Usually, it's the other way around. I kind of like your technique better."

"Oh, I've just started," Julie purred and straddled his good leg. Full red lips dropped over his.

Colby pulled her close and nearly devoured her. Physical therapy was brutal, but he had to admit that Julie made the pain of therapy bearable. She massaged in all the right places.

Drugged

The phone sounded like a cannon going off in Samantha's ear. She bolted from bed, feet on the floor, before the receiver came to her ear. "Weld County, Samantha McFitzroy speaking," flew from her mouth out of habit.

As her mind rose above several layers of sleep, Samantha glanced around the room. "Where am I?"

"Sam? You must have been dreaming. This is Ivar."

"Okaaay." Samantha tried to get her bearings in the dark room. She turned, tripped over the leg of the over-bed table, and caught a bouquet of roses before they toppled. A small card fell at her feet. "I'm a little sluggish around the edges. Was I admitted to the hospital?"

"Yeah, three days ago," Ivar said. "Don't you remember my visit last night?"

Samantha laughed. "Yeah, right after Detective Cage left my room."

"What?" Ivar asked. "Now I know you were dreaming. Surely you remember last night."

She didn't answer.

"Look at your left hand."

Samantha glanced at her fingers. A sparkle caught the hall light filtering into the room. "Ivar? I'm wearing a ring. Is this a real diamond?"

Ivar chuckled. "That's right, honey. You made me the happiest man in the world. We'll make our wedding plans once this blows over."

"Wedding plans?"

"Sam. Don't you remember last night?" He sounded upset. "*I* put that ring on your finger. Not *Colby*!"

"No, how could he? He's dead."

"Whatever you say, Sam."

Wondering what that meant, she picked up the card from the floor. She sat back on the edge of the bed and switched on the overhead light. *It's dated June 26th. Did he say three days ago?*

A sob erupted. "What day is it?"

"Seriously, you don't remember, do you?" Ivar asked. "That gas was more powerful than I thought. I'll be right over." Dial tone buzzed in her ear.

Putting down the phone, she turned the card. The squiggle-printed scrawl on the envelope looked familiar. 'Get well soon. Love, Maddog.'

Maddog was here? Not again. Fear clutched her heart, squeezed a firm hold, and pulled it into her throat.

She opened the card and read, 'Sam, need your help. I didn't do it. Please talk to Ivar. I'll always love you, but I'd never hurt you or Pops.'

Crumpling the card, she threw it into the trash. *He's asking for my help? Some nerve after all the pranks he's pulled.*

Why don't I remember anything? Her cheek throbbed. Running her fingers over the side of her face, she noticed her eye was swollen and painful. *Maybe, I got a concussion when I fell in the ED.*

She felt dizzy and ran her hand along the wall until she found the bathroom, turned on the light, and looked in the mirror. A dark purple shiner peered back at her. "Great. That'll make a beautiful wedding picture. One I'll avoid the rest of my life."

The last time she was at her parent's home flashed through her mind. At first, she thought the bullet had shattered the living room window, but now that she reflected, she never heard a shot, just a soft popping noise. *Maybe the gun had a silencer. She remembered* something silver had landed at Ter's feet before his body flew backward, and she accidentally crushed it with her knee. *I wonder if Ter survived.*

Samantha left the bathroom and closed the door. A blue, hospital-issued robe hung over a wing-backed chair. She draped it over her shoulders and found a pair of white slippers under the bed. Her head throbbed when she knelt to put them on.

She glanced at her wrist. Her watch wasn't there. Pulling aside the curtain, she noted it was twilight. Either dusk or dawn, she wasn't clear since she had no idea which way her room faced. *Ivar mentioned his visit last night. It must be dawn.* As she passed a trashcan, an empty bottle of champagne caught her eye. *How much of that did I drink?*

Glancing into the hallway, she noticed her room number was 457 or maybe 459. The numbers were blurred. However, according to the fire escape plan posted inside her door, she was on the fourth-floor orthopedic unit. She thought ICU was on the third floor.

No one was in the hall, so she padded toward the elevator and pushed the down arrow. A deep voice echoed from the stairwell. "She's in room 457. I'll take care of the guy in ICU."

"My room?" Samantha ducked into a linen closet across the hall and cracked the door.

Two men walked by. One was the male nurse with the tattoo from the ED. His dark eyes glanced up and down the hallway then he cocked his head in the direction of her room. "I'll only be a minute."

The other man wore green scrubs, a disposable surgical hat, and a mask over his face.

The elevator arrived and startled the man in scrubs. He wiped his brow when no one got off and blew out a deep breath.

Samantha watched in horror as the tattooed nurse slipped a hand in his coat pocket, pulled out a syringe, and edged his way into her room.

Has he been drugging me? Samantha pondered. *No wonder I can't remember anything. What has he been giving me?*

A few moments later, he poked his head out of the door. "I think she's in the bathroom."

A middle-aged, dark-haired nurse pushed a medication cart down the hall toward them.

The tattooed nurse ducked back into Samantha's room.

"You're here early." The nurse smiled at the guy in scrubs. "I haven't finished the pre-op on Mr. Green yet."

"That's okay," his deep voice boomed. "I'll come back in a few minutes." He turned and pushed the elevator button and entered when the doors opened.

Unsure where to go, Samantha found a set of scrubs in the closet. The pants were too long and covered her slippered feet. Her right arm wouldn't fit into the sleeve.

The cast was duct-taped, soaked in dried blood, and chipped at the elbow. As awful as it looked, she wondered why no one had replaced it. *This is a hospital, isn't it?*

She ripped away at the duct tape and removed a large chunk of plaster, making the cast at wrist level instead of her elbow. The sleeve tore slightly as she forced her wrist through the opening, but she managed to get the scrub top on. In an equipment cart, she found an arm sling, plucked it out of the plastic wrapper, and slipped it in place, hiding the broken cast. A surgical scrub cap hid her red locks.

A door slammed, bringing Samantha's attention back toward the hallway.

The tattooed nurse darted her way and nearly collided with her as he entered the room.

She moved behind the supply cart to hide her black eye. Lowering her voice, she said with as much authority as possible, "May I help you?"

"Sorry, wrong turn. I was looking for the stairs." He stepped into the hallway.

Samantha heard his retreating footsteps. The coast was clear, so she went back to her room. *The guy in ICU* sped through her mind. "Ter?" She glanced down the hall.

The medication nurse emerged from the room next door.

Standing tall, Samantha mustered her courage and stepped up to her. "What floor is ICU on?"

"Third, but use the other elevator," the dark-haired nurse pointed. "This one opens at the wrong end of the hall."

"Thanks." Samantha headed in the direction given.

The nurse returned to her task at hand.

Samantha rounded the corner. Not wanting to wait for the elevator, she took the stairs down one flight and hoped she wouldn't run into either of the two nurses who were drugging patients.

A Chance of a Ghost

Pops frowned at Tommy, who stamped his feet.

"The sun's out, and I'm not staying here another day," he announced and grabbed his sister's hand. "We're leaving right after breakfast."

The swelling in Pops's ankle had gone down somewhat, but he was in no condition to hike a long distance. He hobbled to the couch. "Before you kids run off, how'd you like to meet a ghost?"

Tommy laughed. "There's no such thing as ghosts."

"Maybe not in your world, but there is one in mine. I'll see if I can make contact."

Bridget peered over at Pops. "Don't make any promises that you can't keep. You know Tobias would have come to our rescue by now if he could."

Pops smiled. "I have a secret. I'll share it with you after we eat."

Lisa pulled away from Tommy. "Can I sit in your lap?" She crawled onto the sofa and scooted onto his knee. "Whisper the secret in my ear. I won't tell anyone, even if he tickles me."

Bridget chuckled and flipped the French toast. Venison sausages sizzled in another frying pan.

"That smells good." Tommy rubbed his tummy. "When do we eat?"

"Soon. Would you set the silverware on the table?"

"Maybe we can have a picnic outside in the woods." Tommy looked hopeful. "I'd like to pick some berries, too. Mom lets us go down to the brook. We have raspberries sometimes with our pancakes."

"It's still damp outside," Pops said.

"Don't worry. I'll fix everything." Tommy climbed onto the counter and took out a wicker basket.

Bridget helped him down.

"I'll get the old canvas from the storage room." Tommy dropped forks and knives into the basket and left the room. He returned with a bucket and a tarp.

Bridget packed the toast and sausages on top of a few paper plates and laid them in the basket.

Lisa slid off Pops' knee and held out her tiny hand. "I'll help you, so you won't fall."

"Thank you, young lady." He scooted forward.

"Ready?" Lisa pulled on Pops' arm. "I'm starving."

"It's only seven-thirty. Where did all that spaghetti you ate last night go?" He laughed and pushed himself to his feet.

A loud whirring sound came from outside.

Pops moved to the window. "There's a chopper flying over.

Maybe we can catch their attention."

Bridget headed for the door with a red dishtowel. She ran into the yard and waved it over her head, but the chopper flew out of sight. "Maybe it'll come back. We'll be ready for it next time." She draped the towel over the waistband of her apron.

Tommy trudged behind her with the tarp. "I hope Mommy is okay."

"I'm sure she is." Bridget carried the pail and basket over the crook of one arm. "I heard on the radio that the police are looking for Walter and the two of you. Maybe that chopper is looking for you right now."

Pops asked, "Where to?"

"Over by the water." Tommy pointed and ran ahead. He dropped the canvas.

"Maybe if we build a fire, they'll come find us," Tommy smoothed the tarp across the ground under a tree.

Pops shook his head. "That's dangerous. We already have a fire burning out of control in Colorado. We don't need another."

"Then it's a good thing that it rained the past two days," Tommy said.

Lisa let go of Pops' hand. "I see berries." She ran over to pick one. "These have stickers."

Bridget set down the basket and brought over the pail. The bushes were filled with plump red raspberries.

The children helped. Lisa scooped up a handful.

Before she could get a mouthful, Tommy grabbed his sister's arm. "Don't eat them yet. Mommy says we have to wash them first."

"That's right." Pops knelt on the ground. "Maybe we can save them for dessert. I'm hungry."

"Me, too." Lisa dropped the berries into the pail and ran to sit by Pops.

Tommy handed the bucket to Bridget. "Okay, but we can't leave them in the sun. They get mushy."

Bridget set them in the shade under the tree and joined the group for breakfast. When they finished, she washed the berries, and they had dessert back at the shack.

"Okay." Tommy stood with his hands on his hips. "Where's your ghost?"

Pops sat on the couch, leaned forward, and crossed his arms. "Tobias, Tobias, Tobias." Then he blinked.

"Is something supposed to happen?" Tommy asked.

Pops scratched his chin. "I'm not sure, but it worked for Beetlejuice."

"Who's that?" asked Lisa.

Bridget shook her head. "I told you not to promise something you can't deliver."

"It's been three days," Pops said. "I thought he had time to rest by now."

"You're just spoofin' me." Tommy grabbed his jacket. "I knew there was no ghost." He headed for the door.

A gust of wind blew through the broken window.

Bridget pointed toward a light mist. "Tommy, I'd like you to meet Tobias."

Tommy's eyes widened. "Really?"

A cell phone dropped at Bridget's feet. The wind gently ruffled the boy's blond hair and disappeared.

Pops nodded. "What's that?"

A siren sounded in the distance.

Bridget flipped open the phone to a text message. "I called 911. Someone will be here soon. Too weak to do much more. Tobias."

Mr. Strong

Ivar's on his way echoed in Samantha's mind. *I sure hope so.* She entered the stairwell and spied the tattooed nurse on the third-floor landing.

His hand rested against the door. He leaned over the railing and studied the stairway below. Then his head lifted. Samantha ducked, held her breath, and hoped he didn't see her.

She waited until she heard the door open and close, and she chanced another peek. He had disappeared, so she darted down the steps to the landing where he'd been. She opened the door a crack.

The ED nurse with the tattoo stood inside the door, talking with a stranger.

She caught a glimpse of his nametag. Steve Walters. A gasp escaped her lips. She dashed upstairs. *Ter called him Walter, the man holding Ter's wife. Why didn't I notice that before now?*

The door burst open. Walter headed her way and grabbed at her ankle.

Samantha kicked free and took two steps at a time.

The fourth-floor door slammed above her with such force that she heard the echo reverberate—the guy in scrubs headed down the stairs toward her.

Caught between the two, she leaned forward and slid her cap over her black eye.

"Good morning," deep voice said and passed beside her.

Walter yelled, "Grab her. It's McFitzroy. See her cast?"

The man turned in time to get a face full of the fractured cast as Samantha swung her right fist with all her might.

The man fell backward onto Walter.

Samantha bounded up the stairs, threw open the door on the fourth floor, and screamed, "Code Blue Stairwell! Code Blue."

Someone must have heard her because the alarm bonged across the intercom overhead and repeated her warning.

Within seconds, the stairwell flooded with hospital personnel. Samantha ran to the back elevator and took it to the third floor. Pausing in the ICU waiting room, she grabbed the phone and dialed Ivar's cell. "Pick up!"

The call went to voice mail. "It's Samantha. I need help.

Walter is here in the hospital."

Commotion erupted in the hall outside the ICU. Walter headed her way.

"Hurry!" Samantha slammed down the phone and scooted into ICU.

"Ma'am, you can't come in here," a nurse said.

She pushed past and zigzagged through the unit in search of Ter.

"If you don't leave, I'll have to call security," the nurse called out.

Rounding bed E, she halted and ducked behind the curtain. From the corner of her eye, she saw Walter walk over to the end of the hall.

Three bells rang as a warning overhead.

Walter took a syringe from his pocket.

She ran for the man as he inserted a needle into Ter's IV port. She yanked the IV out of Ter's arm and leapt onto Walter's back.

"Mr. Strong, ICU," sounded over the intercom.

"Stop!" Samantha called out. "Someone call the police," was drowned out with a repeated, "Mr. Strong, ICU."

Blood dripped onto the floor from Ter's arm.

"Look what you've done." Walter rammed against the wall nearly knocking her off his back.

Samantha clung around his neck. "Call security!" They both shouted.

Some thug peeled her off Walter's back.

"Hold her until I can sedate her," Walter said with authority.

"No!" Samantha rammed her cast into the thug's gut and faced three equally large men standing outside the door.

Emit rounded the corner. "Sam! What are you doing here?" "Oh, Emit, Thank God. Walter has been drugging me. I think he drugged Ter, too. Check his pockets."

"She's crazy," Walter said. "You know me. I work in the emergency department. I come up here all the time."

Walter confidently pushed his way from Ter's room into the main ICU.

"Check Ter's blood work," Samantha said.

"Yeah, do that," Walter called out. "I'm sure you'll find morphine and phenobarbital. That's what you're giving him, right?"

The thug groaned and then grabbed Samantha's wrist.

"Emit!" Samantha cried.

Emit grabbed her cast, and the thug let her go. "What have you gotten yourself into now?"

"Just listen to me." Samantha inched toward her colleague. "Call Ivar. I'm sure we can work this out."

Emit shook his head. "This has gone far enough. Ivar put me in charge. Take her to her room and stay with her," he said to the man in scrubs who just walked into Ter's room.

"No, not him! He's with Walter."

"It'll be my pleasure." The guy in scrubs wrapped his grubby fingers around her arm. "Come on. Do as the Sup says."

"Sup?" Samantha grimaced. "Emit? What's going on?" *Is he their supervisor?*

The three men in the doorway converged on her.

"Room 457." Emit checked on Ter. "I'll be there shortly. I have a few things to do before I see you again, Missy."

Detoured

Ivar barely left the office for the hospital when his police radio blared. "Two children and a woman were spotted in a field not far from Highway 85." *Wonder if it's Ter's family.*

Believing he'd failed Ter the night of the shooting, Ivar vowed to rescue his wife and kids. Somehow. Some way. He debated, but he knew that Sam was protected in the hospital. He'd see her soon.

A 911 call for the same area cinched his plan. Ivar phoned his partner. "Brody, I'm picking you up early." He explained why.

"Catch me at the corner by the bakery," Brody said. "While I'm here, I'll get you a latte and your favorite bacon and egg crescent sandwich."

"Sounds great." Ivar hung up and switched on the car radio to a surprising newscast.

"…our station's report of Pamela Rodriguez's rescue was in error. It was a case of mistaken identity. The woman is still missing. Although we have an inside report that the children escaped their captor, their whereabouts are unknown."

Recalling Sam's cryptic message a few days ago, he wondered if Tommy and Lisa really did escape. Ivar pulled up to the bakery and gratefully accepted the large latte passed through his window.

Brody slid into the passenger's seat and handed him the sandwich. "Have you heard from the hospital recently?" He buckled his seatbelt, and they headed for Highway 85.

Ivar took a sip. "Only from Sam. Why do you ask?"

"Rotten news about Colby." Brody gave a sidewise glance at Ivar.

"Yeah." *Does Brody suspect I'm covering for Colby?*

"Investigation shows someone tampered with his brakes."

"I wonder who did that." Brody bit into his large glazed doughnut.

"Good question. He was at Vickers' all day."

"I think it's time to retire. This small town is getting too rough for me." Brody shook off the flakes of sugar that landed in his lap. "Do you think they found Ter's kids?"

"Hard to say, but what are a couple of children doing out alone so far away from town?" With a sigh, Ivar added, "Ter's still unconscious, but records show he has a hunting lodge close to that area."

Brody licked his fingers. "Do you think the kids are there?"

"I don't know," Ivar said.

"We've never had such a rotten month." Brody frowned and took another bite. "Why us?"

"You're asking too many questions. I need sleep." Ivar clutched the steering wheel until his knuckles ached. "Something's going on with Samantha, and sleep is the last thing on my mind."

"But you saw her last night, right?" Brody grinned.

"Yeah, and this morning, she didn't even remember seeing me."

"The night you proposed to her?" Brody asked in surprise. "What woman wouldn't remember that?"

"Sam," Ivar said. "I thought she loved me."

"You know she loves you."

"She just doesn't remember." Ivar tapped his fingers on the steering wheel. "Why?" His cell beeped a warning that he had a voicemail. "I wonder who called. I didn't hear the phone ring."

You must have been on the police radio with me," Brody said. "You know how loud that speaker gets."

Ivar checked his message. "It's from Sam." His heart leapt as he heard her voice and played a tug of war with his mind. "I can't think straight. My mind's gone."

Brody grabbed his arm. "Then let's make a change of plans."

"Turn around and drop me off at the station," Brody said. "I'll take another car, and you go to the hospital now. Something doesn't add up. You'd never forgive yourself if anything happened to your fiancée."

"I can't let Ter down again."

The least you can do is call Sam. Tell her you'll be delayed," Brody insisted. "If you can't reach her room, leave a message at the nurses' station."

"All right, that's a good idea." Ivar dialed Samantha's room. The phone rang until it automatically forwarded to the nurses' station.

"Orthopedics, Grace Landers speaking."

"Hello, Grace. This is Officer Rexall. I'm trying to reach Samantha McFitzroy. She doesn't answer her phone."

"Sorry. I can't give you any information," Grace said. "Patient confidentiality."

Fear crept into his soul. "This is police business," Ivar lied. "Do I have to talk with your supervisor?"

Grace hesitated. "No. I guess not…"

A commotion in the background made it difficult to hear Grace. "…she transfer…seizure…"

"What? She was transferred… Where to? When?"

"Patient confid—"

Ivar slammed his phone shut. He flipped on his siren and sped in the opposite direction.

"What happened?" Brody asked in surprise.

"I had no idea that she'd gotten worse, but I think she had a seizure."

"Good thing you called."

"They're transferring her," Ivar said.

The police radio crackled to life. "Ivar. It's Emit. We need you at the hospital ASAP."

"I'm on my way." Ivar took the corner on two wheels.

Brody reached for the dash. "I'd like to make it to the hospital alive."

Ivar ignored the comment. "You call the office and send another officer to check on Ter's children. Make arrangements to hide them away at the retreat. You know the place. I'll call dispatch."

"If 911 responds, I'm sure Ter's family will have plenty of help."

Ivar glared.

"I'm right on it." Brody grabbed the radio. "The retreat? You are worried."

When Ivar reached dispatch, there was no record of a transfer from the hospital. "What's going on?" He flexed his fingers. "She was taken in plain daylight."

Ivar squealed into the emergency lot, parked, and the men ran inside.

As usual, the ED was busy.

Ivar tracked down the secretary. "Did an ambulance leave here within the last thirty minutes?"

"No. I've been here the whole time, but that doesn't mean one wasn't sent from another unit in the hospital."

"Brody, stay here and make those arrangements. I'm going upstairs to talk to the orthopedic nurses." Ivar bolted for the door.

He found Grace at the orthopedic desk and flashed his badge. "What happened to Miss McFitzroy?"

"She had a seizure before I came on duty," Grace said. "I guess it happened before shift change. At least, that's what the nurse told me during report."

"Can I read her file?"

Grace frowned. "I'm not sure about that."

"Can you at least read the chart to see what happened?"

Grace sifted through several folders inside an outbox. "It must be in medical records."

A dark-haired nurse walked up to the desk while rummaging through her purse. She bumped into Ivar. "Sorry. Rough night. I didn't see you."

"Were you here when Samantha McFitzroy had her seizure?" Ivar asked.

"Seizure? That's news to me." She moved down the hall and stopped. "Is that the patient from 457?"

"Yes." Ivar stepped closer.

"I don't think she had a seizure, but some incident happened in ICU. They called a Mr. Strong, and three orderlies brought her back to her room. I tried to talk to her, but the men wouldn't let me in the room."

"Men?"

"When I saw them leave, she was very cooperative."

Ivar turned back to Grace. "Who gave you the report on Miss McFitzroy this morning?"

"A nurse who floated from the ED. His name is Steve Walters but he goes by Walter."

"Walter?" Ivar asked with a jolt. "Are you sure?"

Grace nodded.

"Thanks, Ma'am." Ivar turned to the dark-haired nurse. "Do you know where they took her?"

"Down the elevator to OR, I think. At least the men were in scrubs. Wait! I answered a Code Blue in the stairwell. That same man was there. Come with me."

Ivar dashed down the hall after the woman. She took him down the back elevator to OR. "There's a room down here that leads outside. If anyone needed a quick escape, it would be from there."

Ivar stepped onto the freight dock. An ambulance pulled out from the back door. With one glance through the ambulance window, he spied a redhead in the back. He grabbed his phone and called highway patrol. "This is Officer Rexall. Get me the chief." He gave the ambulance plate number while he dashed to his car. "Have him call me back."

Brody must have seen him run past the ED. "Wait. Ivar, don't leave without me."

The two officers slid into the car and squealed after the ambulance.

"Call the ICU medical director and have him check on the status of Ter Rodriguez. I want a drug screen run."

Brody pulled out his cell and made the call. They must have paged the director overhead because it took a while before Brody made the requests. "Call me as soon as you get the results."

"Highway patrol," came over the car radio.

"We're looking for a Weld County ambulance." Ivar gave the license number. "I need roadblocks set up throughout town."

"I'll get right on it," the patrolman said. "They won't get too far."

Sirens Everywhere

The radio came to life from the dashboard of Ambulance 21 as it pulled out from the back dock of the hospital. "Are the cops following you?"

"Is this a secure line?" Emit asked.

"Of course it is. I won't let anyone know my identity, especially some hick cop and his partner. Now, are they following you?"

"It looks that way," Emit said.

"Merge into traffic along 16th Street."

Three ambulances joined them at the intersection.

"Go south on 8th Avenue. Highway patrolmen are setting up a roadblock on Highway 85. Overtake one ambo and get lost in the crowd."

"Do we want to be caught going out of town?" Emit asked.

"Not if we don't have to," the man over the radio said.

Sirens echoed from every direction.

"Run code 3, red lights and sirens, and head toward Canal Road."

The other three ambulances did the same. Emit passed the rear ambulance and wedged it in the middle.

"Are you still being followed?" came across the radio.

"We got out ahead of them. I'm not sure if they can keep up."

"Then slow down, you fools! They need to believe they're chasing the real Sam."

Walter scratched the side of his head. "Couldn't you have gotten a better wig? This itches like crazy."

"How did I get stuck with so many incompetents?" the radio came back.

"Where to now?" Emit asked. "I see them about three cars back, and we're surrounded by cops."

"Good time to put 'plan scatter' into action."

"10-4." Emit pulled away, heading south.

The first ambulance continued north. The second went west, and the rear ambulance made a U-turn.

People stood on the sidewalks, covering their ears.

Cars lined the streets, some blocking traffic as the cop cars tried to follow in each direction.

Ivar's squad car honed in on Ambulance 27.

"We lost him," Emit said.

"You idiots! That hick is following number 27. Sam's in there. Abort. Do you hear me? Abort!"

"I thought you wanted him to get lost." Emit made a U-turn and followed Ivar's car. "Walter, stand up by the window as I pass him. Look as if you're trying to break out the back door. Wave as if in panic. Do anything to draw his attention to us."

Walter sprang from the gurney, pulled the red wig down over his eyes, and waved frantically at Ivar as they passed him.

Ivar's car swerved, nearly hitting the ambulance and now followed Emit's ambulance.

The radio blared, "Turn right. We need him to go south."

Emit did as he was told.

"Listen to this." The radio opened into utter chaos as the police channel played.

"Which way do we go?" one officer asked.

Another said, "I pulled over an ambulance. There's an unconscious woman with a black eye and multiple bruises. The driver says they're en route to the hospital."

"Give them a police escort," the chief said.

"Officer Harold, what's the status on the ambulance heading east?"

Harold replied, "Still running Code 3. Do you want me to continue following?"

"Yes. Report back when they get to the hospital."

"Officer Rexall, what's happening?"

"We're heading north. No, make that west. No, south," Ivar said in confusion. "We're going around in circles. I'm following Sam."

"What happened to the fourth ambulance?" the chief asked. An officer replied over the radio, "Lost it. No, wait! Two more are heading this way. How many vehicles do we have? Are there any left at the station?"

The chaos snapped off. "I guess we got their attention. Sam's sequestered safely. Implement the exit plan. Repeat. Implement the exit plan."

"Walter, get rid of that red wig." Emit turned the ambulance around and headed for Platte Valley. Ivar followed.

"Get the kid on the gurney," Emit said to Walter. "Start an IV and look official. I'm calling in to dispatch."

"He's my boy. I know what to do," Walter snapped back.

"Emit," came across the speaker. "You need to ditch that hick cop. Run through the next light and go to our meeting point. The boss will take care of everything."

Emit turned off his red lights and siren and slowed until the next light turned yellow. He flashed his lights, fired up the siren once more, and ran the red light as instructed.

Ivar followed across the intersection.

Two shots rang out, blowing out the cop's front and back tires on the passenger's side. Ivar's car spun out of control and came to a stop when it hit a light post.

Emit kept driving. "Forget calling dispatch. We're home free."

"You're doing great, Son." Walter hugged his boy. "I love you. The boss promised, Mommy will be home tonight."

Donations

It was mid-afternoon when the trucks rolled from I-25, taking the 20th Street exit into crowded LoDo Denver. The Rockies were playing at Coors Field. Parking was at a premium. The old warehouse came into view, abandoned until last year when a Colorado banker purchased the structure. Now it housed donations, those orphaned even from the local ARC, Salvation Army, and Goodwill stores across Colorado.

The metal doors opened with a low groan. The lights flooded piles of second-hand clothing, overloaded trash bags, pierced by heels of cheap shoes and hideous purses. A whole section of used books lined the back wall. Beds, microwaves, TVs, and other small appliances were stacked neatly along another.

"We need the basement," the driver said to the wiry old woman at the door.

She greeted him with a salute. "You're looking fit as always. Of course, ex-soldiers have that look. Clean cut and standing ramrod straight."

He returned the salute. "Where to?"

"Pull down that aisle. There's a freight elevator at the end. Hit B5 to get to the lowest level. That's where you'll find his man cave. The garage is waiting."

"Thanks." He removed a folded, white handkerchief with the initials GG embroidered in royal blue in the corner. The driver wiped his brow, closed his window, and cranked up the AC.

"Afternoon, Gary." A cheerful Pacific Islander met the truck as it exited the elevator on B5. "Boss wants these babies handled with care. Park 'em at least four feet apart so the doors won't ding one another."

"Right. I'm familiar with his routine." Gary pulled up to the garage and opened the back of the truck.

His partner climbed from the cab and jingled through a set of keys. "I don't mind driving these classics, even if it's only for a few feet."

The back ledge hovered a moment and then dropped to the floor, making a ramp. Gary climbed out and joined his partner.

"Wow. Look at this 1955 Chevy Bel Air." His partner climbed inside. "My dad owned one of these years ago. It's a shame he got rid of it." He closed the door and drove it off the truck, parked it next to a roadster, and headed for the next car.

"I love the 1939 Lincoln convertible," Gary said as he backed it off the truck. "They don't make them like this anymore."

"Where'd he get the 1910 red Model T Ford?" His partner waited inside the cab while Gary cranked the engine.

"That was a steal," Gary said. "We went to Mississippi for an antique show, and this guy couldn't afford the trip back home. I would have bought it if I could afford the airfare. Boss gave him a first-class ticket to California. Amos refused to return the car."

"I bet they're insured to the max," his partner said. "Vickers won't lose his shirt over the loss of these babies." He grinned and moved the Ford into the garage and then joined Gary as they closed up the back of the truck.

"Linda's going to be royally pissed when she learns we actually burned her Mercedes but saved his classics," Gary said. "We needed hard evidence at the 'crime scene'. I spent a whole month finding old parts to match the guts of these vehicles to plant in the fire."

"You're pretty spry for being dead," his partner climbed into the cab.

"I'll cry at my funeral. Linda scheduled it for next Tuesday. I don't have any family now that my twin brother took my place. You're planning to attend, aren't you?" He started the truck and drove into the elevator.

"I'm being well paid. You better believe I'll make it a very sad event."

Visit to Tobias

Tobias felt his fingers itch to get out of this hole in the ground, but his spirit only fluttered. It refused to rise.

Tobias felt the energy of a live person aboveground. 'Ivar, is that you?' No sound came forth.

"I can't believe I'm here, but what choice do I have? Everything's going to shit. At least I'm still alive." Footsteps trod over the grave with an uneven gait. "Tobias." Someone dropped to the ground. "I got your note. Come out and let's talk."

Tobias concentrated with all his might, but he couldn't lift. Not even a breeze stirred.

"Am I supposed to see you?" Ivar called out. "Of course not. You're a ghost!"

The lad must have gotten to his feet. Tobias couldn't feel the body heat any longer. 'The card by the headstone.' Tobias couldn't project his words. He tried again. 'Don't leave before you get the card.'

"I can't wait around forever." Ivar sounded peeved. "I'm swamped at work. Sam's missing, and I can't find her. She's counting on you."

Rage ripped through Tobias. *Don't you think I know that? It's why I broke down and asked for your help!* Still unable to make his words roil. Tobias felt locked in his dead body.

Footsteps rustled over dried grass. "I must be crazy. Why'd I think you could help? Just shows how desperate I am."

'No. Don't leave.' With one last blast of air, Tobias blew with all his strength. The cracked tombstone shifted and a chunk of stone landed on the ground. A thud came from overhead.

Tobias pulled the hairy roots to wiggle the plant above.

"Ouch! Stinking thistles." Ivar said. "What's this? A thank-you card?"

Good. He found my note, now find Sam. Relief flowed through Tobias as he succumbed to a deep sleep.

Meeting Pam

Samantha's head throbbed, and a dull ache nudged the shoulder where Emit injected some drug into her arm. She rolled to her other side and tried to rub the area, but her fingers couldn't quite reach the spot. "I can't believe I trusted that schmuck."

"How are you today?"

Startled, Samantha had been unaware of the woman sitting on the edge of her bed until she spoke.

A high-cheeked, raven-haired woman leaned over her with a cold compress in her hand. A greenish bruise surrounded her right eye and looked almost like make-up, shadowed to complement her hazel irises.

Samantha ran a hand over her face. "Who are you?"

"Pam Rodriguez." Her smile wasn't full, but she looked relieved.

"You're Ter's wife?" Samantha asked.

Pam's eyes widened. Her mouth gaped. "You know him?"

The room spun as Samantha tried to sit up, so she leaned on her right arm. It felt different. "Not really. I've just run into him a time or two." She ran her left hand over the cast. "No duct tape. Someone changed it."

"Changed?" Pam leaned closer.

"My cast. Someone put a new cast on my arm. The old one fell apart when your husband shot it."

Pam jumped to her feet and dropped the compress. "What? Ter would never…When? Have you seen him lately?"

"Don't worry." Sam reached over to pick up the cold cloth. "He didn't hurt me. We had a misunderstanding." Placing the rag over her forehead, she leaned back. "I saw him this morning in ICU."

Pam lifted a corner of the rag. "You couldn't have. You were here. I thought you must be exhausted. You've slept almost continuously."

Samantha uncovered her face. "What day is it?"

"I've lost track of time, but they brought you here late one morning a few days ago."

Samantha squinted at her wrist. *Oh yeah. Watch is gone.*

"Where are we?"

"I don't know." Pam faced Samantha. "Did you say ICU? What happened? Did Ter get hurt? Are the kids with him?"

"I'm sure they're safe." Samantha had no proof, but she saw fear in Pam's eyes.

"You said Ter was in ICU." Pam worried her lip.

Samantha wanted to distract her and definitely didn't want to tell her that her husband was on a ventilator fighting for his life. "My mind's fuzzy. I was the one in ICU." She studied her surroundings. A high ceiling loomed overhead. The white walls had no windows, and two unfinished wooden doors were all she saw.

Samantha moved slowly to a sitting position. The dizziness eased. "Where does the door on the right lead to?"

"A sitting room and the kitchen. I have a bedroom, too." Pam pointed. "It's through that door to the left. There's a bathroom between our rooms."

"No windows?" Samantha asked.

Pam shook her head. "But the kitchen is well-stocked with food and drinks. It's a good thing, too. The building doesn't have any running water. It went off earlier today."

"Any clue where we are?"

"None."

"I heard the chimes when I replayed Ter's messages." Samantha gingerly swung her feet over the edge of the bed.

"I used to hear chimes, but they moved me after the children escaped. Are you working with Ter?" Pam asked. "I don't understand what's going on. Is he safe?"

Samantha wanted to shout, "No!" Instead, she asked, "Do you know who's doing this?"

"Walter used to come by every morning and night to check on me, but since you came, a guy named Everett or something like that comes every few hours."

"Emit?" Samantha asked.

"Maybe. I didn't pay attention. He told me to take care of you."

"Is he a paramedic?" Samantha held her forehead.

"Maybe. I stay away when he comes near me. He brings food and puts it in the kitchen."

"Did Walter give you that shiner?"

"Not exactly." Pam gently patted her eye. "I tried to escape and fell down the basement stairs. At least, that's what he told me. I don't remember."

"You don't remember, and I can't either," Samantha said. "Do you have an IV?"

"No. Why?" Pam asked.

"Never mind." Samantha patted her hand. "It must be in the food. Have we had anything to eat lately?"

There's a thermos of coffee." Pam smiled, and then it faded. "I've been feeding you as directed. We also shared some fudge that Walter brought earlier in the week."

"Did we eat any dinner?" Samantha asked.

"Not that I recall. Maybe I slept through it."

"Breakfast?"

Pam nodded. "I made eggs and bacon this morning. It felt good to cook for someone."

"Was Walter here at the time?"

"No." Pam hesitated. "I told you. Walter hasn't been here since you arrived."

"Oh. That's right. You did tell me. Mind's spinning."

Pam nodded. "You know this sounds daft, but I think we're in a city somewhere."

Samantha stood. The room spun for a moment before coming to a halt. "Why's that?"

"I keep hearing muffled beeping noises like trucks backing up. Sometimes, they sound as if they're below us, but I've called out several times. No one comes to the door."

"When was the last time Emit stopped by?" Samantha frowned. "I don't remember seeing him."

"About an hour ago. He asked about you but didn't go in to see you this time."

"Don't drink any more coffee or eat anything." Samantha licked her dry lips. "I think it makes us forget."

A noise came from below. Samantha dropped to the floor and listened. Something slammed. "Was that a car door?"

Pam joined her on the floor. "Something's moving down there."

"Good. We're not alone. How long do you think you've been here?"

"Maybe a week." Pam frowned. "It could be longer. I'm not sure anymore. They took my watch."

"Mine, too." Samantha got off the floor. "Show me around. I need to get the lay of the land. Then we'll make a plan to escape."

Another Failure

Unable to concentrate, Samantha couldn't come up with a viable plan to escape, so she turned in for the night.

A few hours later, she shivered and pulled up her comforter.

"Wake up. I have to talk to you." The mist crept around her face and lifted the curls from her cheek.

"Go away. I'm sleeping." Samantha rolled over.

The ghost refused to leave.

"Tobias? Get off my bed. I'm freezing." She pulled the pillow over her head.

"Get up. My energy is nearly gone." Tobias blew cold air at the pillow. "Let's get out of here."

"What?" Samantha sprang from the bed. "You're here to free me?" She turned on the lamp by her bed.

"Someone has to." Tobias hovered near the door. "It wasn't easy tracking you down. I tried to phone Ivar, but I can't text anymore."

"I'll get Pam." Samantha dashed toward the bathroom door. "Whew, it stinks in there."

"Wait," Tobias said. "I just wanted to be sure you're all right."

Samantha hesitated. "You're fading."

"I know! I'm barely a mist anymore. All I can do is use the wind."

Samantha felt a tingle as he crossed the room. "Wait, you can't blink me through walls?"

"No. Maybe, in a week or two, after some more rest." Tobias' voice grew dim. "Got any ideas?"

"Do you know where we are?" Samantha asked.

"In an old warehouse in Denver."

"Is anyone else here?"

"Probably somewhere in the building."

Samantha's stomach growled.

"Don't they feed you?" Tobias shimmered.

"I'm fine. Don't burn out. Can you get a phone?"

"I can't get it through the walls."

Samantha rubbed her chin. "Right. I need you to get the keys to the front door. Emit has them. Do you know Emit?"

"Does he work with Ivar?" Tobias asked.

"No. He's an EMT." Samantha glanced at her bare wrist and frowned. "What time is it?"

"Around three in the morning." He disappeared.

Samantha looked around the room. "What day is it?"

"July first." His voice cracked. "I'll be back," sounded in her mind.

"Tobias, are you still here?" He didn't reply.

"Who are you talking to?" Pam stood at the bathroom door. "I thought you were having another nightmare."

"Sorry. It's late. Go back to bed." Samantha climbed under the covers. "We'll talk more in the morning."

Pam left the room. "I swear I heard someone else in the room."

"Good night." Samantha turned out the light and whispered, "Hurry back, Tobias."

Followed

Foul-smelling sweat dripped from Steve Walters' face. Walter, the name he went by, ran a sleeve over his brow. His heart thudded against his ribcage. If his boss found out what he planned to do, he'd pay, but Walter couldn't do this anymore. *Today was the last straw.*

The boss promised to free his wife. Days passed since he'd delivered Samantha. Since then, the boss found one delay after another. *No more!*

Walter turned off his headlights. The car crept along the curb across the street from an old apartment building and parked. He'd followed a rusty truck to this ghost town earlier today, but it was too risky during daylight. Now, as the sun set over the mountains, he returned to claim Carmen.

The truck sat empty in the driveway alongside the apartment.

A light flickered through the upstairs apartment window.

Walter hunched down for one last look, removed the keys, and got out of the car. The door closed with barely a click. Crouching in the shadows, he watched and waited.

Getting up his nerve, he darted across the street and peered into the truck. As he suspected, no one was inside. He ducked against the side wall and inched his way to the back corner of the apartment to take a look. Dressed all in black, he blended with the night.

A dark-haired giant stood near the back door, smoking a cigarette.

A gasp slipped past Walter's lips. *There he is. The man who shot Ter.* Walter didn't know his name, but he called him Ogre. The dim patio light made his skin appear yellow.

Ogre blew out a ring of smoke. "Did you shut her up?"

"She's a good girl. She no make any noise. Let her be," came from inside.

Walter hoped no harm came to his wife.

The screen door opened. "When you comin' in?"

"When I'm damn well good and ready." The tip of Ogre's cigarette glowed brighter as he inhaled and looked away.

Walter dashed behind a cluster of trees past the corner of the building. A lump caught in his throat. *Can I truly kill a man? Yes, if it means saving Carmen.* His breath quickened when the man turned his way.

Ogre's voice grew deeper. "I saw something in the shadows."

"Don't get kilt." The man's accent sounded like he came from the same region of Columbia as Carmen.

"Just follow orders!" Ogre dropped to one knee and peered around the yard.

Yeah, follow orders. See where it gets you. For the past month, Walter had done everything the boss said to do. He ordered Ter to do horrendous crimes. Walter even kidnapped Ter's wife and children to ensure compliance. When the children broke free, Walter did nothing to prevent their escape. Maybe that had been the turning point. Staring into Tommy's eyes reminded him of his own son. *Wonder if Pam's still alive.*

A shudder ran through him. He'd drugged Samantha. Ter and Pam, too. Walter shifted his weight.

"I know something moved out there." Ogre crushed out his cigarette.

"What you see?"

"Hush, Emmanuel," Ogre hissed.

That man's a murderer. He shot Ter. *He might even shoot Carmen. I have to save her.*

Walter's side cramped. Holding his breath, he watched the huge man creep toward him. First, the shiny barrel of a pistol followed by extended hands, and then the rest of his body appeared. The gun swept from side to side.

His silent soles left the concrete and stepped into the yard. Kneeling beside an old lawnmower, Ogre aimed at the tree. "I see you. Come out with your hands in the air."

Walter crouched lower behind the thickest portion of the tree trunk. His dark-barreled Beretta tracked Ogre. Unblinking, his vision narrowed, refocused, and tunneled onto the man.

An owl hooted overhead.

A shot sliced a limb from the tree.

The bird lifted and then cratered to the ground.

"Emmanuel, what did you do that for?" Ogre cried.

"Owl's bad omen. Brings death to house." Emmanuel went back inside. He reappeared without his gun, ran past Ogre, and climbed into the rusty truck. "I'm not staying here."

Ogre turned his pistol on Emmanuel. The first shot splintered the windshield, but Emmanuel backed out of the drive. Tires squealed. Ducking low, he turned. The second blast slammed into the driver's door. He kept driving.

Ogre swore and turned his gun back to the tree.

Taking a life wasn't as easy as Walter thought it would be. He aimed and pulled the trigger.

Ogre flew backward and shot wildly into the air. "Damn, I knew someone was out here!" He rolled up onto his knees.

Walter leveled the gun at the ogre's head this time, but another bullet split it open before he could fire.

A scream came from inside the building.

"Carmen!" Without thinking, Walter ran for the back door, grabbed it, and flinched. Blood splattered the door. It dripped down his arm. Searing pain burned his chest. Inhaling, he grabbed the wound. The warm flow pulsed a few times as he crumpled to the ground.

Carmen threw open the door and dropped the gun. "Scott!" she yelled. "No! I didn't know it was you."

He felt her cradle him as darkness took him.

Secret Meeting

Ivar settled into a leather wing-backed chair across the coffee table from Detective Colby Cage.

"Thanks for the private nurse." Colby sorted through a stack of files and pulled one marked Vickers' Estate. "Rehab is grueling, but I refused to cancel this meeting. What did you find so far?"

"Someone tampered with your car." Ivar placed the investigation report on the coffee table facing Colby. "Punctured brake line made a slow leak, so they worked until the fluid pumped out."

"I figured as much." Colby perused the details.

Ivar flipped through his notes scribbled on a legal pad. "Probably cut the emergency brake line, too."

"Must have happened at Vickers'." Colby repositioned his injured leg. "Now that I think about it, I skidded to a stop when I found Mrs. McFitzroy's Honda."

"That was a terrible day." Ivar ran his hand through his hair.

"After I spoke to you, I sped toward town. Rounded the corner to pass and pumped the brakes, but nothing. I'm thankful that semi stopped me from going all the way over the cliff. Not that it was a soft landing."

"The paramedic said you died at the scene." Ivar leaned closer. "What happened?"

Colby shrugged. "My head hit the steering wheel. It knocked me unconscious. When I woke up, my car had landed on the ridge below the highway. A foot more, and I'd be history."

"Were you thrown from the car?" Ivar asked. "I didn't get the details. Brody worked the case. He said you died."

Colby nodded. "That's what they thought, so the rescue team treated the others. Then Emit arrived. He shook me until I thought my teeth would fall out. He insisted I contact you immediately."

"When I heard your voice, I nearly jumped out of my skin. Sure, I was going crazy, talking to another ghost."

Colby chuckled then sobered. "Guess that's how Bridget felt talking to Pops after his shop blew up."

"Yeah. I'd have been more empathetic if I'd known what it felt like." Ivar rubbed at the headache lurking behind his eyes. "For some reason, your death seemed to play right into our hands."

Colby sighed. "I know I fought you on the idea, but my mind was in a fog, and I couldn't think clearly."

"At first, it was a precautionary measure," Ivar said. "I didn't know what to expect or who to trust. The best thing was to remove all doubt and have you go underground. I hate to say it, but I think Tobias planted that gem."

"Samantha's ghost? You think he planted the idea?" Colby's brows came together. A crease formed across his forehead. "I don't believe in spirits."

"I never used to either, but this one won't leave me alone." Ivar's jaw clenched. "Tobias thinks we're working together to solve this case. I don't have a clue how he got that idea, but he left me a note."

"Right." Colby rolled his eyes. "So, did you talk with this… this spirit?"

"Are you kidding?" Ivar asked. "I visited his tombstone. Even called out his name, but nothing. Then I found a soggy thank-you card tucked under a corner of the stone. It was addressed to me."

"Someone's playing a prank," Colby smirked.

"I don't think so. Sam swears by him. Letters in an old English scrawl covered the page. It felt spooky just reading it. I kept it as evidence."

"What did this soggy, suspicious card say?" Colby rolled his shoulders.

"Tobias thinks someone's searching for Fang Parker's old silver mine. It caved in years ago, but he believes it has something to do with a lode of silver hidden near the mine. The map shows the location. Unfortunately, we can't find the map."

"Did *Tobias* have any ideas where to find this relic?"

"In his wife's diary," Ivar said. "The one Ter's partner stole from Pops' office when they ransacked McFitzroy's."

"So theft was the motive?" Colby asked. "Did they find the map?"

"I'm not sure." Ivar felt heat rush to his face. "Sam mentioned a map, but I was preoccupied at the moment."

"Meaning?"

"It's another topic we need to discuss before I leave."

Colby fidgeted. "Could you hand me a couple of Vicodin?"

Glad to drop the topic, Ivar got up and searched the label of two bottles on the counter. Finding the pain medication, he handed the bottle to Colby. "Still causing fits?" Ivar poured a glass of water and set it on a stand next to Colby's chair.

"Yeah."

A tinge of guilt nudged Ivar, but he shoved it aside and sat down. "I have to admit, Tobias led us to Pops and Bridget. And Pops found Ter's children. I have them in a safe place."

"Okay, so maybe Tobias exists." A muscle in Colby's cheek quivered as he clenched his teeth.

"What did you find at Vickers'?"

"The Mercedes is toast, but I'm not sure about the Classics. I found some parts that could be from those old vehicles, but not enough to convince me. Something's fishy."

"It's a shame about Gary," Ivar said. "We found his bones in the ashes. He was still in bed."

"Wait a minute." Colby leaned forward. "You know it wasn't Gary, don't you? Angela said she'd informed you." He thumbed through his report. "Here it is."

Ivar got up and read over Colby's shoulder. "Investigation shows body found at the Vickers' estate is not Gary Gordon's."

"Angela didn't notify me." Ivar pointed a finger. "And neither did you."

"I just did." Colby smiled and turned the page. "I hushed the evidence until further investigation. He pointed again to his report. "See?"

Ivar picked up the file for a closer look. "It also says there were two bullet wounds. One to the head, another to his right arm, and they came from two different guns. Maybe the fire was to cover up a murder."

"A lot of extra work, don't you think? Wouldn't it have been easier to bury the guy?"

Ivar rubbed his chin. "DNA has a familial match, but the dental records are different."

"Yes. About that, do you think the break-in to the warehouse had anything to do with dental records?" Colby asked. "That's where they store old files."

"My thoughts exactly," Ivar said. "His dental X-ray might have been tampered with."

"Vickers has enemies," Colby said. "During my investigation, I found out that Amos refused to return that antique, red Model-T to the owner. Maybe he put a hit out on Amos."

"What's that got to do with Pops?" Ivar asked.

"Good question."

"And somehow, the diary enters in." Ivar tapped his chin and paced. "Back to Pops. I don't see anything at Vickers to tie to the other crimes. Different MO."

"True, but made to look similar. Vickers' was arson, not a bomb. It appears to be an amateur job."

"Yeah." Ivar worked a kink from his leg. "Off the record, do you think Gary had smarts enough to pull off this job?"

"Do you mean, does he have a reason to get even with his boss? Probably. Would he? I don't know, but if he did, it backfired big time. The fire destroyed his home."

"Gary might have planted another body to free himself from blame." Ivar sat back down and cupped his chin in the palm of his hand. "Where would I find another identifier for Gary?"

Colby listed on his fingers. "Medical records, X-rays for broken bones, maybe other ailments?"

"We discovered more than 40 medical and 20 dental records missing between the years 1962-1988. His is one of them."

"Any idea who the warehouse victim is?" Colby asked.

"I got a call today from an FBI agent, Jump Sweeny. The body matches the description of his former partner, Max Wright."

"What was Max doing in the warehouse?"

Ivar pulled out an e-mail from Sweeny. "He says Max was tracking Wendell Gordon."

"So Wendell *was* in town. Pretty suspicious."

"Yeah," Ivar said. "My gut says that one of the Gordon brothers' ashes were in that fire."

"Sweeny's FBI, huh? Wonder if he'll come to Colorado."

"I, for one, will welcome the help."

Colby leaned forward. "He's not coming, is he? I mean, you haven't heard that for a fact, have you?"

"No. Sweeny's out of the country at the moment."

Colby yawned and stretched. "Pain pill's kicking in. Anything else we need to cover?"

Ivar pursed his lips, moved to the edge of his seat, and placed his hands on either side of the chair. Ready to bolt, he blurted, "You probably should know, I proposed to Sam."

"That was a coward's way of taking advantage of my injury," Colby said.

"I'm no coward! However, when it comes to Sam, I'm not taking any chances."

"I should be ticked. You locked me up for two weeks, so I couldn't see Samantha." Colby's eyes narrowed. "Truth is, I like her. She's bright, attractive, and there's never a dull moment with her around. She deserves the best."

"Yes. She does," Ivar said.

"And you think you're the best for her?" Colby laughed. "Be honest with me. You owe me that."

Ivar scooted back into the chair. "Maybe not, but she doesn't deserve a cad like you."

Colby playfully lifted his crutch, swung it toward Ivar, and halted mid-swing. "As luck would have it, I think I'm falling for my therapist. She's fixing me dinner tomorrow night."

"Good. At least you've taken your eyes off Sam." Ivar grinned. "I can't get my mind off her. I've canvassed the area for days, studied every crime scene until they've etched every detail into my memory, and still nothing. Where's Sam?"

"She's safe." Colby put his crutch back on the floor. "Unlike when you tried to protect her."

"Wait a minute." Ivar leapt to his feet and glowered over Colby. "How do you know?"

"Emit told me."

"Do you know where she is?" Ivar's voice rose. Fists clenched at his side.

"Not me. I'm holed up undercover, remember? I said Emit says, she's safe. He knows where she is."

"How would he know?" Ivar blurted. "He's just a paramedic, and I don't trust him."

Colby shrugged his shoulders. "Why do you say that?"

"During that ambulance charade, I trailed him until someone shot out my tires. When we did track down his ambulance, he was long gone. After a thorough search, I found a red wig. It was a set-up."

"Are you sure it was Emit?" Colby asked. "I didn't hear about that incident."

"No, I suppose not. I didn't keep you in the loop."

"Then we're even." Colby raised his eyebrow. "We both have our secrets."

That infuriated Ivar. "So you trust Emit?"

"He's my undercover agent."

Ivar took a step closer and leaned over Colby. "What? Now you have an undercover agent? Since when?"

Ignoring Ivar's wrath, Colby continued. "Emit had to go to the dark side to get close to the enemy. He followed orders. You trust me, don't you?"

"I don't know who to trust. That's my problem." Ivar frowned. "Sam's gone. We found Pops and Bridget, but they're worried sick. Ter's kids are staying with them, and I managed to hide them away, but for how long? Pam's still missing. Who knows where Walter's wife is? Then Walter and his son disappeared without a clue." Ivar slammed his fists on Colby's chair.

Colby bit his lip. "Yeah. Emit, too."

"What? When was the last time you heard from him?"

"The day they took Samantha."

"That was four days ago. You haven't heard from him since then?"

Colby pursed his lips. "Well, no, but he's playing it close to the vest. If he's caught talking to me, he will blow his cover. How's Ter?"

"He's off the ventilator, but still sedated. He did confirm Tobias's theory about the diary and the old map. Sam's key opened the lockbox."

"So, did Ter's partner find the map?"

"He doesn't think so." Ivar put both his hands up and curled two fingers in the air like quotation marks. "He was only following orders."

"Who's orders?" Colby asked.

"They better not have been yours!"

"Mine? You think I'm behind this?" Colby swung his leg to the floor and struggled to get up. "I'm the victim here." His green eyes glared like a cat. "Locked up in this room for two weeks. Unable to leave. Pretending that I don't exist? They're not my orders."

Ivar took a deep breath. "Who's then?"

"Have you asked Tobias?" Colby chuckled once again. "Samantha's ghost. She's something else—"

"Well, she's my something else, so don't get any ideas." Ivar paced. His knee throbbed. His head ached, and he was exhausted. Thank goodness we discovered someone drugged Ter. Blood work showed evidence of, he grabbed his notes, a drug called Lormetazepam."

"That's a mouth full. What kind of drug is it?" Colby asked.

"A hypnotic, but it's not FDA-approved in the U.S. I think they used it on Sam, too. That's why she couldn't remember anything, even though she answered my questions. They frequently use the drug during surgical procedures."

"Can patients get repeated doses without side effects," Colby asked.

"Angela said it can cause dizziness, fainting, and nightmares."

"If the drug is unavailable in the U.S., where'd they get it from?" Colby asked.

"Europe, South America, or Asia. The best part is that its effects reverse quickly. What I want to know is how they got past the guard you put on Ter."

Colby's head jerked. "Guard? Well, I had Emit watching over Ter."

"What? You sent Emit to do the job? Ter could have been killed." Ivar's phone rang. "Officer Rexall." He moved to the coffee table and picked up a pen. "When?" With a flick of his wrist, he scribbled on his hand. "Where? I'll be right there." He hung up and headed for the door.

"Who was that?" Colby scooted to the edge of his chair and picked up his crutches.

"My partner, Brody. Steve Walters is in critical condition, gunned down outside an abandoned apartment complex somewhere near Ault. An unidentified body's in the backyard."

"That far away? No wonder we couldn't find him." Colby grabbed his jacket. "Wait, I'm going with you. I'm done with being undercover. Agreed?"

Ivar gave a curt nod.

Colby balanced on one crutch. "Now that Emit's missing, I better put a real guard at Ter's door."

Ivar whipped out his cell. "Never mind. I'll take care of it this time. Then you're going to tell me where you're keeping Sam!"

Owl's Omen

It took thirty minutes to get to the apartment complex. By then, a small crowd gathered. Red and blue lights flashed through the dusk. Police pushed back the onlookers and marked the area with crime-scene tape.

Brody greeted Ivar outside the back door. "Walk around the chalk outline. We found Steve Walters lying there. The paramedics took him already."

A bloody handprint smeared the door. A pool of blood lay across the threshold.

"Hope you haven't eaten in a while. I nearly lost my lunch."

What about Mrs. Walters?" Ivar asked.

"She's in shock and rode in the back of the ambulance with her husband. You can talk to her at the hospital."

Ivar stepped around the pool of blood. "Do you know where their five-year-old son is?"

Brody shook his head. "I haven't heard any mention of a son."

A generator roared to life and lit up the backyard.

"Over here." The coroner said.

Ivar headed toward a crumpled body on the grass.

The coroner knelt with his fingers on the man's neck. "He's a goner."

"Cause of death?" Ivar asked.

The coroner rolled the man over. "A bullet wound to the chest and one to his head. Injuries are from two different guns. I believe the chest wound is from the Beretta we bagged as evidence. The head wound from a pistol. Mrs. Walters admitted to killing the man. I think she accidentally shot her husband with the same gun."

Colby stepped up to the body and balanced on his crutches.

Brody's mouth dropped. "Detective Cage. You're alive!"

"I hope so." His grin blossomed.

Roxy, the photographer, came from the back door. Her hand flew over her mouth, and she darted back inside. A retching sound echoed. She returned, paler and wobbly on her feet.

"Who found the victim?" Ivar asked.

"We got an anonymous tip," Brody said. "Not many neighbors. The first witness on the scene denied reporting the incident, but 911 said the male caller had an accent."

"We're you the first officer to arrive?" Ivar asked.

"Yeah," Brody said. "No one answered the front door, so I came through the back. Mrs. Walters lay across her husband sobbing, holding him to her chest."

"We're fingerprinting the place," an officer said.

"I understand the wife went missing for four weeks," Colby said.

"Are you sure it's been a month?" Ivar felt like Colby blamed him for their lack of progress.

"Certain of it." Colby repositioned his crutches to pull out his cell phone. "I have a message from a daycare in Brighton where she taught kindergarten. Dated June 15th. She hadn't been to work for two weeks, so they let her go. That was nearly two weeks ago. Is this where they held her captive?"

"We don't know yet," Ivar snapped. "I'll let you know *after* we investigate."

Colby shrugged. "Okay. Don't get defensive."

Ivar scratched his jaw. "Isn't Walter the guy with a flag tattoo who works in the emergency department?"

Colby cleared his throat. "Yes, he was Emit's contact. Now I'm worried."

"About Emit or Sam?" Ivar's fists clenched. "You don't really know where he's keeping her, do you."

"As I said, it's been four days since Emit contacted me." Colby scrolled down his cell's contact list. "I've tried to reach him, but no luck."

Ivar paced, then paused. "Maybe Walter turned him over to his boss."

Colby tried dialing again. "Call went to voice mail."

Ivar turned to the medical coroner. "How long ago was he shot?"

"I'd say within the last ninety minutes." The coroner ran his hand over his balding head. "His body temperature is 97 degrees. The ambient temperature registered 58. I'm done here. Let's load him up." He grabbed the gurney. "We'll have more information after the autopsy."

Roxy made her way outside and kept her video recording as they moved the body. "What happened to the owl? Did it get caught in the crossfire?"

"I'm not a vet," the coroner said. "Let's get a move on it."

Ivar caught Roxy's glare. "Better take the owl, too. Knowing Angela, she'll be upset if you don't."

The coroner bristled. "Oh, so now you're saying that I can't do my job? I'm good enough to cover during her vacation, but when it comes down to the wire—"

"That's not what I'm saying," Ivar cut in. "We want all the evidence before it gets destroyed, and she'll want to compare that bullet that killed the owl to the rest of the crime evidence. I'll look for your preliminary report in the morning."

"Autopsy won't be done until the afternoon. Angela's instructions were that she'd do any autopsies. She'll be back after the funeral."

"Oh, that's right, Gary's funeral. I'll see her there."

Colby whispered in Ivar's ear, "It's not Gary."

Ivar frowned and turned to Brody. "Interview any witnesses you can find while we head over to the hospital. Maybe we can talk to Mrs. Walters even if her husband is unable to speak."

"I'll go with you." Colby hobbled down the driveway and shuffled past the shattered glass. He stopped and pointed to a piece of metal on the street. "Roxy, more photos over here and then bag this as evidence.

"What did you find?" Ivar asked.

"Bullet fragments."

A rusty truck pulled up behind Ivar's car. A caramel-skinned driver opened the door, glanced around, and slammed it shut again. He stared at the apartment building and stuck his head out the car window. "What happened?"

His thick accent caught Ivar's attention.

The driver's eyes widened as the medical coroner pushed the covered body down the driveway. He made a sign of the cross over his chest. "Never argue with an owl." The engine gunned. The truck nearly hit Colby as it backed up and then swerved around Ivar's car.

"I've seen that truck before." Colby climbed into the passenger's seat. "It was at the Vickers' estate the day my brakes failed." Colby pulled a pen from his shirt pocket and scribbled something on his palm.

"The driver mentioned something about an owl." Ivar slid into his car. "I think he called 911."

Colby said. "Follow him. "I'll report the license number."

Gathering Information

Samantha's mouth felt like cotton. Her dry tongue licked her lips to moisten them. She'd refused to drink or eat anything all day. *Tobias, where are you?*

No response from her ghost.

"I'm starving. All this food and nothing to eat." Pam paced from the kitchen to the sitting room. "We could at least eat the eggs."

"I'm not taking any chances," Samantha said. "Maybe something is on the shell."

"I'll check for pinholes or cracks before I cook it." Pam marched into the kitchen and opened the fridge.

"Count me out," Samantha said. "I don't trust anything."

Pam slammed the fridge. "Where's Emit?" She clenched her fists. "Usually, he's here two or three times by now."

"We're not ready for him yet." Samantha pulled open another kitchen drawer.

Pam stood in the doorway. Her arms crossed, and she tapped her foot. "What are you looking for?"

"I'm trying to find something to pick the lock with."

"Yeah, I already tried that." Pam shrugged. "No hangers, wires, or paperclips."

"Maybe this will work." Samantha held up a table knife.

"What do you plan to do with that? Stab the lock?"

Samantha moved to the door. "No. Maybe I can wedge open the deadbolt."

"Good luck." Pam sat on the couch. "I'm tired and hungry."

"And crabby." Samantha laughed.

"Yeah, well, in my defense, I didn't sleep most of the night after you woke me."

"Okay." Samantha wedged the knife between the door and the jamb. "Sleep now. I'll wake you when I get the door open."

"Like that's gonna happen." Pam stormed out of the room. "We'll die of starvation with a kitchen full of food."

Samantha sighed. "Not if I can help it." She forced the blade up against the deadbolt, but it wouldn't budge the lock.

"I wonder what happened to Emit," Pam called from the bedroom.

"I'm sure he's ordering a gourmet delight for our next meal."

A ding came from outside the door. "Shh, someone's coming." Samantha moved away from the door.

Footsteps approached and stopped. The knob rattled. Something jingled in the lock.

A cold draft blew against the door, causing it to rattle.

"Oof!" Something bumped against the wall outside.

A breeze slid under the crack below the door, but no mist. "Tobias, is that you?" Samantha whispered.

A key lay on the floor at her feet.

"Sorry. It's the best I can do." The breeze disappeared.

Samantha darted toward the door, caught her hip on the knife handle, and broke off the tip. "Pam. Come quick!"

"Is it Emit?" Pam whispered.

"I don't know, but look what I found." Samantha held the key in the palm of her hand and then slipped it into her pocket.

Samantha motioned to Pam and moved to the wall to listen.

Pam scampered back into the bedroom.

All seemed quiet.

"Tobias?" she whispered. "Is someone out there?"

Still no answer.

Several seconds passed. Samantha dug the key from her pocket. "Come on, Pam. Let's check it out."

Pam poked her head around the bedroom door and looked about the room. "Are you sure the coast is clear?"

"No, but there's one way to find out." Samantha inserted the key into the deadbolt and turned it. The bolt slid from the jamb. She moved the key to the locked door knob.

"I'll stand behind the door, just in case." Pam dashed across the room, backed up against the wall, and held her breath.

Samantha twisted the key. "Now." Without waiting, she yanked open the door.

Emit lay on the floor holding his head. A tray of food lay scattered across the floor. His leg snapped in her direction, trying to block her. "Where do you think you're going?"

Samantha hopped out of the way just in time and ran forward through the hallway. "Pam, lock the door!"

Pam slammed the door. "Run, Sam, run." The deadbolt clicked.

Emit ran after Samantha as she raced by several closed doors 314, 316, 320. The elevator was to her right, but she didn't dare wait for it. She pushed the button and ran past.

Emit grabbed her shirt as she reached the stairwell.

Samantha spun around in time to see his fist. She ducked, and he slammed it into the wall.

"Damn it, Sam!" Emit yelped.

She didn't wait and headed down the stairs at full speed, hopped over the railing, and dropped to the next landing.

Footsteps pounded after her.

She threw open the door marked 'second floor' and darted over the next railing. Holding her breath, she hugged the wall.

Emit took the bait and ran onto the second floor.

Samantha blew out a lungful and scooted down to the first floor. Muffled voices met her ears. *Are they friend or foe?* She chanced a peek.

The room bustled with activity. A teenage boy sifted through plastic bags filled with used clothing.

An elderly man put together metal shelves lining the wall by the door.

Samantha walked into the room and pretended she belonged there. She picked up a black scarf from a plastic bag and wrapped it around her head to hide her red curls.

An elevator dinged at the back of the room. A teenage girl got off. She pushed a laundry basket filled with sheets over to an aisle and parked it.

Without hesitation, Samantha walked to the basket and glanced down the aisle.

The girl stood on a ladder, rummaging through a top shelf.

Samantha moved the container to the freight elevator, pushed the down button, and waited.

Emit appeared on the first floor. Out of breath, he leaned his arms onto his knees and heaved a sigh. Then his head jerked from side-to-side.

The old man building shelves asked Emit, "May I help you?"

The freight elevator opened. Samantha moved the laundry basket inside.

The B5 button lit up, and the doors closed.

Unsure where the elevator was headed, her mind raced. A lattice panel on the ceiling rattled. Samantha overturned her basket, stood on the metal rung, and grabbed the grid. She pushed a tile aside and pulled herself up into the ceiling, barely replacing the grate when the elevator came to a halt.

A man got on and tapped a button.

Samantha bent down to peek through the grid. *Thank God. It's Amos. I knew he was investigating on his own.* She nearly called out to him when she saw a familiar, leather-bound book in his hands. *Great-grandmother's diary. Where'd he get that?*

The elevator stopped, and the doors opened. Amos stepped out.

B3 lit up over the door. Samantha waited until the doors closed and hopped from the ceiling. She stood along the wall, pushed the open button, and peered into the corridor. Out of the corner of her eye, she caught a glimpse of Amos. He stood inside a windowed office down the hall on her left.

No one else seemed to be around, so she kept low and crept closer.

The elevator motor whined as it left the floor. It appeared to be heading up.

Samantha tried a couple of doors. *Locked.* As she neared the window, she heard two men talking. One was Amos. The other voice, she didn't recognize at first.

"You told me there was a map," Amos said.

"There was. I saw Pa put it there, but that was many years ago. I figured he found the silver and cashed it in."

"You're sure the silver is still outside the mine?" Amos asked. "Could you find it without the map?"

"Believe me, I've tried."

"Why'd you wait so long to ask for my help?" Amos sounded upset.

"I figured it was gone by now, but Pa mentioned it again on his deathbed. That's when I brought it to your attention."

"But you took a step further than I planned." Amos scolded. "Things have gotten deadly. I refuse to take the heat on your behalf."

"I understand. I'll disappear right after my funeral."

What? Is that Gary? He's alive. Samantha heard the elevator ding behind her. She moved across the hall from Amos and pushed through an unlocked door. It opened into a small office.

"Amos!"

Oops. That's Emit.

"I'm in a private meeting," Amos shouted.

Emit knocked on the glass window. "Sam broke free. I can't find her anywhere."

"Don't worry," Amos said. "She won't get far. Gary, take care of things. I'm leaving for Columbia right after your funeral."

Samantha gasped. *My God! Amos?* She felt her knees go weak. *Amos!* Her fists clenched.

"What about Pam?" Gary asked.

"She's still locked upstairs." Emit moved into the doorway. "What should I do with her?"

"Gary, you've made a mess of everything. You, too, Emit. Tidy it up. I don't want to know what happens, but don't hurt Sam! I only wanted the map. And Pops."

"Pops? Amos did this to Pops? That bastard! I can't wait to get my hands on him. I have to tell Ivar. He'll know what to do.

Samantha peeked through the crack in the door and saw Amos leave the office.

"Where are you going," Gary asked.

"To my office. Don't call me."

"Come on, Gary. We've got work to do." Emit motioned from the doorway.

"How did Sam escape?"

"You won't believe it. A faint mist gathered in the hallway, and a wind whipped up like a tornado. It blew me against the wall, and I hit my head. I think this place is haunted."

Gary sucked in his breath. His face paled, and his eyes widened. "Wendell? Is he haunting me?"

"Of course not. I know deep down there's no such thing as ghosts. Are you going to stand here all day?" Emit grabbed Gary and pulled him into the hall. "Come on. We have to find Sam."

Chaos Erupts

The boss strode through the office where a small army of heavily armed agents worked on his latest project. "Evening, Charlie."

The security guard saluted. "Evening, Boss. Heading to the tower?"

A curt nod was his answer.

Charlie opened the door to the boss's office. Wall-to-wall state-of-the-art security technology hummed in the background.

The boss wandered to the bay window. "I don't want to be disturbed."

"Yes, sir." Charlie closed the door.

Things are heating up around here. It's time to bail. Boss placed his thumb on the ID pad. "Get me, General Gonzales."

The computer took only a few seconds to respond. A sultry female voice replied, "I have the general on the line, sir."

"Patch him through." He adjusted his silver-rimmed glasses and opened his laptop that sat on an antique writing table.

"Good evening, Boss. To what do I owe the pleasure?"

"General Gonzales, I have good news and bad."

"Give me the bad news first," Gonzales said.

"An earthquake erupted near the coast of Columbia in Armenia. Inmates broke down the prison walls and escaped. At least ten warlords and members of the drug cartel remain at large."

"What's the good news," the general asked.

A wicked smile curved his lips. "Amos Vickers, the great philanthropist, is leading an effort to relieve suffering and curb chaos. Supply ships are already en route. He's sending $15 million in humanitarian aid. The cargo includes food, shelter materials, and hygiene kits. Also, a medical team is flying to meet the ship.

"So Columbia is back on the map?" the general asked. "What's our next step?"

"Not so fast. Let me bask in this opportunity. I've come up with an infallible plan. One so brilliant that not even you can guess."

"Sounds interesting. Fill me in on the details."

"Tonight. The area lies in ruins. No electricity. No clean water. No food and plenty of looting."

"Where shall we meet?" the general asked.

"The usual place. At dusk. Bring no one."

"Yes, Sir." The general disconnected.

"Ah, yes." Boss rubbed his hands together. "And they'll all be there to meet Amos the Great. What a fanfare."

What's Amos Up To?

Samantha moved across the hallway into the glassed-in office. The diary lay on Amos's desk on top of several manila folders. She slid the book into her pocket and flipped through the top file labeled "Columbia Rescue." It held several account numbers with large sums of money, an inventory list, and a map. *It must be one of his charity accounts.*

Taking a closer look, Colorado Rockies was on the map, listing the times of every in town game. Amos had jotted the same note alongside a few games—Strike during third inning. *Wonder what type of strike.* She reviewed the dates. The first note appeared on the date Pops Fountain was bombed. The second date coincided with blowing up her condo, and the third date was the same day of the fire at Amos's. *That can't be a coincidence.* The next folder contained detailed instructions on some form of a robot. Samantha had no clue what that meant and shrugged her shoulders.

A small chirp came from the phone on Amos's desk, and the dial lit up. When the light went out, Samantha picked up the receiver to call Ivar. No dial tone. "Shoot!"

A half-eaten turkey sandwich and a bag of peanuts sat on the desk. Samantha devoured the sandwich and then felt guilty. *Pam hasn't eaten either.* Pocketing the peanuts, she heard the elevator ding.

A shiver raced down her spine. *I should have left while the coast was clear.* Her eyes darted around the room. *Too late to run back across the hall.*

The elevator doors opened.

Samantha pushed behind a set of metal filing cabinets and held her breath. She peeked through a crack between them.

Gary entered the office and checked the desk. "I thought I left it here." He picked up the phone and entered two numbers. "Amos, I know you told me not to call, but did you take the diary?"

"Then who did?" His voice sounded irritated. "No, I didn't call you a moment ago. I just got back." Gary's head snapped in her direction and then toward the door. He stepped into the hallway and glanced up one side and down the other.

Samantha took a deep breath.

"No. There's no one here." "Yeah, I'm sure."

Her heart leapt as he headed back into the room.

"Emit? Aah. You won't be bothered by him anymore. I'll take care of Pam in the morning. Right after my funeral." He paused. "I'll need time to dispose of her body."

"No. I haven't seen Sam, but I'll find her." Gary gently set the phone back into the cradle. "Shit! If Amos didn't take that book, Emit must have it." Gary dashed back out of the office. "And now, I can't ask him where he put it."

Why? Did Gary snuff Emit? Samantha waited until she heard the elevator doors open and close and then she darted to the stairwell. She grabbed the banister and sped up the stairs to floor three. Her breath came out in jagged puffs. Her heart pounded in her chest.

The elevator rumbled to life. *Where's Pam's room?* Room 314 came into sight as the elevator dinged. *Two more doors.*

"Pam?" She whispered and yanked the key from her pocket. "Hide. Someone's coming." Samantha quickly unlocked the door. She slid inside Pam's room as the elevator opened.

A few moments later, someone knocked on the door. "Pam? You in there?"

"It's Gary," Samantha whispered. "Don't let him know I'm back."

"That you, Emit?" Pam called out. "I hope you brought food. I'm starved."

"Sorry. I forgot. Is Samantha with you?"

"No. Why?" Pam asked.

"Okay. Just wondered. I'll bring food next time."

"Hurry back," Pam said.

No one answered.

Samantha stood with her ear against the door and waited until the elevator dinged then blew out a breath. "That was close. You did well."

"I'm still starving." Pam moved into the kitchen and opened a cupboard.

"Don't eat anything from in there." Samantha dug out the peanuts and handed them to Pam. "I have a gift for you."

"Thanks." Pam ripped open the bag. "Why didn't you escape?"

"We will tonight when everyone has left the building."

Things Don't Add Up

"How could I be so stupid?" Samantha ranted. Her fists opened and closed as she paced. "He knew I'm a hostage. I bet he stole Great Grandma's diary. That blasted man probably ordered the bombs, too. Why? What does he have against us?"

"What burr got up your ass?" Pam asked.

"You're observant." Samantha fired back. "We've been set up by my uncle."

"Uncle?"

"Yeah. My Uncle Amos." Samantha stomped her foot. "Well, he's not really my uncle. I *thought* he was Pops' best friend. Ha, ha. The laugh is on me."

"The only Amos I've heard of is Amos Vickers. I don't know him, but I know of him. He's one of the richest do-gooders on Earth."

Samantha nodded her head. "Yeah, that's the same, Amos."

"You call him uncle? How lucky can you be?" Pam gushed.

A puff of air escaped Samantha's lips causing her bangs to flutter in the air. "Yeah, lucky. Listen, you're not going to believe this, but he just ordered Emit to 'take care of you.' And I mean, blow you away." She pulled out a chair and straddled it.

"Amos, the charity king?" Pam leaned forward. "You're right. I don't believe it."

"Okay, I'm going to tell you the facts. Ivar always wants facts, so here goes."

"Calm down," Pam said. She flinched at Samantha's glare. "Okay. I'll pretend I'm Ivar and play devil's advocate."

"That's just what he'd do." Samantha nodded. "Don't make any rash judgment about my sanity, but I think I've figured out why Pops and our family are on his hitlist."

"Hitlist?" Pam's eyes flew open. "You mean he ordered the bombings?"

"See, I knew you'd think I've lost it." Samantha stood.

"Go on. This is interesting. Tell me everything." Pam got up and poured a cup of coffee. She found a pen and paper and sat back down. "I'll make a list."

"That's a good idea, but put aside the cup."

"What?" Pam asked. "Oh yeah, it may be spiked. I need to focus on the list. Fire away."

"I told you what I saw. I can't believe it took me so long to figure it out. Amos was one of the first to check out the bomb at the fountain shop. I heard him say that no one could have survived."

Pam scribbled on the paper. "Next."

"He came by the day after my condo was destroyed to check it out." Samantha gnawed on a nail while walking back and forth.

"Because he was concerned. You said he is Pops' best friend."

"Was. I said he WAS his best friend. But why did he put on a great front?"

Pam shook her head. "What happened at your condo?"

"He acted…strange. He offered to go through our safety deposit box. Then he made a comment about someone looking for something in my condo."

"Why bomb it if they're looking *for* something? Won't it *destroy* whatever they're looking for?" Pam tapped her fingers on the table apparently mulling things over. "I'm not convinced."

"No, I suppose not." Samantha chewed harder on her nail. "That threw me for a loop, too. Just hear me out."

Pam shook her head. "He can't be the one. After all, someone burned down his garage. He lost his expensive cars."

"That's another part I don't get…unless he wanted to dispel any suspicions." Samantha walked around the table and back. "Then there's the key."

"What key?" Pam asked.

"Uncle Amos gave me a short red, white, and blue key two years ago when my grandpa died. He told me to keep it near me always. He asked if I still had it."

"What's the key to?"

Samantha paused and shook her head. "It's supposed to open the back door to the garage."

"What's so odd about that?"

"It doesn't work." Samantha went back to pacing. "I tried it one night when the automatic garage door opener refused to work. I guess the electricity had gone off, and Pops had to reset the code. Anyway, I went around to the back door, but the key wouldn't even fit the lock. That's why I wasn't too worried about giving it to Ter."

Pam tapped a finger on the cup handle. "Maybe someone replaced the lock."

"Nope. And there's more." Samantha said. "Amos is in this building, and he knows we're here. He was talking with Gary."

"The chauffeur?"

"Yeah. He is alive."

"Stop pacing. I can't follow you and write, too." Pam patted the seat of the chair next to her and picked up the mug.

Samantha gently placed a hand over the cup. "You're not going to drink that, are you?"

"I just need to hold it," Pam said.

"Then dump out the coffee so you don't absently take a sip.

If it's drugged, you won't be able to get away."

Pam sighed and set the cup down on the table with a thud. The coffee splashed onto the tablecloth staining it a slight blue tinge.

"Whoa, that can't be good. I wonder what drug causes—" Footsteps outside the door caught her attention. "This is it," Samantha whispered. "Gary's back."

"It's probably Emit."

"I don't think so. Gary said Emit won't bother Amos anymore. Whatever that means."

"I think you're a little crazy." Pam dashed toward the couch and lay down, pretending to be asleep as planned.

Samantha grabbed the sheet of paper and stuffed it in her pocket. She dashed into the kitchen, grabbed the frying pan, and moved beside the door.

"Don't kill him!" Pam whispered and gave a nervous twitter. "Oh, never mine. Gary's already dead."

Samantha motioned for Pam to be quiet and raised the pan above her head.

A key jiggled in the lock. The knob turned, and the door opened.

Samantha shut her eyes and swung the pan.

A crutch flew across the room as someone fell to the floor beside her.

Opening one eye, she squinted down at Detective Colby Cage lying on his side. A smile radiated from ear to ear. "You're a real spitfire."

"Oh, my God. You're alive!" Samantha dropped the pan and knelt beside the man rolling over in a fit of laughter. "Colby, did I hurt you!" She checked his head for any bruises. When she didn't find any, she grabbed his crutch from the floor.

"You were right, Ivar." Tears rolled down Colby's cheeks.

Ivar stepped past the detective and entered the room. His ice-blue eyes twinkled. "When you fall for a girl, you really fall. Lucky, she's mine." He wrapped a possessive arm around Samantha. "Are you all right?"

"Is *she* all right?" Colby asked. "The frying pan never had a chance." He fingered the dent in the pan where it hit his crutch.

Samantha scowled, checked the hall, and then closed the door. "Stop joking. I could have killed you."

Pam bounced from the couch. "Do you know these men?"

"Let me introduce you to our mighty heroes." Samantha made the formal introductions.

Ivar grabbed Colby's arm and helped him back on his foot.

"Did I hit you or just the crutch?"

"I'm fine," Colby said. "This crutch saved my life. If I hadn't shoved it in the door first, it might have been my head that you whacked."

"How did you find us?" Samantha clung to Ivar. Her legs felt like noodles.

"We caught up to a superstitious South American," Colby said. "He told us where to find you."

"Did you find Pops?" Samantha asked.

"He's fine. So is your Mom," Ivar said. "They can't wait to see you."

"What about my children?" Pam asked.

"They're safe with Pops and Bridget." Colby hobbled over to the table and sat down. "I haven't had this much action in weeks. Is that coffee I smell?"

"Don't drink it," Both Samantha and Pam shouted.

Colby glanced at the blue coffee stain. "Better test this."

"I'll call in the team and then we need to talk," Ivar said.

Samantha ran her eyes over Ivar, the width of his shoulders, all muscle covered with golden skin. He'd risked his life to find her. Well, it was Colby that she'd almost killed, but her heart thudded for her fiancé. *How could I have thought about another? What I have to say will tell all, but will Ivar believe me?* "Get us out of here," Samantha said, "before Gary kills all of us."

"Gary Gordon?" Colby asked.

"He's not dead," Samantha said. "However, I don't want to wait around until he shows up. You're not going to believe what I've found out. Pam's already heard most of it."

"Does this have anything to do with your ghost?" Colby asked.

Pam's eyes widened. "Ghost?"

"Guess not," Colby said.

Ivar studied Samantha's face. "Are you really all right?"

"That depends." Samantha crossed her arms over her chest. "You might not think so after you hear our story."

Pam's News

"Where's Ter?" Pam opened the police car door before Ivar could pull to a full stop outside the hospital.

Ivar slammed on the brakes.

Pam rushed to the curb. "Where's my husband?"

Colby zipped down the electric window. "Pam. Get back here. It's not safe."

"I'll get her," Samantha threw open the passenger door and caught Pam by the arm.

"How in the world can I protect both of you?" Ivar snapped.

Colby climbed from the car and hobbled toward the girls. "Let's go inside and wait for Ivar to park.

The wheels spun as Ivar took off for the visitor's lot.

"I'll see you upstairs." Pam marched inside and down a narrow hallway in search of an elevator. "What room is he in?"

Samantha pulled her back. "We're not in the lobby." She turned toward Colby. "What part of the hospital is this?"

Ivar rushed through the door and blew out a breath. "Why didn't you stop her, Colby? She was sitting next to you."

Colby frowned. "Stop complaining. We're safe."

Pam wiped her forehead with the back of her hand. Voices dimmed into the background. She staggered.

Samantha firmed her grasp. "Pam? Are you okay?"

"Please take me to my husband." Pam leaned against the cool wall. *That's better.*

"Should I get a wheelchair?" Samantha asked. "You don't look well."

"Just take me to Ter!" Pam snapped. She shook her head to clear the cobwebs.

Ivar moved them down the hall to the back elevator. "This is where Emit whisked you away from the hospital."

Samantha stopped in her tracks and released Pam's arm. "Are you sure no one's around?"

Colby punched the up arrow of the elevator with the tip of his crutch. "I'll protect you."

"I feel much safer," Samantha retorted.

A door slammed down the hall as the elevator arrived.

Pam darted inside ahead of the rest. "What floor?" Her finger hovered over the numbered buttons.

"Second." Ivar motioned Samantha inside and then glanced up and down the hall. "I don't see anyone." He joined them. "Don't be alarmed when you see an officer stationed outside Ter's room. We're not taking any chances."

"Good." Pam pushed the button, and they went up.

When the elevator door opened, Samantha whispered into Pam's ear, "Act natural."

"I see the officer." Pam dashed ahead.

The officer was startled and flexed his hand over his gun. He relaxed when he saw Ivar. "That's the second time today that I nearly pulled my weapon."

"When was the first?" Ivar asked.

"Half an hour ago. I could have sworn that therapist was Gary Gordon. The officer leaned toward Ivar. "Of course, it couldn't have been. He's dead," he whispered. "No ID and no nametag. He fidgeted so much that I reached for my gun. When he saw it, the lad turned and left. Gun shy, I guess."

"I want to see Ter." Pam didn't wait for a formal introduction. She pushed the door open and gasped. "What have they done to you?"

The officer rushed forward. "Who are you?"

Ivar stepped between them. "She's Ter's wife."

Ter swung his feet over the bed and sat up. "I'm glad to see you, honey. How are the kids?" His voice sounded raspy, but he smiled.

Pam swayed.

Ter reached out and caught Pam's arms as she stumbled forward. "Are you okay?"

She dropped to her knees. "Fine. I think. What about you?" She eased herself to a standing position, held his face between her hands, and gazed into his eyes. "What happened?"

"Someone shot me, but I'm much better," Ter said. "The doc said I can go home in the morning."

"You look much better," Samantha said.

Ter smiled. "Thanks, Sam. You saved my life."

Pam stood and turned toward Samantha. "You were there?" The room spun. Her fingers tingled. Black spots formed before Pam's eyes. *Did someone shoot him?*

"Pam, what's the matter?" Ter's voice grew distant and sounded garbled. Her stomach clenched. "I don't feel…"

The next thing Pam knew, she was lying down.

"She's coming around." A damp cloth brushed across her forehead. Her vision cleared.

Samantha hovered over her. Concern filled her eyes.

"What happened?" Pam asked.

"You fainted, and you've been out for quite a while." Samantha turned toward the door as the doctor walked into the room.

"I don't know what came over me." Pam stared at the tube in her arm.

"You are dehydrated," the doctor said. "We started an IV to give you some fluids."

"I want to see my family," Pam said.

"If you feel up to it, I'll bring Tommy and Lisa home in the morning," Ivar said. "They will be glad to see both of you."

Pam sat up on the cart. "I'm fine. Can't I see them now?" The room started to spin. She leaned back on the pillow. "Maybe not. I'm feeling a little dizzy."

The doctor put his hand on Pam's arm. "Perhaps it would be better to wait until morning."

Pam said, "At least I want to talk to them."

"Okay." Ivar nodded and turned to Samantha. "Stay here until I get back. I'm going upstairs to see Colby. He's checking out the officer's story. We'll call Pops and the children when I get back." Ivar left the room.

The doctor leaned closer. "I have some good news, but this is private."

"It's okay," Pam said. "You can tell me in front of Sam."

"Okay." The doctor smiled. "You're pregnant. We'll keep you overnight for observation. I'll tell admissions to put you in the same room as your husband."

"Pregnant?" Pam gasped. "I can't wait to tell Ter. We've been trying for over a year."

"We better find out what drugs they gave you," Samantha blurted.

Pam's mouth flew open. "That's right." Her eyes darted between the doctor and Samantha.

"We'll draw a drug screen," the doctor said. "And in a few weeks, we'll do an amniocentesis. I'm sure we can flush all the toxins from your system."

Growing Evidence

Samantha gazed out of the passenger's window as Ivar drove to the police station. Although she was uncharacteristically quiet, her mind worked overtime.

Ivar asked Colby, "What do you think? Was the therapist, Gary?"

"I doubt it," Colby said. "If he's alive, he'd be a fool to show his face."

"If he's alive?" Samantha asked. "You still don't believe me?"

"We need proof," Colby said, but I've suspected for a while.

"I believe you, Sam," Ivar said. "Let's swing by the deli and get something to eat. You must be starving."

"It's getting late." Colby rubbed his leg. "Can't we do this in the morning?"

"There's not enough time," Ivar said. "We need to get Sam's parents and the children home before the funeral."

"Oh, the funeral. Amos, the viper, will be there." Samantha felt the snake's fangs sink into her skin. "I don't want to go."

"Why not?" asked Colby.

The venomous betrayal leapt through her bloodstream. Samantha slammed her fist on the dashboard. "My whole world is crumbling. Everything I believed in is a lie. I can't face Amos right now."

Ivar squeezed her hand. "I'll be right there with you. Won't he be surprised to see you, but together, we'll end this."

Samantha returned his squeeze. "Let's trap him in his fine lies and show the whole world what a snake he is."

Colby nudged her shoulder. "Are you going to make accusations in front of the whole church?"

"Hush." Ivar pulled into a parking lot. "I'll be right back. What do you want to eat?" He took their orders and returned shortly.

Ten minutes later, Samantha entered the police conference room and collapsed into a chair.

Ivar brought three mugs of coffee to the table. He set one down, handed one to Colby, and placed a cup in front of Sam. "Let's get to the bottom of this."

"Yeah," Colby said. "Why are you so upset? You're free. Pam's free. Pops alive."

Samantha turned and glared at him. "Upset. Upset? I'm more than upset. I'm furious! I thought Amos was a friend. How could he do this to me? Worse yet, how could he do this to Pops? He's utterly shattered our lives."

"I get that," Colby said.

"Then there's poor Pam and Ter." Samantha's tears threatened to spill. "I'm glad we stopped by the hospital. Ter looks much better, but I didn't expect Pam to collapse. We have to find out what drugs they gave her. Her baby's life may depend on it."

"I got back Ter's lab results a few days ago. He was given a hypnotic," Ivar said. "My guess is, that's what Walter gave you and Pam, too. I told the doctor the name of the drug. He said the short exposure shouldn't harm the fetus, but they'll put Pam in a high-risk OB clinic."

"What's the name of the drug?" Samantha asked. "I want to see for myself."

Ivar dug out the report and handed it to Sam.

She frowned. "They don't use this drug in our country."

"I know." Ivar wrapped an arm around her shoulders and then sat down. "We're running tests on everything."

"All this happened because of Amos." Samantha was ready to rant again.

Ivar gave her hand a squeeze. "Pam and Ter will go home in the morning."

Samantha took a sip of coffee. *Isn't that like Ivar, he changed the subject. Well, I want to know all.* "What about Walter? Did you find his son?"

"Walter's in rehab, and the son is back home with his mother." Ivar gulped his coffee. Back to Ter, We'll pick up the children first thing tomorrow. You want to go along, don't you, Sam? We'll bring Bridget and Pops home, too."

"Absolutely," Samantha said. "It was great to talk to Mom and Dad over the phone, but I can't wait to see them again."

Colby stretched out his leg on the opposite chair. "Let's get started." He chewed a bite of his turkey and cheese sub sandwich and swallowed. "Take it from the beginning."

Samantha put her hands on her hips and glared. "Beginning of what? The first explosion, Pops' disappearance, the massive bone mystery, or the destruction of my condo? Pure history. We've already gone over that."

"True. Let's talk about the hostage situation. You got a key from your *ghost*." He chuckled. "Then what?"

"Oh, you want current events," Samantha grumbled and pulled out her list. She launched into the allegations against Amos.

When she finished, she took a sip of cold coffee. Eying those around the table, based on Colby's comments, Samantha knew that he refused to believe Amos was behind the bombings.

It irritated her that Ivar kept chewing his gum. He didn't eat a bite of his sandwich, nor his chips. At times, he nodded or cleared his throat but never came out with his true thoughts. *Oh, he said he believed me.* However, she knew he was looking for proof. *He always needs physical evidence.*

"Where do we go from here?" Colby asked.

"We keep searching," Ivar said. "Something's bound to surface."

Samantha tossed up her hands. "We go after Amos. I'm sure he's behind this."

"Really?" Colby asked. "Who's going to believe you when I can't even wrap my head around the allegations?"

Ivar held the back of his neck and flexed. "Honestly, Sam, *I do* believe you, but we *can't* just arrest Amos. We're small fish in his vast ocean."

Samantha glared. "We can question him. He knows more then you think he does."

"Right." Colby shook his head. "I'm not going to be the one to accuse Amos as our number-one suspect. He's the richest, most generous charity sponsor on this planet."

Samantha slammed her fist on the table. "So are you just going to fart around until the next major blow-up? And I mean that literally."

Beneath the darkened scruff, Ivar's face had thinned. He reached over and caressed her hand with compassion that seemed to speak from his soul. "No. I do believe you, Sam. We'll check this out. Together, we'll find a way."

Samantha hopped up from the chair. "Then we'll talk with him, right?"

"Count me out," Colby said. "It's late. I'm in pain, and I'm tired."

"Bombs are your specialty," Ivar reminded him.

Colby heaved a deep sigh. "What do you have in mind?"

Ivar rubbed his chin. "Based on the sophistication of the hits, I'd say we're dealing with someone with a military background. Contracts don't come cheap."

"Gary fits that description." Samantha sat down and leaned forward. "I know he's alive, even if Colby doesn't believe me."

Ivar gave a sideways glance at the detective. "Colby *knows* he's alive, don't you?"

"Yeah. I think so." Colby raised his index finger and pointed at Ivar with more enthusiasm. "Now, Gary is in our league, but I can't come up with a motive for Amos."

"Money comes to mind," Samantha said. "Oh, I know Amos doesn't need any, but his charity foundation could launder a lot of funds. And Gary certainly can use the money."

"How does that brain of yours come up with these ideas?" Colby asked.

"I haven't quite figured everything out yet."

Colby laughed. "Check it out with your ghost. Maybe he'll think of something."

"Maybe he will." Samantha snapped back.

"I heard from the investigative team while we were at the hospital," Ivar said. "That warehouse downtown has five floors. The penthouse was locked up tighter than the Pentagon."

"There are at least five basement levels as well," Samantha said. "But you can't get to them from the front. There's a freight elevator on the first floor. I can show you the private staircase."

"I don't want you going back there. We'll get the floor plans from the city," Ivar said.

"I wonder who owns the building," Colby said.

"Goodwill or maybe ARC, I'm not sure, but we'll find out soon." Ivar took a sip of coffee. Exhaustion radiated from his every move. Even his chewing seemed an effort.

Samantha tapped her fingers on her cup. "I bet good old Uncle Amos's corporation owns it? He has property everywhere."

"Samantha! That's ridiculous!" Colby said. "Vickers?"

Ivar glared at the man. "Now, Colby, we don't have the facts, so we aren't ruling out anything."

Colby dropped his gaze. "This is a waste of time, and I need to rest." Colby swung his leg from the chair and stood up. "I'll call my brother. Jared will give me a ride home." He headed for the door. "Amos Vickers, a bomber? Who will believe it?"

Samantha hopped up ready to pounce.

Ivar tipped his chair as he bounded forward and caught her. "Let him go. He's not going to help."

Samantha melted into his arms.

Ivar brushed his lips over her hair. He whispered, "Keep these thoughts between us for now, until we can prove what you witnessed. You've been through a lot in the last month, and I'm not sure the public will believe you. Amos is such a high-profile figure. I can't risk people turning on you."

Samantha stared at him. "So you do believe me?"

Ivar gave her a squeeze. "Of course I do." He pulled a file from a pile stacked on the corner of the table. "Maddog said something about Amos, too, and Gary Gordon is no friend of his."

"Maddog?" Samantha asked. "He sent me a card. He thinks he's being framed."

"Let's plan on attending Gary's funeral," Ivar said. "You never know who will show up."

Samantha struggled for breath. "What about Amos? I know he'll be there, and he knows I was rescued."

"Then let's be sure he sees you," Ivar said. "I'll be right by your side. Act like nothing has changed between the two of you."

"Won't he be furious?"

"Not if he thinks you don't know his part in this whole plan," Ivar said. "We'll see if we can't set him up."

"Good idea."

Going Home

Velvety clouds welcomed dawn's light. Samantha bounded down the front steps to meet Ivar. She leapt into his open arms, planted a kiss, and then pulled away. "Let's get Mom and Pops."

"Not so fast." Ivar crushed her to him.

His lips met hers. Their tongues played a slow, seductive dance. She devoured his taste.

Ivar backed away and studied her face. "I love you." His voice sounded mellow.

Samantha placed her finger over the dimple in his chin and traced the curve of his jaw. "Old news, darling, but it's good to hear it again. I adore you."

He traced his hand down her arm and clasped her fingers. "I'll be glad when they remove that cast so you can hug me again."

"Uh-huh," Samantha murmured. His warm breath made her tingle. "We better go before I drag you inside."

"That would be okay with me." Ivar grinned.

"But it won't take us to Pops."

"Right." Ivar straightened and opened the passenger door.

Samantha slid in. "Where are you keeping them?"

"You'll see." Ivar closed the door and went around to his side of the car.

"I called Pam," Samantha said. "They'll be home by noon."

"Then they'll be home in time to meet the children." Ivar started the engine and headed for the mountains.

An hour later, an officer greeted the car as it drove up to the private hideaway.

Ivar rolled down his window, flashed his ID, and spoke to the man. The gates opened, and they passed through.

"Where did you find this place," Samantha asked. "I didn't even see it from the road until you turned off a half mile back."

"That's the beauty of this hideaway." Ivar drove past luscious gardens and a spring-fed pond. Aspen trees provided the area with shade. He pulled in front of a two-story cottage made of various shades of gray stone.

Pops sat outside on the porch in a wicker rocker, reading a book. A small blonde-haired girl sat on his lap.

She giggled and turned the page.

Samantha asked, "Is that Lisa?"

"Yup." Ivar climbed from the car. He darted around the front and opened her door. "Pops looks as if he's enjoying himself. Bet he'll make a great Gramps."

"Sam!" Pops lifted the girl and set her down. "I thought you'd never get here. I've read Peter Pan five times this past week. I can recite the story with my eyes closed."

Like Tinkerbelle, Samantha flew into his outstretched arms. "Pops, I'm glad you're alive." She pushed back and studied him. "Are you all right?"

"I should be the one asking you that question. Look at that shiner."

"It's nothing. Samantha looked toward the door. "Where's Mom?"

"She went with Tommy. He took a dip in the pool."

"Have you heard about Amos," Samantha asked. "He's behind everything."

"Come inside," Pops said. "Tell me all about it."

An officer rounded the corner. Bridget and a young boy walked behind him.

Lisa wrapped her small hand around Pops' finger. "I want to go home."

"That's why I'm here," Ivar said.

"Yippee, we're going home." Lisa hopped up and down and clapped her hands. "Hurry up and get dressed, Tommy."

"I'll get my stuff." Tommy dashed inside.

"Change into regular clothes," Bridget called after him.

The door slammed.

Two suitcases sat by the door. "I'll load these," Ivar said. "We can talk on the way."

"Samantha!" Bridget scooped her into a fond embrace.

Tommy returned dressed in jeans and a shirt. He carried his socks and shoes. "Let's go."

The officer motioned to a car. "I'll take the children in my car and follow behind you."

On the drive back to town, Samantha told of her ordeal with Amos and then became silent when Pops started to cry. "I'm sorry, Pops. I know he was your best friend."

"I just can't understand," Pops sobbed. "We've known each other since high school."

Bridget held his hand and rubbed his knuckles.

"Let's drop it for now," Samantha said. "Tell me what happened while you were away from home."

Pops brightened. "Let me tell you about Tobias…"

Before Samantha knew it, they'd pulled in front of the Rodriguez residence. Pam rushed outside to greet the children.

Ivar climbed out of the car and escorted Lisa and Tommy into the house. He returned shortly. "It's after eleven. Not quite three hours before Gary's funeral. Do you want to meet at the station, or go home? I'll have a police officer posted outside the house."

Bridget placed her hand on Pops' shoulder. "Let's go home."

Heart To Heart Talk

Samantha took Pops' outstretched hand as they sat across the kitchen table sipping lemonade. "I know how much you enjoyed being with Amos. I couldn't believe it at first either, but he proved to be a villain. There's nothing that can erase that image from my mind."

"I had no idea Amos was so bitter." Pops cleared his throat. "I guess I should have tried harder to understand his moods. There were times that he was miserable to be around, but usually, we enjoyed each other's company."

"I wonder what got under his skin." Bridget put her hand on Pops' shoulder. "What happens next?"

Ivar ran his hand through his hair. "That's just it. What can we do? We need more proof. Solid evidence that he's behind the bombings, Ter's attack, and who knows what else."

Pops frowned. "I can't believe he'd go to such lengths. Tobias swears the bombings had something to do with that map of the silver mine. How does that tie to Amos? Gary, yes, but not Amos."

"I got an e-mail from an FBI agent," Ivar said. "His name is Jump Sweeny. I asked him to come to town. Maybe he'll help."

Samantha peered over at Ivar. "When did this happen?"

"Before we found you at the warehouse. Sweeny claimed the body we found at the medical records storage unit was his ex-partner. He believes Wendell killed him. Our investigation proved he's right."

"What did Colby think of the idea?" Samantha asked.

Ivar tapped his fingers on the table. "I haven't told him yet. I'll wait to see if Sweeny says yes."

"Amos put all of us on the spot," Pops said. "I want to see his face when I confront him."

"No!" Samantha said. "At least not until after the funeral. Oh, speaking of the funeral, we need to go."

Pops stood. "I better put on my suit."

Ivar held up his hand. "Please, sir, I'd rather Amos thinks you're still missing. I can't wait to see his reaction when he meets Sam. He doesn't know she's free."

"I bet he does," Samantha said. "He knows everything."

Bridget gave Samantha a hug. "Be careful and give my best to Linda. This will be hardest on her."

Gary's Funeral

Linda Vickers stood at the door to the Presbyterian Church and greeted everyone as if family. "Good afternoon, Mayor. I'm glad you could make it. Gary would be proud that you took the time from your busy day to be here."

"Amos always spoke highly of the lad," the mayor said. "I know he'll be lost without his beloved chauffeur. Gary used to accompany him everywhere he went."

"Yes, nothing's the same since the fire. Amos is so busy; he barely made it back to town for the funeral."

"Where is our host?" The mayor stepped into the sanctuary. "Oh, never mind. I see him talking to the reverend."

Linda looked down the aisle.

Amos smiled, gave a slight wave, stepped forward, and shook the mayor's hand.

Linda ran a finger over her cheek to catch a tear.

Colby gracefully hovered in the doorway using only a cane. "My, the church is packed. I think the whole town showed up and then some."

"Amos made an open invitation to his constituents, clients, and investors. Gary met most of them over the years." Linda put a hand on Colby's shoulder. "I was afraid we'd have to attend your funeral, too."

"Honey, that's a terrible thing to say." Amos strolled between the two. "Please excuse my wife. She has been under a lot of stress lately."

"I understand." Colby shook Amos's outstretched hand.

"I hope your leg is feeling better. I couldn't believe someone tampered with your car. And you think it happened on my property? Terrible, just terrible."

"News travels fast in a small town. I only heard about it yesterday." Colby moved from the door and joined Ivar and Samantha sitting in the back row.

Linda stepped over to the pew. "Sam, you must sit up front with Amos and me. With your mom and Pops missing, we'll be your new family."

"Thanks, Linda." Glancing at Ivar, Samantha smiled. "There's hardly any room up front. And I'm already where I want to be." She clasped Ivar's hand.

"Oh," Linda's eyes brightened. "I see you're engaged."

"Yes. That shouldn't be a surprise. I love Ivar. I've always loved him, and I wish Pops was here so I could tell him, too."

With a laugh, Linda held out her hand and beckoned with her fingers. "Show me that diamond."

Samantha held up her ring finger.

"It's a beauty." Linda glanced at Ivar from the corner of her eye. "You're a lucky man. When's the wedding?"

Ivar cleared his throat. "Sam says I have to ask Pops, first."

Linda laughed. "Excuse me for being crass, but that might be difficult under the circumstances."

Sam's eyes darted between Ivar and Linda and back again. "Aah, yes, well, this funeral is a sad occasion. Mother will be disappointed that she couldn't comfort you during your hour of need."

Linda's mouth quivered. Her eyes filled with tears. "I know. I miss her a lot."

"Linda!" Amos stepped up and slid an arm around her shoulder. "People are lining up at the door. You best get back to them."

"Right. I'll talk to you later, Sam." She moved into the aisle to greet guests rather than going to the front door. *I wish he wouldn't always tell me what to do.*

A scowl crossed Amos' face and then brightened. "Sam, we need to talk. How about after the funeral?"

"I don't know Uncle Amos." Samantha leaned closer to Ivar. "I'm rather busy today. Can we meet for breakfast in the morning?"

A frown flashed, but he nodded. "I'll clear my calendar for six o'clock. I have to fly out of town at one, and you know what it's like flying out of DIA."

He's leaving town again? News to me. Linda inched closer.

Amos ran a hand through his ever-tidy silver hair. His navy pinstriped suit with razor creases made him look younger.

"I'll be up," Sam said. "Will you come to Mom's, or should I drive over to your house."

"I hate to say this, Sam, but your mother's house is a mess."

"It's not so bad."

"I'm sure after they broke into the place." He waved his hand in the air as if brushing his thought aside. "Well, you've boarded up the front window, so I don't really know. I mean, I stopped by there to check on you after I heard about the terrible event. You'll need to tell old Uncle Amos everything that happened, but this isn't the time or place."

"I have a few questions of my own." Samantha sounded angry.

"I'm glad you're home safe and sound." Amos tugged at his tie. "I thought we'd meet in town. We can have a cup of coffee and a bagel at the bakery."

Sam paused and smiled. "The bakery at six. I'm looking forward to it."

"I'll be coming with Sam," Ivar said as Amos stepped back into the aisle.

He turned. "That won't be necessary. Will it Sam?"

Linda watched her husband move away with an attitude that said, "Don't mess with me, boy." She leaned toward Amos. "I didn't know you were leaving town in the morning. Where are you going this time?"

Amos laughed. "Duty calls, love. Duty calls." He motioned to the organist.

The opening notes of "Amazing Grace" filled the church.

The congregation stood as the reverend led the song.

Since the body was only ashes, an honorary pallbearer wheeled a large color photo of Gary down the aisle to the front of the church.

Amos glanced up to the balcony, brought his hand in front of his chest, and gave a thumbs-up signal.

Something or someone moved.

He grabbed Linda's elbow and smiled. They followed Gary's photo down the aisle of the church and moved into the front pew.

Leaning close to Amos' ear, Linda whispered, "Who was that in the balcony?"

Amos wrapped his arm around her shoulders and pulled her closer. "Now honey, I know it's been a rough morning. I'm afraid you're seeing ghosts." He patted her hand.

Linda stepped back and muttered, "I'm not blind, and I'm not stupid. What's going on?"

***

Samantha recognized only three-quarters of the people in the church. "Where did they all come from?" she whispered.

"Shh, we'll talk later." Ivar ran his thumb over her knuckles. "I have Roxy taking video from the balcony. I want to know who attended and why."

Colby leaned over Samantha. "I want to see that video, too. Gary would be proud of this crowd."

Samantha whispered, "I have a feeling that Gary is laughing at the whole event."

"Are you still sticking to your story?" Colby chuckled. "Or is he a ghost, too."

"Knock it off. This isn't funny." Ivar grabbed Colby's lapel and whispered, "You already admitted he is alive."

"I know what I saw." She shifted her gaze to Ivar. "By the way, I don't want you to come with me to the bakery in the morning. I'll be safe. He's not going to harm me, especially not in public."

"I'm not taking any chances," Ivar said. "If I don't go, you'll wear a wire. I'll be right outside, ready for action."

"Shh," Colby said. "Not here."

The crowd hushed as Amos got up to give the eulogy.

A shuffling noise came from above Samantha's head.

She leaned over and whispered in Ivar's ear. "Roxy better keep quiet, or everyone will know she's on the balcony."

Amos's eyes stayed focused on the congregation, but his voice grew louder.

A thud echoed through the church.

Amos kept talking over the noise. His voice grew raised another notch.

Not wanting to raise suspicion, Samantha moved out of the pew and stood in the aisle. She dabbed at her eyes with a sleeve and dug through her purse for a tissue. Finding one, she blew her nose and moved to the narthex.

Amos' voice boomed, "All rise while we sing "Peace in the Valley."

Samantha turned to see the congregation rise as one. Amos nodded to the organist and then headed toward her. She ducked around the circular staircase to the balcony.

Amos reached the narthex. His head jerked to the right and left, and then he went downstairs.

Samantha didn't wait around. She ran up to the balcony.

Roxy lay on the floor holding her cut lip.

"What happened?"

"I must have tripped." Roxy sniffled. "I thought I saw someone up here, but then I realized it was that black curtain. The window must be open because it moved."

The curtain wasn't moving now.

Samantha tiptoed in the back of several chairs and looked behind the black drape. "Turn the camera this way," she whispered. "It's not a window, but a door, and it's locked." She leaned her ear to the door. "I don't hear anything."

Roxy got up and swung the video camera her way.

Amos appeared at the top of the stairs. "What's going on up here?"

Roxy turned the camera in his direction. Amos gasped and then darted back down the steps.

Samantha followed and caught up with him. "Ivar wanted to video the funeral, but Roxy tripped and cut herself. I went up to check on her. Let's go back inside."

Amos gritted his teeth. His Adam's apple bobbed as he swallowed and he plastered that toothy grin on his face. When the silence got thick enough to cut, Amos marched up to the front. "Sorry, about the interruption." He glared at Samantha. "We'll all miss Gary. Please join us in his life celebration with refreshments in the basement."

The organist took her cue. "When the Saints Go Marching In" echoed through the rafters. The audience filed out of the church to the music.

Ivar and Colby met Samantha outside on the church steps.

Most of the people made their way to the basement.

Samantha's stomach rumbled. She blushed. Food had a way of pulling people in its direction, especially during times of grief, but she knew now was not the time to sate her hunger.

Roxy carried the tripod and video camera out to the car and tugged on Ivar's sleeve.

"What happened?" Ivar asked.

"Let's fingerprint the balcony," Roxy said. "Something's fishy.

"We don't want to make a scene during the funeral," Colby said. "Can't it wait?"

"That's up to Ivar, but I want to know who tripped me," Roxy said.

"Let's go back to the station and watch the video." Ivar headed for the car.

Samantha stormed out of the police department after watching Gary's funeral video. "Nothing. There's nothing to prove Gary's alive."

Ivar dashed behind her and grabbed her arm. "You know that I believe you."

Cage yelled over his shoulder. "You're crazy. You can't even prove Gary's alive. How are you ever going to take down Amos?"

Ivar gave a defiant glare at Cage. Then he brushed Sam's cheek. "You're not crazy. We'll find something."

"Thanks for trusting me. I love you for that, but right now I need some time alone."

Her curiosity drove her back to the church. "Someone was in that balcony with Roxy when she fell. It had to be Gary."

Most of the people had eaten their fill and only a few cars remained at the church. A red convertible pulled out of the lot and drove past her. "Amos?" She followed the car down the block to get a closer view of the driver.

The person had a dark hooded sweatshirt pulled over his head.

"Not Amos. He wore a suit to the funeral." She nearly turned around when the driver glanced her way and sped up.

"I bet that's Gary." Following at high speeds through town was dangerous, so she drove to the city overlook and parked.

Rummaging through the glove compartment, she found a pair of binoculars and got out of her car.

The convertible's engine roared below, and the driver slacked off, drove around the block a couple of times, and turned through the commons. She tracked the car as it drove through the cemetery and parked outside the old high school. The driver climbed out of the car. His head turned, searching in each direction before running toward the back of the school.

Why would anyone go there? It's been abandoned for years. Samantha climbed into her vehicle. She drove within a block of the school, parked, and followed at a distance on foot.

At first, she thought she lost him. The car hadn't moved, but he was gone. She darted to the school grounds and dropped to the grass under the merry-go-round.

Something caught her eye. The sun's reflection against the window shadowed briefly.

A man in blue jeans crept alongside the school's wall. His head turned from side to side as he slithered toward the gym. He seemed nervous. Once he reached the back, he managed to open the door, took out some duct tape, and wrapped a piece around the lock.

Samantha waited until he went inside before following. She peeked through the window and saw the man walk across the gym. When he moved into the hallway, she eased open the door.

Gravel crunched from behind her. Samantha didn't wait to see who followed her. She slipped inside and hid behind the dark burgundy curtain on the stage.

***

Even at twenty-six, Maddog feared his old man. *I shouldn't have come today, but I need answers.* It had been a rough week. His father drilled him every day, preparing him for the upcoming trial. *Father will tan my hide if he finds out about this meeting with Gary.*

Shivers ran through him as he approached the two-story building. The building hadn't seen a student for nearly a decade once the county built the new school.

The door to the large gymnasium was ajar. *Gary's already here and waiting.*

Maddog peered around the schoolyard before sneaking inside the gymnasium. The dank odor made his skin crawl. The stage still stood at the end of the room. He remembered playing trumpet in the band. Samantha sat next to him during most of his senior year.

Moving toward the hallway, he looked up at the torn basketball hoops. The old court held fond memories. He'd mastered the game by the time he'd finished eighth grade. Football was another matter. That blasted Ivar out-kicked, out-ran, and out-classed him in everything he did. He even stole his girlfriend. *Well, Sam was never really mine, but she's still the girl of my dreams.*

Heading down narrow steps, Maddog reached a hallway lit by dirty windows above the brick walls. It felt as if they closed in on him. Cobwebs hung from the ceiling's light fixtures. Many had missing bulbs.

***

Maddog! Is he following me again? Samantha tiptoed from the stage into a dark hall. *Well, this will be the last time.*

Maddog crept along the edge of the hall. His feet shuffled.

Hope he doesn't mess this up. I need to get proof for Ivar. Samantha called out in a loud whisper, "Hey, Maddog."

He turned and frowned. "Who's there?"

"Psst. Over here." Another voice came from behind him.

Maddog whipped around. A rusty locker door opened, and Gary stepped out. He reeked of the sweet smell of marijuana. "Being dead is harder than I thought."

Colby is going to believe me this time when I have proof Gary is alive. Samantha grabbed her cell phone and hit record, but she couldn't get a good view. *At least I'll have an audio recording.*

"You got me into a heap of trouble. Why'd you slip me some pot?" Maddog moved down the hall and stood by the lockers. "I've never touched the stuff my whole life, and I'm not planning to take up the habit now."

Samantha crept along the shadowed wall and ducked into the library. The door creaked, but the men didn't seem to notice. She left it open a crack to watch, trying to capture video.

"How'd you become such a prick?" Gary asked. "Your father's a highly-respected citizen and the top attorney for the greatest philanthropist on this side of the ocean."

"I guess he took after my ancestors."

"Fang?" Gary asked.

"You could say that." Pride radiated in Maddog's voice.

"Then you must have taken after your mother's side of the family." Gary sneered. "It doesn't matter. I need you to swear you'll never say that I'm alive. Your life depends on it. I'll be gone by the time you go to court, but it won't bode well if you mention my name."

"I'll tell the truth," Maddog said. "My father wouldn't have it any other way."

"Are you itching for a fight?" Gary pulled out a bone-handled switchblade.

Samantha gasped and hit the phone icon. *No service.* She looked around. *Of course, there's no service in a building like this.* She went back to recording, "Careful with that knife." Maddog stepped away.

Gary flicked it open.

"Okay." Maddog held up his hands. "I finally understand. Sometimes I get a little dense."

Gary darted toward Maddog. "What else?"

He's going to kill Maddog. As much as I can't stand the man, I don't want him killed. Samantha set down her cell phone near the door and searched for a weapon among the old books. The largest one she could find was an algebra book. She headed toward the door.

Maddog said, "I last saw you when you kindly filled a gas can for my old Ford. You told me I could bring the can back in the morning. The weed must have been in the can without your knowledge. I can't possibly tie the marijuana to anyone at Amos's household."

Gary took a step closer. His dark eyes narrowed. "I don't think you saw any weed in my gas can. It was on you all along. Better yet, you found it in your jacket. The one you accidentally left in the park a week ago. You got an anonymous phone call letting you know someone found it."

"Yes, that's exactly what happened." Maddog backed up another step.

"You know, no one would find your stinking body if I killed you right here."

"No!" Samantha shouted.

Gary turned toward the library.

Samantha grabbed her phone, backed away from the door, and hid behind a bookcase.

The library door slammed shut.

Samantha listened intently and realized she'd turned off the cell's recording. She hoped she had captured most of the action and hit the record button once more.

Maddog said, "No, Gary, don't hurt her. You don't want to damage your fine record. After all, you're already an angel in heaven in most people's eyes."

After a few minutes, Samantha peered around the bookcase. No sight of Gary, so moved and tried to open the door. It wouldn't budge. *Did Gary lock it?* Studying the room, she noticed the upper window above the door slightly ajar. She set down her phone on an old warped library table. Grabbing a wooden chair, she stacked it with several moldy books, and climbed up to peek through the transom into the hallway.

She held her breath, tried to reach her phone, and toppled from the chair. Dusting herself off, she restacked the books, clutched the cell, and mounted the chair once more. She restarted the video once more and held up the cell.

Gary moved the switchblade from one hand to another as he stepped closer to Maddog. His jaw tensed. His shoulders rolled. "You have the map, don't you?"

Maddog gasped. "What map?"

"It wasn't in the diary," Gary said.

"What diary?" Maddog's voice got louder. "What are you talking about?"

So, Gary stole Molly's diary.

"Hey, dork, I'm beginning to believe that you really don't know what I'm talking about." Gary lunged at Maddog's throat. The blade caught his chin and raked his neck. Blood soaked his collar.

Samantha yelled, "Stop it!"

Maddog's howls must have hidden her cry. Neither man glanced her way.

Maddog sidestepped Gary's next lunge. Clenching his teeth, Maddog's eyes narrowed. He grabbed Gary's arm and twisted it away.

Samantha could almost feel the adrenaline spur him into action.

In one fluid motion, Maddog's hard muscles bunched, hands clenched, and his foot connected with Gary's crotch.

"Ugh," Gary dropped like a stone and rocked in pain. The knife clattered against the cement floor. Palpable fear shone in his round eyes. His white face managed a grimace.

Maddog kicked the blade under the lockers, aimed his cell toward the windows, and called 911. Blood dripped from his neck. Hardly able to breathe, he gasped, "Old school, knifed by lockers. Gary's alive!" His voice ricocheted through the hall and faded.

Samantha jumped from the chair. She jiggled the doorknob. "Let me out!" Unable to budge the door, she climbed back on the chair, her book ready as defense.

Maddog grabbed the edge of his shirt and held it to the neck wound. "Hurry." The cell fell from his bloody hand.

Gary crouched and fished under the lockers for his knife.

Samantha clenched the cell phone with her teeth, grabbed the heavy book, and tossed it.

Gary didn't see the old algebra book fly toward his head, but he grunted as it made contact and then collapsed.

Samantha tried to pull herself up through the slotted window, and the chair toppled over. She hit her head on the bookcase, and her vision dimmed.

Truth Revealed

Ivar spotted a red convertible leaving the church later that afternoon. It matched a stolen vehicle from Amos Vickers' collection. He wondered why it showed up, today of all days, after Gary's funeral.

Following at a distance, he lost sight of the car. To get an overview, he drove through the park and up to Lover's Leap. As he neared the peak, he saw Sam drive away. He clenched his fists. "She's doing it again. Why can't she trust me to solve this case?"

Ivar peered over the hill and spied the red vehicle down below, parked among the weeds next to the abandoned high school. He took the path on foot. Rounding the corner at the bottom of the hill, he was surprised to find Maddog's Ford parked at an angle beneath an oak tree.

The playground looked deserted, so Ivar tried the front door.

It wouldn't open.

Going around to the back by the gymnasium, he found the lock duct-taped. He drew his service revolver, pushed through the door, and went inside.

Garbled voices echoed through the abandoned building. Long-forgotten school days drifted through his mind like sifting through ashes. Something clattered from in the hallway.

Ivar dashed through the gym and reached a windowed door facing the corridor by the old library. Lockers lined the walls along the hall. The opposite wall had tall, frosted windows that let in filtered light.

"Now you've done it," a harsh voice snapped. A locker door slammed shut.

A young man lay sprawled across the floor. Blood dripped from his neck. "Maddog?" Ivar ran toward the man.

"Don't move!" Gary's hand came up with an open blade. "I'm warning you. I'll kill him if you move one-step closer. Drop the gun."

Ivar nearly swallowed the wad of gum he'd been chewing. "Leave him be, Gary. It's me that you want."

"I said, drop the gun." He hovered over Maddog.

Ivar held out the pistol in two fingers, placed it on the floor, and then stood.

Gary eyed Ivar. "I need that map. Sam doesn't have it. We've searched. I even had the old diary, but the map is missing."

"What's so important about a map?" Ivar asked. "It can't be worth people's lives." He raised his hands and took a step closer.

Gary knelt next to Maddog and placed the knife against his neck. "This time, I'll cut through the carotid, and I'll throw the blade straight through your heart. You know I can do it, too."

"What's with the map?" Ivar asked again.

"It's a silver mine, and it belongs to me. Pa left me a cache of silver hidden away. I must have that map!"

"Did you bomb the soda fountain?" Ivar asked. Something across the hall rattled.

"No harm in building a bomb, as long as I didn't set it off." Gary sneered. "Whoever did, he can't tell time."

"What do you mean?"

"Shut up. I'm thinking!" Gary shouted.

Maddog's eyes fluttered, but Gary didn't seem to notice.

"That's a unique knife. We found one just like it in the rubble with your name on it. I'm curious. Does that one have your name on it, too? Or does it have Wendell etched on the handle?

Instead of slamming the knife into Maddog, Gary raised his head and focused on Ivar. Gary lifted the knife and studied the bone handle. "Yeah. But Wendell doesn't need it anymore."

"Why? What did you do to your brother?" Ivar took another step.

Gary seemed to be in a trance. His eyes glistened. A smile crossed his mouth.

Ivar heard sirens in the background and knew he had only a few minutes to get the knife away from Gary before he killed Maddog.

"I'm sure he deserved whatever he got," Ivar said.

Gary's nostrils flared. He stood and waved the knife in the air. "Damn right, he did!" Spittle flew from his mouth.

Maddog's eyes opened, and he quickly closed them while he inched himself toward the lockers.

Gary jerked toward the man.

"That's not your brother," Ivar said and lowered his right hand toward his back.

Maddog's chest rose and fell in short pants.

Gary shifted the blade toward Ivar, adjusting his grip by placing his thumb on the knife spine, and extended his arm. He briefly glanced back at Maddog.

Ivar turned slightly and moved his right hand around to the back of his waistband. His fingers wrapped around the handle of his spare gun. "Gary."

Gary's head shot back up to focus on Ivar, who held up his left hand, palm out in front of his chest, and locked eyes. "It's okay. You did the right thing." Continuing to empathize with Gary, he motioned with his foot for Maddog to slip under the lockers. "He tormented you, didn't he? Did you do the same to him?"

"No, I couldn't do that. I had to make it quick to let the evil out." His fingers clenched the handle.

"Yes, you made him pure again so he could love his brother." Ivar's sweaty hand inched the gun from his waistband.

Gary nodded with understanding. "Yes, I shot him!" His right hand drew back over his head. His left arm came up at a ninety-degree angle to the floor.

Maddog rolled to his hip.

Gary's weight shifted from the right foot to his left as his right arm swung the knife overhead.

Ivar pulled out his gun. "Drop it, Gary!"

Maddog kicked out with a vengeful force, catching Gary in the gut as the knife left his hand.

"Ivar, look out!" It came from above him. A book flew overhead.

Ivar fired.

Blood splattered as Gary flew backward and hit the lockers. His body moved as if in slow motion and slid down to the floor in a pool of blood.

Ivar screamed as the blade bounced off the book and hit his chest. To his amazement, the knife grazed his badge, broke, and fell to the floor. His hand clutched his chest. "I'm still alive."

Maddog leaned over Gary. "Why?"

"Amos…" The rest died on his lips as the paramedics rushed down the hallway.

Maddog glanced toward Ivar. "You've been injured."

"So have you." Ivar trembled. He dropped his gun. "Is he dead?"

A paramedic leaned over Gary and nodded. "He's really dead, this time."

"Great kick," Ivar slumped to his knees beside Maddog. "He would have killed me if you hadn't knocked him off his aim."

The emergency crew descended on the men.

Ivar chewed frantically on his gum in time to his heartbeat. He wouldn't forget the horror of Gary's madness and cruelty for a long time. Nor could he nudge from his mind Maddog's bravery.

Abby ran up the hallway. "At least it isn't Sam this time."

Ivar ran his fingers along Maddog's neck and chin, still dripping blood. "Take care of my friend, Duke Parker," Ivar said. "I'll talk to you after they treat your wounds."

Abby ripped open a gauze sponge and made a pressure dressing over Maddog's wound. "That's going to make a scar on your handsome face, Duke." She smiled down at the man.

Another paramedic unbuttoned Ivar's shirt and peeled it off his shoulders. Blood trickled along the edge where his badge had been. He cleaned the wound. "Where'd that book come from?" the paramedic asked.

Rattling continued from across the hall. Now, there was loud pounding and a muffled sound. "Ivar get me out of here!"

"Sam?" Ivar moved past the paramedic. He turned the knob and pushed the door. "It won't open."

"Up here!" A redhead popped over the window vent. "I'm trapped. The bookcase fell in front of the door, and I can't move it.

"What are you doing here?" Ivar asked.

"Um, I followed my instincts." Samantha pulled herself up and managed to get one leg over the window then the other. She dropped over the outside edge of the window vent and hung onto the ledge.

Ivar reached up and caught hold of her waist. "What happened to your other eye? Now you have two shiners, one green, and one purple."

"It'll match that bruise on your chest." Samantha slid down his body to the floor. She didn't let go, but leaned into him and kissed him deep and long.

Maddog cleared his throat. "Samantha, I'm happy for you and Ivar, but can we leave now?"

Samantha knelt beside Maddog and gave him a peck on the cheek. "Thanks for saving his life, and I recorded most of what happened here today. That should prove your innocence. I'll send a copy of the recording to your father as evidence in court."

Maddog blushed. "Thanks. I owe you. Ivar, take good care of our girl."

Ivar nodded. "You can count on it."

Angela Clayten headed their way. "So, we finally found the real Gary Gordon."

The crime scene investigation crew followed in her wake.

"Now that we have our medical records straightened out, I'm certain it was his twin brother's body that we found after the Vickers' fire." Angela knelt beside Gary. "Both boys dead. Such a pity."

Regrets

Amos rolled over and kissed Linda. "It's time to go, honey. I'll take the jet. You sleep in."

Linda flipped on the light. "What time is it?"

"Two-forty. Sorry, change in plans. I can't meet Sam for breakfast, but I left her a message."

"Why not?" Linda swung her feet over the edge of the bed.

"The rescue ship lands in Columbia in eight hours. I told the ambassador that I'd be there. They need me."

"I was shocked to see Pops and Bridget, and I'm thrilled they are alive," Linda said. "You should have seen Pops' disappointment when he found out you weren't home."

Amos got up and dressed. "I know, sweetheart. I heard the regret in his voice when I talked to him on the phone." *And that's not the half of it. I've never heard Pops so angry in my life.*

"It's a shame about Gary. I would never have guessed that he was so dangerous."

"He made such a fuss over a little map." Amos shook his head. "Terrible, just terrible.

Linda brushed a curl off her forehead. "Then you heard that Bridget found the map in her apron pocket. She had thrown it in the laundry."

"Yeah. Pops said it didn't survive the wash." Amos laughed. *Good thing, too. My stash is safe.* "We'll have dinner together next week when I get home. You can count on it."

Linda put on a robe. "I'll make you some coffee before you leave."

"Thanks. I'll be down in a minute. I need to pack."

Linda greeted Amos in the kitchen with a steaming mug. "It's not right what Gary did to all those poor people. Steve Walters is in rehab, and Terrance Rodriguez spent weeks in ICU. He finally went home yesterday to be with his wife and children."

Amos sat at the table. "Write whatever checks you see fit." Linda frowned. "Me? Since when do I write checks?"

Amos laughed and rubbed her cheek. "There's plenty of money. We should pay their medical bills ASAP, and I'm tied up for a few days."

"We should reimburse Pops for the Fountain Shop," Linda said. "Sam's condo and repairs to the house, too."

Amos gave her hand a squeeze. "Buy yourself a new Mercedes while you're at it. I feel like a new man. Charity for all."

Linda studied his face. "You do look different. More relaxed.

Maybe we can get away for a while when you come home."

"Sure, sounds wonderful." Amos gazed into her eyes. "I love you, Linda. Remember that."

She put her hand on his. "Our little Samantha's getting married. I can't wait to help with the wedding."

"A Christmas wedding would be lovely." He gulped down his coffee and set the mug on the table. "Give me a hug before I go."

He kissed her long and deep. "I hope that holds you until we meet again."

"Good-bye, Amos." Linda set the mugs in the sink. She yawned and headed upstairs.

"Get some rest." He picked up his bag, went into his office to get a few files, and left the house.

Hijacked

Eight hours later, Amos Vickers stepped through the door of a private jet and waved to the crowd below. Unable to reach the devastated coast after the earthquake, Vickers landed at El Dorado International Airport in the Republic of Columbia. From there, a military helicopter, located outside of Bogotá, would airlift him to his destination.

The Republic of Columbia's president heralded Amos Vickers' arrival with great fanfare. Ten cars lined into a motorcade, which also included an ambulance, two press vans, and dozens of motorcycles. A red carpet ran from the bottom step of his private jet to the mayor's personal black limousine.

Amos squared his shoulders and moved down the steps to the waiting car. His smile widened.

A man in a black uniform opened the door. A faint odor of tobacco wafted from the interior. "Welcome to our beautiful country. Mayor Diego, our previous commander of Columbia's FARC rebel force wishes to speak with you."

"This is a pleasant surprise." Amos climbed into the back. "It's an honor to meet you." *Where have I met this man before?*

"Mr. Vickers, it is I who am honored. The president sends his regrets for his absence, but he wants to show our appreciation. You have done much for our country."

Two secret service men drove up alongside the vehicle on motorcycles.

The limo pulled forward.

"I've received overwhelming support from donors," Amos said. "A 'Doctors Without Borders' emergency team landed a few hours ago. They should have reached the coast by now."

"Yes, I heard from the U.S. ambassador a few minutes ago," the mayor said. "They've already started treating victims. How can we ever thank you?"

Amos grinned. "I'm only on this earth to serve."

"Shelter is the main problem." The mayor frowned. "Over a million people have lost their homes during the earthquake. The United States sent thousands of troops to help distribute food and keep looters from ransacking the area, but they have their hands full. Our men barely found shelter for 25% of the needy, and they've worked 'round the clock' for two days."

"I will send caravans filled with tents and supplies," Amos said. "Soon, everyone will have a cot to sleep on."

As the motorcade reached the security gates, people cheered. Hundreds lined the route. They waved U.S. and Columbian flags. Many threw flowers and confetti as the motorcade drove by.

En route to the military field across town, the mayor pointed out the window. "The crowd hopes to get a glimpse of the 'King of Charity.'"

Amos laughed. "Or perhaps they wish to see their esteemed mayor."

"Perhaps." Removing his shades, the mayor slid them into his pocket and pulled out one of his famous cigars. He offered it to Amos. Then he lifted a bottle. "Aguardiente, my friend? It tastes like anise but with a kick."

"I'd love one." Amos pocketed the cigar and took the ornate crystal shot glass set before him. He tapped it against the mayor's. "To your health, your country, and our friendship."

"To your future," Mayor Diego replied.

The motorcade slowed as it pulled into the military airfield and stopped near a helicopter.

General Gonzales opened the car door and saluted. "Buenas tardes, Señor Alcalde. Good afternoon, Mr. Vickers. I know you're busy. Please follow me."

Turning, Amos pumped the mayor's hand. "As always, an honor, sir."

"We'll meet again, soon," Mayor Diego said.

Amos stepped out of the motorcade and waved to the crowd.

The Mayor's car sped around the helicopter, followed by a trail of black limos, and then drove away.

"Do you have a place for these fine people to congregate?" Amos asked. "I'd like to talk to them."

"I have orders to fly you directly to headquarters," the general said. "Things are not going well on the coast."

"Surely, we have a few—"

"Now!" The general left no doubt this was a command.

The rear car of the motorcade swerved and pulled behind the general. The doors flew open, and six agents piled out. They surrounded Amos, a cache of automatic weapons strapped at their side.

Amos eyed the general. "What's this?"

"A change in plans." The general nudged Amos toward the helicopter. "We move without delay. Your life's in danger, and I'm assigned to your protection. This could lead to a world-changing event."

The guards marched Amos forward.

Sweat dripped down his back, but he refused to show fear.

The general whispered into his ear. "Better not let the people know there's a problem. They admire you."

"Right." Amos boarded the waiting helicopter, turned, and waved to the crowd once more. He put a hand along the side of his mouth and whispered to the general, "Where are we heading?"

"You have a date with the boss." General Gonzales nodded to the pilot, and the helicopter lifted. His raspy voice sounded as if he'd been breathing smoke for years. "Then, who knows, but I doubt you'll need a return trip home." A waxed mustache lifted. His square teeth formed a smirk.

Who's the Real Boss?

A date with the boss? That's me. We'll have to see how world-changing this event could be. The tension heightened Amos's senses.

The general's voice seemed curt, gruff, and at times insolent.

His eyes shifted between the pilot and the two guards.

Amos had always trusted Gonzales, but something dreadful was playing out. Stretching to his full height, Amos pulled his shoulders back and stood toe-to-toe with the general. *Better clarify what's going on.* "So, we're seeing the boss? How can that be? He's standing in front of you."

"Things are not always as they seem." Gonzales ran his hand across his throat. In a whispered voice, "Be careful."

The pilot turned around. "General Gonzales, take control of the plane."

The general scrambled into the co-pilot seat.

"Amos, we meet again." The uniformed pilot stood. His puffy cheeks sucked a sharp inhale of his cigar. Smoke curled through his nose and mouth. "I told you we would see each other soon."

Amos gasped. "Mayor Diego…But how? You drove away in the lead car."

"Yes, they delivered me to the front of this plane before driving away." Diego smirked. "How does it feel to call another, Boss?"

Amos resisted the urge to flinch. "I don't know what you mean."

"I think we understand each other perfectly. Right, Boss?" Diego sneered. "But sadly, no more. That title belongs to me." He inhaled once more and then stubbed out the cigar on the sole of his boot. "This is my country. My land, my drugs, and my trade. You no longer exist."

"What do you mean?" Amos took a step forward. *Play him for all he's worth. Let him think he has the upper hand.* "I suppose you envy me and my tremendous deeds for mankind."

"Fortunately, your death will be quick and painless, unlike what you did to my family. All I wanted was to deal in a little cocaine, but you put an end to that."

Amos glanced at the two guards and then back to his enemy. "What family? I don't know what you're talking about."

There was a little incident at the Castrini house back in June.

A gasp gave away his fear. "Santiago Castrini?"

"My father. He was innocent. My brothers and extended family. All massacred. "I survived because I love to smoke." He shook his head.

"What do you want?" Amos cringed at his words then calmed. "I have money, power, contacts—"

"You think you can buy your freedom? Think again." The rotund man let out a belly laugh. "The president ousted me from power. Said I'm corrupt. I'll be on trial if he catches me. I'm no longer mayor. Now I'm Boss."

"What happened to the president?" Amos felt his gut flip. "You have him, don't you? That's why he didn't meet me as planned."

"You can save his soul with yours," Diego said. "Where's the map? I know you tried to destroy it. Even got a couple of Columbian immigrants to help you. I suppose you gave them a great deal on a home loan—CEO of your own bank. Once they got in too deep, you helped them raise funds through a few odd jobs. They bombed your best friend's shop and his daughter's condo then raided his home. No luck finding the map?" His dark eyes narrowed. "Your chauffeur thought you were helping him find it but that was also a lie. You want the mine for yourself."

"What interest do you have in a collapsed silver mine in Colorado?" Amos asked. "It doesn't make any sense."

"A private investigator kept Wendell Gordon under surveillance. You found out and informed Wendell. He killed the agent in that old warehouse. Then you killed Wendell in place of your chauffeur, right? They were twins, after all. Who'd know the difference?"

Amos gasped. "What are you saying? My chauffeur died, and I didn't kill him. You don't have the facts right."

"Maybe not, but I do know you're running drugs out of that mine."

Amos recoiled. *Too near the truth for comfort.*

"Don't worry. The only ones who know your flaws are aboard this helicopter." Diego laughed once more. "Soon, all your sins will be forgiven. I'll take over your drug operation at the mine as repayment for my family's massacre. Should be an even trade, No?"

Diego nodded his head to the two guards. "Dump him into the ocean. We're landing soon."

The guards moved for Amos, one on each side, and headed to the door.

Amos turned his head toward the cockpit and saw Gonzales give him a salute.

"Boss, I have the president on the radio." Gonzales didn't wait for a reply. The speaker blared.

"… got word our ex-Mayor Diego's aboard," the president shouted above the mayhem. "Blast that helicopter into oblivion."

Diego dashed for the radio and grabbed the handset. "Amos Vickers is on board. Repeat Amos Vickers is on board."

"Look below," Gonzales said. Army tanks with machine guns lined the shore. They opened fire. Smoke filled the air. A Blackhawk took off and headed in their direction.

Diego, now back in the pilot's seat, took over the controls. "Let's get the hell out of here." The chopper lifted and swerved.

Amos felt like a million bucks. Make it a trillion. Gonzales had his back. Adrenaline pumped through his pores. Nothing could stop him now. His alter ego took over. He shoved a guard against the door.

It gave way as Amos grabbed a strut overhead and kicked him through the opening.

The second guard reached for his comrade, but he lost his balance and clung to the ledge as the chopper maneuvered.

The Blackhawk opened fire. The man's body, riddled with bullets, dropped. As the chopper turned, the door slammed shut.

A sound like firecrackers popped at the front of the chopper.

Amos hopped from the strut.

Blood splattered the control board. Diego's body lay over the stick forcing the chopper into a dive.

Gonzales dropped his gun and shouted into the radio. "Retreat. Mayor's dead. I have Vickers." He pushed Diego's body out of the way and pulled the chopper out of the dive.

The president came on the speaker. "We will retreat. Thanks, General Gonzales. The country salutes your bravery."

The Blackhawk turned around.

Gonzales shouted over the noise of the engine, "Where to Boss?"

Amos chuckled and moved Diego's body. He strapped himself into the pilot's seat. The clouds opened into a downpour as they lifted toward the Andes. Amos maneuvered around the mountains like a pro.

"I thought you were a goner for a minute until I took control." Gonzales gave a shit-eating grin. "Must feel good to be boss again."

Amos glanced at the black hole in Diego's temple. "Did you do that?"

Gonzales grinned.

"And you rescued the president." It wasn't a question.

"My men freed him." The general brushed a sleeve over his medals. "We can't let the people know that a madman ran the country for the past week."

"I'm proud of you."

The general beamed. "Where did you learn to fly?"

"Vietnam." Pain surged through Amos.

"You sound bitter."

"A grenade took my little brother's life. Pops didn't save him. He promised to watch over him but ended up a POW. I was in Seoul when I heard the news. It changed my life. I vowed…never mind. It hurts too much to talk about."

Gonzales put a hand on his shoulder. "I understand."

"I thought take a life for a life, but it didn't feel right." Amos slammed his fist on his knee.

General Gonzales said, "My shrink tells me every action is a part of a bigger plan."

"I don't believe in shrinks?" Amos made a U-turn mid-air. "Let's finish this!"

The sky brightened over the shoreline. Amos felt it was destiny. Like his life's journey from darkness to fame. "Time for the parachutes."

"What?" General Gonzales tugged at his thick mustache.

"My life is too complicated," Amos said. "I'm taking a new identity."

"You are a good pilot." Gonzales scratched his head. "You can land this. We don't need parachutes."

Amos chuckled. "Good. I'll wear one, and you go down with the chopper. It makes it easier to disappear."

"That's not funny." Gonzales unbuckled and got up from the co-pilot's chair. He swore in Spanish under his breath.

A parachute pack dropped in the seat next to Amos.

He peered up at the decorated general. "So you're wearing one, too. That's more like it."

"Yes, Boss."

Amos' smile widened. "You transferred the charity money to my Swiss bank account?"

"Of course. I always do as you ask, don't I?" Gonzales glared down his nose and flashed a small grin.

"Minus 20%." Amos chuckled. "However, you're worth it."

"I'm surprised you didn't take your personal millions, too."

Amos frowned. "I can't. I'm making a fresh start and don't want Linda looking for me. I need to start over." He rubbed his forehead.

"You feel guilty?" Gonzales asked.

Amos slipped into his parachute. "Not for everything. I ordered the bomb at the Fountain shop, and yeah, I wanted Bridget's key to get the map. Gary said it was in Molly's diary, but Gary didn't stop there. He blew up Sam's condo. I'd never hurt her. She's my Godchild. Well, I did have her kidnapped, but for her own safety, you understand."

"Whatever. Is this your final confession?" Gonzales stood between Amos and the co-pilot seat staring out the window. "It's too late. We're going to—"

Amos spotted his private jet below the chopper. He forced the stick forward, and the chopper nose-dived.

"Sorry, general. We part ways here." A crisp crack of the general's neck breaking against the control panel signaled Amos to evacuate.

Amos leveled the chopper for the mountains, flipped on the autopilot, and jumped to freedom.

Forewarned

The light was still on in Linda's bedroom when she reached the top of the stairs. A hint of Amos' aftershave lingered in the air. She pulled back the covers of the now-cold bed and her throat tightened. Her eyes filled with tears. Amos' wedding ring lay in the indent of his pillow where his head usually rested.

Deep down, she knew but refused to listen to her fears. "I'll call him later today, and tell him I don't want a divorce." She put his ring on her finger, gathered his robe in her arms, and fell asleep in his scent.

The radio alarm woke her with a news flash. "The famed philanthropist, Amos Vickers died when his helicopter crashed over the Andes Mountains. There were no survivors."

Linda heard her phone ringing, but she didn't pick up. "You knew. Didn't you, Amos?" It wasn't a divorce you wanted, you were afraid for your life, and didn't want anyone to hurt me."

For some reason, she felt relief flow through her. She got up, showered, dressed, and made coffee. A thought crossed her mind. Unsure of what she was searching for, she took her coffee into Amos' office. The desktop reflected the overhead light from its polished sheen.

Linda's gut clenched. The neatly stacked files that usually lay across the left side of the desktop were missing. Only their wedding photo, a phone, and a clock sat at the back of his desk. She set down her coffee, pulled out his plush leather chair, and went to work.

Linda's hands shook as she pawed through every drawer. A sinking feeling clutched her soul. She opened the file cabinets. Facts bubbled to the surface, but there were huge gaps. Like a string of dominos, they formed a straight line to her husband. "Oh God, Amos, what have you done?" His death caused a chain reaction to crash around her.

"Her first phone call was to Bridget."

The Map

Samantha noticed that Tobias became weaker as time went on. Even after weeks of rest, he wasn't able to blow into town as he once had. Well, he didn't relax completely over that stretch of time. He'd managed to call 911 to rescued Pops, Bridget, and Ter's children. Then he helped Samantha escape. Now he seemed pleased just to be in her company.

Deep in thought, she sat in her old bedroom and stared at the gold necklace Tobias had given Sara a century ago. She'd polished the chain, and the monogram SM gleamed in spite of the low light of her lava lamp. Glancing at the old ghost, he didn't even make a dent at the end of the bed.

Samantha treasured her time with Tobias. "I don't get it. Why did the last hour I spent at the clinic crawl by, but when I'm with you, time flies?"

"Try hanging around for a century," Tobias said.

She picked up her journal. Over the past two days, Samantha interviewed Tobias while he still had the strength to share lost information about her past. "What do we need to do, so you can have eternal peace?"

"I don't know. Pops is home. Gary's dead. Maddog's cleared of all legal charges, and you're safe. So why *am* I still here?"

"Why did Gary want the map?"

"His grandfather worked the mines alongside my son, Jacob," Tobias said. "Fang was their boss. Marion was his sister. She used to bring lunch for the workers. Gary's grandfather fell in love with her, but so did Jacob. A family feud erupted when she chose my son. The hate lasted for decades."

"Maybe the reason you're still here has something to do with Fang," Samantha said.

"Hmm." Tobias hesitated.

Samantha gasped. "Do you think Gary continued the family feud?"

Tobias rumbled. "Well his father did smuggle silver from the mine and that map shows where it's located.

Samantha slammed her fist against the bed. "I was sure it was Amos that blew up the store."

"Well, Gary built the bomb, but he never planned to set it off and destroy the map," Tobias said.

"That makes sense." Samantha jotted a note in her journal. "He needed the map to find the silver. Who ordered the hit on Ter? Was it Gary?"

"No, Amos is the boss. He ordered the bombs. I'm sure he orchestrated everything. Maybe things got out of hand as Gary got desperate to find the map."

Samantha went back to her journal. "So Marion became your daughter-in-law?"

"That's right."

"That makes her my…what? I'm confused."

"Great-aunt," Tobias said. "Are you making a family tree?"

"I'm trying to, but it isn't easy on paper."

"I used to be able to type, but I don't think my fingers will make a dent on your keyboard."

Samantha pulled out her laptop. "Then tell me what to type."

"We'll start with you." Tobias moved closer.

"Okay." Samantha shivered and buttoned her sweater.

"Oh, sorry." Tobias backed away a bit. "I forgot what a cool guy I am." A wheezy chuckle escaped the mist.

She laughed and typed Samantha Jean McFitzroy into an Excel spreadsheet. "My parents are Bridget and Pops."

"Right. My youngest son, Rueben John, was Pops' father."

"He died before I was born," Samantha said.

"They all died before you were born. Pops waited so long to get married that I was afraid I'd have no more descendants."

"He hadn't met Mom yet." Samantha said.

"I was surprised when Pops took over the fountain shop, but his elderly mother couldn't keep up with the business."

"So back to Marion."

"Oh, I almost forgot," Tobias said. "I guess you could say, you're related to Maddog in a round-about way. Marion was Fang's sister. She cared for Mrs. Jackson after he buried Spurs."

"Pops told me about that story," Samantha said.

"Everything started with Fang's mine. Well, truth be known; that's not quite right. I got drunk one night at the saloon."

"Do you mean the saloon that turned into Pops' fountain shop?" Samantha asked.

"Yes. That's why I kept coming to the bar…I mean shop. My whole life changed that night. I hoped it would lead me to some clue to get me to heaven. Then I met Pops. He looked just like Rueben, but younger. Then you bounded through the door. I realized my purpose for being on Earth."

"You said that night changed your life. What happened?"

"Fang came into town." Tobias grew colder. The mist roiled and rose higher off the bed. "He had too much to drink and boasted about marrying Jenny. Then he insulted Sara. He said that when it came to fine women, Sara would never marry. Her legs locked at the knees."

"Don't tell me," Samantha said. "I can guess at your reaction."

"I punched him in the gut. He crumpled toward me, grabbed my gun, and we squabbled. The gun dropped to the floor. We both reached for it. I got carried away, grabbed Fang, and threw him over the bar. He crashed into the liquor bottles. The sheriff hauled me away and locked me up. The next morning, I sat in jail while some savage murdered Sara. My Molly never forgave me."

"Did she understand that you fought to defend Sara's integrity?"

"I didn't get the chance to tell her," Tobias said. "She died over the weekend while was searching for Sara."

Samantha cupped her chin in her hand. "Maybe you need to resolve issues with Molly before you can go to heaven. Wait, does Molly's death have anything to do with Fang's mine? Or the stolen silver?"

"Molly died there," Tobias said.

Do you know where to find the mine after all of these years?" Samantha scooted closer.

"I've always known the location. I just refused to go back there after her death."

"Let's get Ivar and find the mine." Samantha hopped from the bed and grabbed her cell phone.

"But the map is destroyed," Tobias said.

"I thought you said you knew where to find the mine. Besides, I pieced together what was left. Parts are still legible."

"I'm not sure I can spot it without searching from the air." Tobias became lighter.

"Rest another day or two," Samantha said. "I'll arrange everything with Ivar." She speed dialed.

"Hi honey," Ivar said. "How's the arm feel without the cast?"

"Stiff, but I'm working out the kinks. I have a favor to ask."

"Okay, but did you hear about Amos?" Ivar sounded rushed. "The military chopper flying him to the Columbian coast crashed. There were no survivors."

Samantha gasped. "When did you hear the news?"

"Not long ago. An emergency broadcast broke over the radio.

I've been on the phone ever since."

Samantha dashed down to the kitchen. "Mom, Ivar's on the phone."

"Shh, it's Linda." Her mother was on the landline. "She's hysterical. I'm going over to console her."

"Yeah. Tell her I'm sorry about Amos." Samantha headed back to her room.

"Sam, are you truly sorry about Amos?" Ivar asked.

"No, but I am sorry for Linda. She loved the man, and I've never had anything against her. Unfortunately, Amos died just as we discovered his lair."

"I'm proud of you, Sam. You've been through hell and back."

"Thanks."

"There's one problem." Ivar sounded upset.

"What's that?"

"I need to talk to Linda about his misdeeds," Ivar said. "This isn't the best time to do that."

"Swing by and pick me up. We'll meet with her together."

"I supposed there's not much we can do now," Ivar said. "Amos will get off free and clear. Who's going to want to charge a dead man, especially one with his clout?"

"What will happen to all the charity money?" Samantha asked.

"I just spoke with Duke Parker Senior. He was Amos's lawyer. According to Vickers' will, corporate control goes to Linda, but Duke hasn't spoken to her either. He called several times, but she didn't answer."

"Everything goes to Linda?" Samantha asked.

"She'll oversee everything, except for a Swiss bank account," Ivar said. "Mr. Parker was shocked that the account balance was zero. It didn't make him happy, but he says the company is still viable. He's driving over to talk to her."

"Then we need to be there to help Linda through this."

"What did you want to ask me?" Ivar reminded her.

"Oh, I almost forgot. Maybe we should wait a few weeks."

Tobias blew a gust of cold air. "No. I think you're right. We need to resolve this. I don't want to stay on earth."

"Right!" Samantha said. "Ivar, can you drive Tobias and me to the old mine? He knows where it is. At least, I hope he does. The map may be of some help, but I'm not sure."

"Now?"

"No. Tobias needs a day's rest before the trip, and we better head over to Linda's for moral support."

"Okay. I'm on my way." Ivar hung up.

Fang's Mine

Two days later, Samantha felt a rush of excitement as they drove to the mine.

Tobias hovered over the back seat of Ivar's jeep. "It's been decades since I visited this ghost town. The mine has changed hands several times since then."

They drove past three log cabins that remained standing. The windows were long gone. The doors hung crookedly. A roof had collapsed into one cabin. Other homes came into view but were in various states of decay.

"That's my old house," Tobias pointed, "but It's destroyed." "Which one?" Samantha asked.

"See over there? Only one wall by the chimney is left. Oh, look. Molly and I got married in that church." Only the steeple remained to mark its place.

"Why is there a paved road through town?" Samantha asked.

"That's new," Tobias said. "Probably since the seventies."

Ivar drove to the end of town. "Is the mine near here?"

"Up that gravel trail. See the ore cars locked at the top?"

"The road is awfully rutted and muddy." Ivar shifted into four-wheel drive. "Are you sure you want to go up there?"

"We've come this far," Samantha said.

"Okay. Hang on." Ivar turned left and drove the incline up the mountain. The mine was further up the Rockies past the tree line. Ivar spun his tires as they neared the top.

Mine tailings spilled out from the mouth. Abandoned ore bins sat on the rusted track.

"That's odd." Samantha pointed, "One rail is shinier than the rest. Does that mean it's still operable?"

"I don't know," Ivar said. "There's a car parked at the entrance. I wonder who is here."

"It's probably been parked there for years," Tobias said. "Look at the license plate. It's dated 1988."

Ivar pulled up to the old Buick. "The front end is rusted out."

They climbed out of the jeep.

Signs posted near the mine warned, "Private property. Off limits." No trespassing signs hung on nearby trees that lined the old railroad trail ending about ten feet from the entrance to the mine's shaft.

More hazardous warning signs were tacked below the others. They told of toxic pollutants, contaminated groundwater, and made it clear, "Do not enter! Will be shot on sight."

Ivar turned to Sam. "I don't think we are wanted here."

"Really? What was your first clue?"

Tobias hovered overhead. "I thought the mine collapsed, but it looks as if someone's been here not long ago. I'm going in."

"We're right behind you." Samantha grabbed a flashlight and headgear.

"Oh, no." Tobias roiled above her. "It's too dangerous. It can't hurt me. Wait here. I won't be long." He disappeared through the rocks.

"Do you smell that?" Samantha asked. "It smells skunky."

"Marijuana," Ivar said. "Probably grows wild out here."

Samantha strapped a headlight over her helmet and switched it on. "Look, the tunnel to the left has been backfilled." Samantha wound around a few beams. "But the one on the right Ys off just after the mouth of the cave. I wonder where it leads."

"Don't go inside," Ivar said.

She turned to him but refused to retreat.

"Sam," echoed through the cave. Ivar switched on his headlight and dashed after her. "Don't touch the walls. They might cave in."

"Careful," Samantha said. "There's water up here. A few beams are rotting."

Ivar slid on some slippery rocks hidden in the water. "Sam. Let's get out of here. It's not safe."

She moved forward. "Look. There's a light ahead."

"And the ceiling has collapsed," Ivar warned.

"I see something that looks like a couple of robots. Mechanical men lined up along the top rung of the rail." She motioned with her flashlight. "I saw a drawing of robots like that in Amos' office."

The light grew brighter then a cold breeze caught her hair.

"Get out. Get out right now." Tobias whipped at her sleeve. "Ivar, get Sam out of here."

Ivar grabbed Sam's arm and pulled her back toward the entrance. A red piece of material blew in the breeze off to their left.

"A flag," Samantha said. "I wonder what—"

An ore car headed in their direction. "Get off the tracks," Ivar shouted.

Before they could move, Tobias roiled and lifted them briefly as the car passed where they'd been only a second before.

The robots' eyes beamed bright lights and blinded Samantha. "They're alive!"

Tobias couldn't hold them any longer. He dropped Ivar, who clung to Sam's leg then lowered to the ground.

Ivar caught her in his arms.

The mist disappeared with a rapid gust. "Get out!"

Ivar set Sam on her feet and yanked her by the hand.

A stitch grabbed Sam's side. She pulled her hand free. "Keep going. I'm right behind you."

The entrance lay dead ahead. Ivar sprinted forward. "We made it."

Samantha tripped over a rock and stumbled to her knees. Her hand rammed against the ground. "Ow!" A sharp pain stabbed the palm of her left hand. She wiped the grit against her pant leg and felt a piece of jagged metal dig deeper into her skin.

Ivar stopped and turned. "Come on."

"Just a minute." She grasped the object and plucked it from her palm.

Ivar shone his flashlight in her direction and ran back to her side. The metal gleamed in his light.

"Let's go!" Ivar leaned toward her.

She shoved the metal in her pocket. "I'm coming."

Ivar pulled her to her feet, grabbed her hand, and ran toward the opening. The walls moved. The tracks shifted.

Samantha sprinted to keep up. "What's going on?"

As soon as they emerged through the entrance, Ivar pulled her off the tracks. "I think we set a trap in motion."

"Why would anyone bother?" She peered around him back into the mine. "Do you hear a whining sound from inside?"

Another ore car headed their way. It was filled with crates.

A heavy mist rode on top of the stack. "There're hundreds of these in the back." Tobias faded as the car came to a halt outside the mine.

Ivar lifted the top crate from the ore car. "I'll be right back. You take care of that wound." He dashed downhill to the jeep.

Samantha pulled a tissue from her pocket and dabbed her palm. It still bled, but most of the grit was gone. Curious, she pulled out the piece of cracked metal, and held it in the light. Her fingers brushed across the surface. She read, 'Little Misty' engraved across its center. "I've heard that name before." She repocketed the item and blotted her wound again. *Colby has been out here in the last month.*

Ivar returned with a crowbar, antiseptic ointment, and a Band-Aid. "Good thing I carry a first–aid kit in my jeep." He leaned the crowbar next to the crate and took her left hand. After doctoring the cut, he wrapped it with the Band-Aid and sealed it with a light kiss. "I guess you'll live."

"Thanks." Samantha moved back to the crate. "Look. Coffee is stamped on the lid."

"I bet this isn't coffee." Ivar inserted the crowbar and wedged the lid open. The crate was filled with small white bags. He ripped open a bag and dipped his finger into the powder. "Cocaine."

Shots were fired from the mine.

Ivar grabbed Samantha, pulled her to the ground and threw his body over her.

Samantha peeked under his arm as grinding sounds came to life. An army of robots marched through the entrance.

"Let's get out of here," Ivar said.

Laser lights lit Ivar's sleeve. He scooted behind the crate as bullets riddled through the wood.

Tobias formed a dark cloud around the robots. A gust of wind, strong as a tornado, knocked the front row backward. Like a string of dominos, the robots fell to the ground.

Ivar rolled to his knees. He took Samantha's hand, and they ran toward the jeep.

The robots seemed to sense their retreat and ceased fire as they righted themselves and marched back inside the mine.

"Drones," Ivar said. "Someone with a military background programmed them."

"I told you that Amos had a file on robots at the warehouse," Samantha said. "I saw it when I found the diary."

Tobias hovered near the jeep. "She's right. He also has an office at the rear of the shaft. It's where Molly used to work, but I couldn't get inside. It's fortified with steel beams. No wonder Amos wanted the map destroyed. He has a fortune in this mine. Not silver but drugs.

"Amos is dead," Samantha said. "What do we do with the mine?"

"Jump Sweeny will be in town tomorrow," Ivar said. "Drug smuggling is right up his alley. I'll gladly let the FBI handle it."

"Wait!" Samantha pulled the piece of metal from her pocket and handed it to Ivar. "You're not going to like what I have the say."

"Try me," Ivar said. "I love everything about you."

Samantha scanned the area then whispered, "That looks like a broken dog tag. I think it belongs to Colby's Husky. I'm sure he was here recently. He mentioned that he bought a new one for Little Misty She had lost it somewhere. It looks like they were both here."

"Now Colby is someone I can go after," Ivar said. "No wonder he refused to believe you. I wonder how he's involved."

"Let's leave that to Agent Sweney." Samantha said.

"Tobias, you found Sara," a female voice whispered through the breeze." Sparks flew around Tobias as the mist landed on the ground. A bolt of lightning flashed through the air and crackled as it touched the mist forming into a second cloud, much like a silver lining.

"Molly? Is that you?" Tobias hovered by Samantha. He became a bright light. "This is Samantha."

The shimmery cloud shot through the air. "You've done well. Thank you, Tobias, for finding her soul. Now Sara is also at peace."

"Sara?" Tobias asked. "You mean she's not in heaven with you?"

"Not until a few moments ago," Molly said.

Amos sounded as if he was weeping for joy. "My family is together at last."

"Yes, and you're free to come home with me." The shimmering lights reflected rainbows around Samantha and Ivar.

A warm tingle flowed through Samantha.

The woman said, "I love you, and thanks to Samantha, we can leave Earth together." The lights gathered into a warm breeze.

A tear slid down Samantha's cheek. To her surprise, she added, "I love you too, Mom."

"Same goes for me," Tobias said. "Tell Pops good-bye and have him take care of our tombstones. Ivar knows where to find them." Two brilliant lights shot into the air, and the sun shone brightly.

"Until we meet again." Samantha waved.

"And this time, we'll meet in heaven," Tobias whispered. The lights disappeared and there was silence.

Samantha leaned over and kissed Ivar. "Let's go home. We have a wedding to plan."

The End

Author's Note

Thank you for reading <u>Until We Meet Again</u>. I loved writing it, and hope you enjoyed reading it. If you did, please tell a friend and consider leaving a review on Amazon. Your sincere feedback means everything to me. I hope to have another story to share soon.

About Author - Jill S. Flateland

**Jill S. Flateland,
RN, BSN, CCRN, MBA**

There is nothing like a good mystery. Suspense novels get my juices flowing. In 2006, I retired and ventured into the wider writing world. In 2011, I published <u>A Lightning Slinger's Tales of the Rails</u> which shares stories of my aunt, Dr. Vera E. Williams, and her life as a female telegrapher during World War II. She worked for the railroad to make enough money to get her Ph.D. in education.

In 2014, we published <u>Ding Dong! The Rural Schools Are Gone</u>, is a story of my two aunts, Vivian V. Lund (age 97 at the time, died at 104 in 2022) and Dr. Vera E. Williams (age 88 at that time, died at age 90 in 2016), who were both rural school teachers in Wisconsin during the early twentieth century. I miss my dear aunts, but their stories live forever in these novels.

I entered my fifth novel, <u>Until We Meet Again</u>, in the 2014 Colorado Gold Contest at the Rocky Mountain Fiction Writer's Contest. The novel became a finalist in the suspense category. *Tobias McFitzroy's old tombstone lay cracked in half and sinking under its weight in a cemetery outside a Colorado ghost town northeast of Fort Collins. The old stonemason had carved his own epitaph. It read, "Until we meet again. 1830 – 1899." Unlike most people, it didn't mean when he'd meet them in heaven. He couldn't. He hadn't made it that far.*

From there, I moved into the Agent Joshtine Cordelia-Hastings series. Sweet Revenge is the first in the series of these action-packed thrillers. Cordy is a peculiar breed. At the age of twenty-three, she is adventurous, quick-witted, and energetic. She's any man's equal, although absolutely female. Her shoulder-length, strawberry-blonde hair is often pulled back in a professional French braid, which reveals a heart-shaped face, ivory skin, and alert eyes the color of a spring pond.

Her Irish-French heritage rings true when it comes to contrasts. Her father's Irish side makes her honest to her core, loyal, and unlike her father, slow to anger. However, once she hits that breaking point, watch out! It gives rise to a heart of a French lion. Just like her mother, she fights for what's right, refusing to admit defeat.

Cordy has honed her skills through past experiences as a research analyst and FBI Intelligence Analyst. Always plotting her next strategy like a three-dimensional Chess game, she figures out five moves ahead of every play.

Her world is a massive planet of asynchronous electronic puzzles to be analyzed, decrypted, and decoded. It's a perfect fit for a woman and job to have risen to lead the U.S. President's cyberspace crisis team.

Her venture continues in Rapid Response, where Cordy fights a bioterrorist attack. An astronaut unknowingly transports a potent virus, created without gravity on the space station, back to Earth. This virus is more deadly than our recent Covid epidemic. Not only does it devastate the lungs, but it also attacks the brain. Risking exposure, Cordy rushes to find a cure when U.S. President Spendorf, his key advisors, and many members of Congress become infected.

Next in the series, <u>Crashing The Grid</u> sends Cordy and her team to reverse a cyber attack on NYC that shuts down the power grid, water treatment plants, and more. Cordy's adventures continue in <u>Combating Chaos: All Systems Down</u>. Cordy and her new husband, JSOC Agent Braun Hastings, hunt down a Russian terrorist, General Okueva. He enlists student hackers to disrupt the New York Stock Exchange and major financial systems. Foreign forces have also attacked London and Rome. Cordy and her team risk their lives to stop the terrorists.

I'm currently writing *Caught Unaware*, where Cordy has been promoted to a new cabinet position at the Cyberspace Crisis Agency. A massive cyber attack on Washington, D.C. challenges the team to pull out all stops to defend the President, especially when drones attack the White House. I hope you enjoy these fast-paced novels.

Although my background is over 40 years in healthcare as a critical care nurse and the CEO of an Urgent Care Corporation, I've been a writer all my life. My husband, Byron, and I live in Colorado, and we travel extensively.

Sales Support a Worthy Cause

Byron and I are actively involved with two Non-Governmental Organizations (NGOs). The first is **Angel Covers**, who helped open Vill-Angel Medical Clinic in the center of a rural farming community in Endebess, Kenya, allowing poor families to receive high-quality healthcare.

As Director of Healthcare Services, my goal is to help expand the clinic to offer maternal-child care. Many families have no car to travel to a hospital, the nearest being 17 kilometers from the clinic. Some have a motorcycle, others have a cart pulled by a donkey, but many walk on foot.

Most women deliver babies at home, but the infant mortality rate in Kenya is six times higher than in the U.S. (Kenya has 30 infant deaths/1000 births compared to the U.S., which has 5 infant deaths/1000 births.) Some women travel up to two hours on foot while in labor to receive care during high-risk pregnancies. Plus, children are at the highest risk for death within the first 28 days. Most die of pneumonia, diarrhea, and sepsis. Our clinic can treat these ailments and provide follow-up care as needed.

The second is **Seeds of South Sudan**, where donations help rescue refugees from Kakuma Refugee Camp in Kenya, allowing orphans to attend boarding school in Kenya. Once these students graduate, they plan to return to South Sudan to help rebuild its economy, infrastructure, and create a stabilized country.

You, too, can help. Part of the proceeds from the sales of these books help support these causes, and I thank you from the bottom of my heart. We know you have many choices for purchasing mystery novels and methods of donating to worthy causes, so I'm grateful that you chose to help support these charities.

Other Books Written by Jill S. Flateland

Thriller Series:

Sweet Revenge

Rapid Response

Crashing The Grid

Combating Chaos: All Systems Down

Suspense Series:

Until We Meet Again

Secret Series:

Secrets & Chandeliers

Family Secrets & Betrayals

Secrets Lost Among Forget-Me-Nots

Secrets of Grayson Mansion

Family Memoirs:

A Lightning Slinger's Tales of the Rails

Ding Dong! The Rural Schools Are Gone

Chugs & Hugs: Growing Up In A Train Station Vol 1

Chugs & Hugs: Growing Up In A Train Station Vol 2

Chugs & Hugs: Growing Up In A Train Station Vol 3